WINTER HEART

WINTER HEART

Winter Heart Series Book 1

H. S. WINTER

Foxbay Vision

Winter Heart by H. S. Winter

Published by Foxbay Vision

First Edition

hswinter.com

Cover by TrifBookDesign

ISBN 978-952-7519-00-4 (paperback IngramSpark)

To all the lonely hearts.

ACKNOWLEDGMENTS

Thank you to all of you who steered me onto the right path and helped me stay there.

To my mother for bringing me bags filled with library books to read as a child.

To the seer who told me to write. To my colleague who handed me the book on creativity. To my friend who discussed cover design with me. My brother who was the first to read the book. My editor who made the editing process a joy. My proofreader who held my hand on the last steps towards publishing. My cover designer who gave life to my vision.

To the indie author entrepreneur and educator who made me a believer and to the supporting community she created. To everyone who has helped me financially and by providing other kinds of support. To the self-publishing community for offering their proven knowledge and new ideas in order to give everyone the chance to shine.

To Finnish nature and wildlife, beautiful souls, myths, and truth seekers of the world for an endless source of inspiration.

CONTENTS

Sharp Frost,
the son of Puhuri,
hard-freezing wintry lad,
when he of his mother first was born,
in summer he was rocked in pools,
on the greatest reach of swamp,
in winter he on fences rode,
he froze morasses, froze dry land,
froze clearings run to waste and dells,
nipped willows by the water-side,
he frost-bit knobs on aspen trees,
he barked a birch's roots,
and nipped the sapling firs;
he froze with ice a river's banks,
made the shore of the sea congeal,
he froze the springs,
he froze the lakes,
and great he afterwards became…

§ 93. Charm for Sharp Frost
Published by Elias Lönnrot in
Suomen Kansan Muinaisia Loitsurunoja (1880)
and translated by John Abercromby in
Magic Songs of the West Finns, Vol. 2 (1898)

1 LIFELESS DARKNESS

White specks sliced through the light.

The falling snowflakes looked like beads on a string. The effect was pretty but irritated her eyes. Sini sighed and turned off the headlamp. The snow-covered ground reflected the scarce light that was left of the day, but she couldn't see the details of the narrow path.

Her walking got clumsier, and she had to slow down until her eyes got accustomed to the dark. It didn't matter. She wasn't in a hurry. She had all the time in the world. In fact, she walked the same path every day.

She wished the sky had been draped in stars instead of dull clouds that kept pouring more of the white. The forest was void of life. Trees and bushes were frozen into dark statues. Every plant and creature living on the ground had been buried. What had been alive had vanished. All colours gone. It was so quiet. Painfully quiet.

Winter had come early, and the soft blanket of snow was already suffocating. At least the overwhelming white was dimmed into a dull grey by the dark. There'd been a time when she lived for the winter season, blessing every bit of snow piling up and making her passion possible. That time was a distant memory.

Her footsteps made no sound in the loose snow as she continued on the path she knew like the back of her hand. She thought of her dog that would always accompany her on the walks in the wood, running somewhere in front of her, scouting for what lay ahead long before she got there. She knew the beam wouldn't be reflected by the dog's eyes, but she flashed the light into the distance anyway.

How many times she'd wished the dog would stay closer to her. She'd tried to compel it to, but it's curious nose and independent ways were too strong a calling. Not seeing the dog in front of her, it was almost like walking alone. During winter, darkness presided over both morning and evening walks, and to be able to locate the dog, she'd bought a red light and fastened it onto its collar.

Sini halted and let her gaze sweep the fuzzy shapes of the terrain. She took a deep breath and exhaled into the cold air. The numbness that was a more and more constant companion caught up with her. There were tears desiring to surface, but there was no point in crying. She wouldn't get relief.

The familiar sensation of a knot in her throat too thick to swallow.

Resuming her walk, she picked up a simple tune. She wasn't afraid of the dark, but hearing her own voice made her less lonely.

She was halfway along the path that encircled the forest in a meandering pattern. She knew she wouldn't encounter anyone. Neither human nor animal. There'd be nothing distracting her from her own thoughts. Her days would continue eventless and lightless for the next few months of dreaded winter.

If only there was another place she could go. Somewhere warm and light and with nothing reminding her of the past. No winters. At times, the thought of escape was the only thing that kept her intact. Other days, knowing it was impossible had her tumbling down a black hole.

The good thing about the dark was it swallowed her up, hid her from the world. A world that had cast her out.

Nothing could reach her through the heavy thickness of dark winter.

Sini picked up the pace as she walked across the field that separated her house from the forest.

Her eyes fell on the little wooden house that lay surrounded by a garden and more forest on the other side. Although Sini was drawn to the little forest and the walks that gave her some relief, she was pleased to see the dim light leaking from the windows of her home. Her steps became more effortless as she reached her front yard. She'd been adamant in keeping the space clear of snow.

Sini opened the front door, brushed the melting snow from her jacket and knitted hat, and stepped inside. She locked the door, leaned against it, and sighed. Thank heavens for a warm and light home in the gloomy season. Why people liked winters was beyond her comprehension. They said the white ground was so pretty and that it lit up the dark time of year. She imagined city-people happily skipping with their skis to perfectly tended tracks, enjoying the short exertion in crisp, sunny weather with good company, feeling uplifted and invigorated as they returned to their comfortable low-maintenance dwellings. They didn't have to live in the ever-present harshness of winter like she did.

Death was what it was—not uplifting light. But viewing the snow-covered ground as something beautiful was an excellent survival strategy. It would have been a totally different situation if the snow had been the colour grey—or khaki.

She took off her coat, padded trousers, scarf, and wool pullover and hung them to dry in the bathroom. Thick yellow curtains covered the windows of the living room. Enhancing the warm light emanating from the lamp in the ceiling and the one on the floor, they created an illusion of a homely atmosphere.

Despite the pleasant temperature, she needed the comfort of a fire. She walked up to the old tile-covered fireplace and oven, leaned into its still warm surface, and pulled out the damper. She took out a firelighter from a box on top and placed it on the logs she'd earlier loaded into the heart of the fireplace. The flame that lit the firelighter caught on to the dry birch wood and searched its way over the rough bark.

Sini pulled up the quaint armchair in front of the fire, sat down, and leaned back against the big, crocheted pillow. Her eyes fixed on the dancing orange-and-white flames. There was something soothing in the way they caressed the wood, loving it into another form of existence. As the fire took charge and filled the space, it broke the silence of her home. Soon warmth radiated from the fire, and although it was pleasant on her skin, there was something cold inside her that wouldn't thaw.

There'd been a time when more people gathered in front of a fire. A time of easy conversation and laughter. She'd been surrounded by friends. She'd been part of a team.

Sini closed her eyes and searched her memories for something that wouldn't feel painful.

Her grandmother.

Sini pictured her grandmother being busy at her writing desk. Even when she got visitors, she wouldn't stop reading books and writing in one of her numerous notebooks. Sini hadn't been that curious about any of it. As a child, she'd rather hoped for her grandmother to spend more time with her.

Her grandmother, Satu, had been aloof and eccentric, but when she did give Sini attention, they'd done fun things together. Walking about in the forest, looking at nature's little wonders. A big black spider spinning its intricate web between tree trunks. The petite but exquisite twinflower thriving where other flowers didn't. And the stone boulders scattered between trees, mosses, and wild rosemary. Sini and her grandmother had pretended the big stones were magical. Every boulder had a portal, and they'd criss-crossed between other worlds through them.

Sini loved those memories, but as with everything else, thinking about the only family she'd ever felt accepted by was an invitation for the sadness to snuggle up. Satu was no longer with her. She'd passed away and left the house to Sini, her only grandchild.

She looked at the painting next to the fireplace. The image made in oil paint was mostly abstract, but she knew it represented her grandmother. Satu had often stared into it, and then she'd asked Sini what she thought about it. Sini hadn't discerned anything special from the circles and shapes she'd interpreted as animals, but she'd liked the colours. Blue, orange, green.

Whenever she looked at the painting, she could feel the energy of her beloved grandmother. But the fact was, she was all alone. She hadn't turned thirty yet, but already believed her best days were in the past.

Sini returned her focus to the dancing flames. If she thought only of the flickering orange, she was able to shut out all things wrong with her life. Her intention failed when the sight of the fire consuming the wood reminded her that the logs in the shed wouldn't last through winter. She'd have to buy more of it—cheap. Wood was expensive if money was scarce, but electricity was more expensive.

Damn! Sini pushed her head against the back of the chair and let out a sharp exhale. The evening would end like all other miserable evenings. She'd wanted to end the harmful habit for so long. She got up, stomped into the kitchen, and grabbed a big bag of mixed candy from the cupboard.

Slumping down in the creaking chair, Sini was relieved she wasn't into alcohol. She didn't need it to numb herself. Sugar had the perfect effect on her senses; new and sweet at first when the pleasure took her mind off things, then the carb overload rendered her senses dull and groggy. Past a certain point, there was no enjoyment—only the ritualistic chewing on the teeth-loosening, gum-sticking nuggets of poison. The fire was the only animate thing to keep her company, and the candy played the part of the consoling companion.

The long list of unsolvable problems recited by her mind tormented her, and the release came in the knowing she didn't have to do anything to solve them.

There was no way out.

Nothing but white.

She should've been blinded by the intensity. As her eyes got used to the beaming light, she noticed subtle variations in the white backdrop. Hues—the lightest of hues—revealed shadows and shapes. The faintest yellow of the ground, the pale-blue shadow of a slight mound. It was pleasant, easy on her eyes.

It was all snow, and it was winter. Looking around, she saw nothing but white landscapes. But she didn't find it dreadful. The never-ending hills and valleys of white had a serene beauty she'd never experienced.

In reflex, her hands rose to pull the lapels of her jacket tighter, but all she felt was the round neckline of a thin shirt. She was wearing only one layer of soft clothing, some sort of simple leisurewear. She exhaled, but no vapour blew from her mouth. For some reason, she wasn't cold. Her hands were warm. She was there, but at the same time, she wasn't.

Maybe it wasn't snow.

She bent down, scooped up a handful of the stuff, and pressed it into a loose ball. It felt like snow, only it wasn't cold. She looked up. The sun was halfway up the clear sky, but she didn't feel the warmth.

A wave of nausea washed over her, making her legs weak. She wanted to sit down, but her body didn't obey the command. Her hand was wet from the snow that had melted. It didn't feel right. A sensation of something gone terribly wrong invaded her. The serene wonder turned into distress.

She looked around to find a way out of the strange setting that was morphing into something opposite, but there was no exit. The pastel hues darkened into ash. She began to hurt. Everywhere. As if every cell in her body was crying. As if everything—including her—was disintegrating.

She tried to scream, but she had no voice. She filled her lungs, trying to force air into sound, but the only thing she heard was the increasing buzzing in her ears. Something collapsed. She couldn't see; she couldn't feel her body. The air vibrated with the scattered molecules of what a moment ago had been solid.

It was over.

Everything.

The next moment, everything was black. Sini didn't know where she was. She tried to breathe, but no air entered her lungs. Fumbling in the darkness, her hands reached something solid. It felt like cool fabric under her palms. She could feel her back pressed against the ground. She had to calm down.

Breathing life into her body, she realised after a while she was in her bed, in her bedroom. She pushed the duvet off her overheated body.

Her nightgown was soaked.

Sini pulled the duvet back on top of her as the moist clothing made her shiver.

She shouldn't have loaded more wood last night. The fireplace was on the other side of the wall behind her bed, and the room temperature was too high for comfort. She remembered having nightmares as a child, always waking up hot and sweating.

Lingering, she tried to dim the horrible ending of the dream by visualising the beautiful landscape. Getting back to the winter fantasy was easy, but no matter how wonderful the impression had been, it wasn't enough to bury the memory of dying in pain.

It was ten in the morning. She usually stayed a while in bed, but gave up, as it no longer brought pleasure. The dream had her wide awake. Although it had turned into a nightmare, it for some reason left her melancholic. As if she'd lost something important, vital perhaps.

The wooden floor was cool underneath her feet, but she didn't want her warm socks. It helped clear her head. She walked over to the kitchen table that fitted a maximum of three people. A third of its surface was covered by a messy stack of local newspaper issues and weekly ads. They conveniently hid a bunch of white envelopes. Out of sight, out of mind. Except every time she looked at the stack, she thought of the bills. She'd minimised her expenses, but there were things she couldn't live without. She'd survived, thanks to unemployment benefit paid by the state. As long as there were no big, unexpected expenses, she should manage the next months—but it was no fun.

It wasn't as if the scenery would cheer her up or that daylight would enter and brighten the room, but she parted the curtains anyway. Everything was covered in white and still gloomy. She turned on the radio on the kitchen counter, and a melancholic schlager played. The radio broadcasted mostly tedious programs, but it interrupted the perpetual silence of her home. She took the oatmeal porridge she'd put to soak the night before and shoved it in the oven of the fireplace. Not particularly filling according to her experience, but cheap and healthy.

She switched on the water kettle and grimaced at the song that came on. Too perky. Was there anything left in the world that could make her feel genuinely good? Her eyes fell upon the dog's bed.

Don't go there, she thought.

She took a glass jar from the fridge and scooped several spoons of bilberry jam onto the heated porridge. Berries were plenty and free in the forest, and she was glad she'd had the patience to pick enough to last through the winter.

The runny black preserve tasted fresh and sweet in her mouth, and it reminded her of summer. Had it been summer, she could've stepped out in her nightgown and had breakfast on the porch. She could've listened to the birds eagerly claiming their territories in preparing for new generations. Her eyes closed, imagining the sun was bright and warm, giving life to the plants and her. Then the sun wasn't warm, and it turned into a white shine as it reflected from a cold, monotone surface.

She couldn't shake the dream.

Not the pleasant part, and not the horrid part.

She was supposed to complete the unemployment status report, but she hadn't felt like it. Taking a walk earlier than usual to catch some of the scarce light was a perfect excuse for procrastinating on the bureaucracy stuff. In the forest, it was easier to pretend she didn't have problems. That she wasn't a part of the world. At least the human world.

She loved the forest.

Sini began following the path where new snow had almost covered her recent footprints. She tried to keep from thinking of where to get money, how to find a suitable job, how to manage alone… Thoughts going in circles instead of bringing solutions.

She spotted it a few metres away. A paw print.

Karo?

Her steps became slow-motion, and her mind emptied as she approached.

What had looked like a dog's paw turned out to be snow from a tree branch that had made an indentation where it had fallen. Sini shook her head. Did she really believe—even for a second—that her deceased dog would leave a paw print in the forest for her, on the path they'd walked almost every day?

Her eyes burned as she stood there, regarding the print she yearned to be Karo's. No matter how long she searched for her dog, she wouldn't see a black shape roaming the underbrush. No matter how many times she called, he wouldn't come running, only to stop and turn and head in the opposite direction.

Her dog had left her, just like the others.

Karo had been her true companion. Someone who loved her, no matter the circumstances. He hadn't cared if she'd made disastrous mistakes in her past. Losing her beloved dog had been the final blow. Without him, she was truly alone.

Sini forced herself to continue walking. As stupid as she felt, she didn't want to leave the imaginary paw print behind. Her legs were heavy. The farther she got, the more unstable her bulky boots became. She wished it was dark already so that she could pretend Karo was with her.

Stubborn and relentless, Sini progressed into the forest when the best thing would have been to return home and crawl between warm sheets. Make herself some hot cocoa, grab a bag of something crispy and salty, and watch a movie. Or just sulk.

Sini walked on. Others would've considered the snow-burdened spruces or the frosted stems of tall grass beautiful. To her, they were a reminder of how winter forced movement into silence. She preferred colour, life, and changing. Without the suffocating white cover, there would've been interesting things to look at. It was a shame her mind wasn't as still as her surroundings.

Sini almost stepped on it before she noticed it and wobbled to a halt. Another paw print. It looked authentic. So real she didn't know whether her mind was playing tricks on her.

It couldn't be real—and of course it wasn't. She turned around to look, but there was only snow and trees sticking out of it. There was no movement, no sound.

She turned back to continue walking. Too late, she realised she was about to step on the print, tried to place her foot past it, and lost her balance. She stumbled, tilted, and fell headlong. She meant to soften the impact with her hands, but they disappeared into the snow and the shrubs underneath. Landing facedown, she felt the cold on her wrists as snow poured into her gloves.

Sini rolled onto her back and became still. She might have laughed at her clumsiness if she hadn't been so miserable about the dog. She tried, and almost succeeded, but the sound leaving her lips turned into sobs.

What she'd held back for weeks, maybe months, attacked her as she'd let down her guard.

She wouldn't get through another winter.

It was the truth. She'd tried to be resilient, tried to believe and prove to herself that she indeed could survive alone in her grandmother's house. Her grandmother had lived by herself most of her life. So what if people had thought she was strange? She'd been a strong woman who'd done her own thing and seemed content with her choices. If she could do it, so could Sini. She had no other choice.

Except she wasn't her grandmother. She had nothing that resembled her resilience, wit, and knowledge. Her grandmother had wanted Sini to visit more, but Sini hadn't been keen on swapping her fun life for a very quiet week in the country. The kind of quiet that resulted from the absence of friends, TV, internet, and other vital things.

The result was that Sini would never see her grandmother again, because she'd passed away suddenly and without warning, and Sini could never ask her the questions she needed answers to. Like, why had she insisted on Sini inheriting the house and living there? If her career as a professional freestyle skier had developed according to plan, she would never— ever—have succumbed to a life in seclusion.

Fate had other plans for her. When she'd learnt of the will, there'd been only a brief moment of hesitation before she'd gratefully taken the offer. She'd thought it would be for a short time, a year max, but there she was, a couple of years later, already understanding she'd never be able to leave.

Tears welled up and began rolling down her temples. She felt the snow biting her skin with its icy teeth.

Her body was numb. She was too weak to get up.

Then again, she didn't want to. She'd lie there until winter had mercy on her, snowed upon her frozen body, and covered her up just like the bilberries and wild rosemary. After a while, the contours of her body would be hidden by the uniform winter blanket. For the first time, she wanted to join the silence. While horrified at her own fate, she felt comfort in that she'd get to be a part of the forest, melt into it. Someone might find her one day, and people might carry her remains away, but her soul would stay forever.

She wasn't supposed to be dying alone in a secluded woodland. She was supposed to be among people. She was supposed to be busy doing important things, going towards a great future with her fiancé. And she was supposed to be valued enough for people to start looking for her immediately—not weeks after they didn't hear from her.

The sobbing got louder until it erupted into violent wailing.

She was a loser, and she had her crazy thoughts to prove it. What hurt the most was that no one would miss her. When they finally found her, there would be no loved ones to mourn her. The tears wouldn't stop.

She refused to feel her body getting colder by the minute.

It was all over.

For good.

Sini let her emotions surface, and as she embraced the sadness she'd tried so hard to repress, a soothing numbness saturated her.

Tears stopped rolling, and her breath slowed down. She closed her eyes and enjoyed the silence, the long-awaited absence of thoughts. Time lost its meaning.

She was ready. She accepted her fate.

The perfect calm was broken by the cold leaking through the clothes and onto her skin. Her mind sought oblivion from the severe environment, but her body wouldn't let her lie there until hypothermia hit. She opened her eyes and was surprised at how blue the sky was.

For no reason, her gaze fell upon a small lump on a pine branch. It was a flecked brown and had eyes. Sini blinked to clear her vision. The strange creature's head was too big for its body. The roundness and the big eyes left no doubt about what it was. An owl! A tiny owl that sat motionless where the branch united with the trunk. It was watching her.

Sini had never seen an owl in the wild. They were secretive animals. Children of the night.

She smiled.

Would she scare it off if she moved? She'd be able to lie there a few minutes more, but then her brain would force her body into movement. She zoomed in on the speckled lump, not taking her eyes off it. It was so motionless she began to suspect her imagination. Maybe she was already hypothermic and hallucinating.

The dark, little square form had a perfect camouflage of deep-brown hues and white speckles that could've been big snowflakes. Only the eyes gave it away. Still, it was surreal. Magical.

She saw it move! Only a tiny bit, but it was obvious. Shivers rippled through her body. The moment was enchanted, and she wanted it to last, but she needed to get up. The little miracle looking back at her snapped her out of her death-wish mood.

Sini grimaced when her already icy hands buried into the snow as she struggled to sit upright and then roll onto her knees. The owl remained still. Perhaps the creature relied on its camouflage instead of flying away.

She leaned forwards and laboured into a crouching position. She had to get off the icing snow.

With her face tilted towards the static owl, she slowly rose to her feet. She shivered again. She hadn't dressed for standing still, let alone lying in the snow.

Sini took a step, held her breath, every second afraid she'd scare the bird off. She took another step, and it inched itself towards her along the branch.

Sini gasped, but it didn't fly off.

The bird appeared as curious about her as she was intrigued by its existence. Standing at a comfortable distance should've been enough, but Sini felt compelled to move closer. She slowly put one foot in front of the other, trying to keep steady. She observed the owl as she did her best to appear nonthreatening.

The oversized eyes followed her as she closed in on it. The head turned slightly to keep her in focus as she reached where the path was closest to the pine trunk. The little wonder looked comfortable on its high lookout spot and was probably not bothered by the cold. Sini thought of her phone. She couldn't remember if she had brought it, but she hoped to take a photo. A memory of the astonishing wildlife encounter that revived her from her spiritual breakdown.

She took off her glove and tried to open the pocket of her jacket. She couldn't get a hold of the zipper pull tab, and she had to look at it to make her numb fingers grip it and pull it down. Slipping her hand inside, she was relieved to feel the shape of the phone.

With her hand still in her pocket, Sini looked up only to see an empty branch. She spun her head in every direction to see where the owl had relocated. There was no living creature anywhere. Only the dullness of the dead landscape remained.

Stupid modern technology. Why hadn't it been enough to just stay present with the animal?

Sini brushed the snow from her clothes and headed back.

Walking home along the same path she'd taken, Sini felt emptier with each step. The encounter with the owl—as short as it had been—had made her feel alive. Walking home alone was admitting defeat. She was walking the thin path between wanting a new life with new hope, and longing to get inside, have a hot drink and a cinnamon roll, and continue like before.

If only she had options.

2 LONGING FOR CONNECTION

A soothing calm had filled Sini.

She didn't know whether it was the release she got from crying her heart out, or the surreal encounter with the tiny owl. She couldn't remember the last time she felt that happy.

Sini sat in her usual spot in front of the fireplace, wrapped in a blanket and with a steaming mug of cocoa. In fear of having another nightmare, she hadn't made a new fire. How strange the last one had been. Although she didn't understand where the dream came from, her gut contracted every time she remembered how she'd felt. She searched for a better memory.

Like so many evenings, Sini thought of her grandmother. How she'd give anything to have her comforting company. Satu might not have been the most expressive person—her presence was rather enigmatic—but she never said a harsh word to Sini or made her feel unworthy. In retrospect, she couldn't understand why she hadn't stayed with her grandmother more often.

The room looked the same as twenty years ago. The chair was the same, and the pillow had always been there. Together with the visual cues, sipping the warm cocoa transported her back to her childhood. If it hadn't been so quiet, she could've imagined her grandmother standing in the kitchen, preparing supper. She'd thought it was her own decision to stay away, but re-examining her reasons, she realised her parents hadn't encouraged her to visit either. It was as though they didn't approve of her grandmother's way of living.

Sini turned and glanced at the writing desk Satu had used for her studies. She hadn't been interested in her grandmother's study subjects before, and she couldn't find a good explanation why. A spark of curiosity struck her, and she stood to walk over to the desk. It had seen better days, and she couldn't date it. She opened the top drawer and found stationary. Pencils, erasers, a wooden ruler... She tried to open the one underneath, but it was as stuck as it had always been.

She pulled at the wooden handle, but it didn't budge. Perhaps the wood had swelled. The stuck drawers hadn't bothered her before, but at that moment, she longed to find something that would shine a light on the mystery that was her grandmother. She wanted to understand the spirit that still dwelled in her home.

She pulled out the chair and sat down. Sitting at the desk felt comfortable. A thought was about to enter her mind, but she couldn't catch it. It might have been the memory of her grandmother. Where did she keep her notebooks? Sini hadn't searched for them, but she didn't remember stumbling upon them either.

She pulled at the bottom drawer, but it was as stuck as the other one. There was no lock that prevented it from opening. She shrugged and attempted to get up, but putting her palms onto the desk top to steady herself made her hesitate. Touching the worn surface of the table, she saw generations of ancestors sitting by it, just like she was. The original colour appeared a dark walnut that suggested value, although the design was as plain as it gets. The only engravings were the lighter-coloured lines and dents spread across the top surface. For all that she knew, it might be ancient.

Sini went to bed early. The forest escapade had her worn out. Despite losing the connection to the ethereal owl and not getting anywhere with strengthening the bond to her grandmother, she was pleased she hadn't needed her usual sugar fix.

If only she'd known Satu better. Not only as her loving grandmother, but as a person.

What had made her so *different?*

The warm air was soothing on her lungs, like a sweet caress on her skin.

She was on her path again, but the ground was a mosaic of dark green and light brown. A deep sigh of relief left her body tingling. Her appreciation of sunlight and warmth rose to a new level. Her feet were weightless while her thin clothes provided freedom of movement.

She inhaled the sweet air scented by pine needles. White flowers covered the ground, and she was about to bow down and pick one when she spotted movement.

A shadow progressed downhill through the knee-high vegetation, closing in on her.

Could it be? It couldn't be…

Karo!

Her face morphed into a gigantic smile. Summer was complete.

Her eyes locked onto the dog bouncing through the underbrush. He wasn't dead after all! He'd just gone missing.

Karo pranced up to her, wagging his tail. He was as happy as she was, but he was always like that—energised. Sini grabbed at his fur. Tears welled up at the familiar sensation of coarse yet soft hair and loose skin. Everything was as it should be.

She was about to tell him how much she'd missed him when he started whining. His movements became agitated. She didn't know if he was in pain or afraid. He'd never been like that before. His bark made her jump.

"What is it?"

The dog glanced at her, only to continue pacing back and forth while making that high-pitched sound. She tried to talk him out of it, but her words produced no effect. She found it hard to breathe as anxiety washed over her. What if there was something wrong with him? She couldn't bear it if something happened to him when he'd returned to her at last.

"Karo! Come here!"

She watched as he ran away.

She wanted to run after him, but her legs didn't obey.

"Karo!"

Tears rolled down her face as she realised he hadn't come back to her.

Reality hit her in an instant.

The iridescent numbers on the clock told her it was nine. In the morning. It was still dark, and it could just as well be evening. She wasn't hot, and she was certainly not sweating.

Was it a nightmare? It had all the ingredients.

Sini rubbed her eyes and felt the moisture of her tears.

God, how she missed him.

She didn't need a nightmarish dream as a reminder of her loss. Turning on the bedside lamp gave some relief from the darkness, but her attempt to get up failed. She turned to her side and grabbed the other pillow. Clasping it to her chest, she squeezed out the remaining tears until she was empty. Hollow.

She wished her dream had been true, that he'd only gotten lost in the forest and would return to her. There was no amount of imagination that could erase the memory of her watching him take his last breath. Although, she was thankful for seeing him again, even if it wasn't for real.

She closed her eyes and reimagined the part where he ran to her and was excited to see her. If only she could have more dreams of him. It had been so real.

Sini sighed as she turned onto her back. If only…

Sini had heard of people who had lucid dreams by will. They knew they were in a dream, and instead of it hijacking them, they were able to direct it. Pick only the fun parts.

Those dreams might be entertaining, but she hadn't been motivated to learn more. But that was then.

What if she could dream about Karo every night and they could go for walks like they used to do? He'd be happy, and she'd be happy. She could build him a doghouse and pretend he spent the day outside. That way, she wouldn't wonder why he wasn't begging for food in the kitchen or lying in his bed.

Sini ran her fingers through her hair. She was going mad. She leaned forwards in her chair and continued eating her lunch. Once in a while, the thick and sticky green mess was fine, as long as it was accompanied by mustard. Pea soup. Another cheap and tasteless meal she'd had too many of—but why would she need anything fancier?

She might give lucid dreaming a try, though. She'd take an afternoon nap and see what happened.

Sini spent the afternoon scrolling the internet.

She was running out of time searching for valid information. Her nap time was fast approaching, but what she'd found was confusing and contradictory, and she wasn't convinced. Everyone seemed to have their own method for entering a lucid dream. Someone recommended trying to fall asleep with your eyes open; another said a mantra about being aware of dreams as they fell asleep. Some did it by inducing a state of sleep paralysis. Then there was setting the alarm to wake up earlier than usual and trying to keep the mind awake while the body reentered a sleeping state. Apparently, keeping a dream journal was important. Meditating people experienced more lucid dreams.

It sounded like a lot of effort. How was she supposed to know which one to try, which one would work? If she lay there doubting, she'd fail. What she needed was calm and conviction.

Sini leaned back in her chair and rolled her shoulders. She wondered about trying just that—getting as relaxed as possible without entering sleep.

She poured another cup of mint tea from the pot. No caffeine or sugar—best to be safe.

After hours hunched on her elbows in front of the computer, Sini turned it off with a sigh. Usually, she had more luck, but convincing facts and lucid dreaming didn't go hand in hand. She knew one couldn't be sure of what was reliable on the internet, but all that effort felt like a waste. Maybe she should just improvise and give it a go?

She wasn't convinced of her own abilities, either. Meditation had never been part of her life, but…training of the mind was common practice among athletes. She still failed to see how controlling her thoughts would help her direct her dreams. Her dreams were most often a mishmash of weird scenes that lacked logic. Strangers and strange places.

Sini stood and stretched her arms towards the ceiling. Her gaze fell upon her grandmother's bookshelf. Reading a book might help her get drowsy, as she wasn't used to taking naps.

Most of the books in the collection were uninspiring and no doubt from one of those book-of-the-month clubs. Stories that lacked adventure, passion, or a way to escape. As a child, she'd read and liked the old tales written from the point of view of wild animals.

That day, she welcomed the calming effect of outdated and down-to-earth stories. As she walked up to the narrow shelf that reached all the way to the ceiling, she felt compelled to search the row of books above her. She let her fingers run along their spines until her hand halted. The title of the book was as uninteresting as she'd expected, but she pulled it out, nonetheless.

Sini sat down at the old desk and flipped the book open. The title page read *The Journey of the Shaman*. She checked the cover again. *The Unintentional Engagement*. She pulled off the dust jacket. The spine had *The Journey of the Shaman* embossed in silver.

She flipped through the pages. The book appeared to be written by someone who called himself a shaman. Weren't those figures from the past? From the time of pagan religion?

Perhaps there were more camouflaged books? She returned to the shelf and picked one. Dust jacket and insides matched. The second one, the same. She pulled out at least ten books—including ones from that particular shelf—but they were all matches.

Sini went back to the book that lay open on the desk and rechecked the cover and the text. How could she have picked the odd one? Was the cover mix-up a mistake, or was there a reason her grandmother had wanted to hide it? Her fingers smoothed the yellowed pages. It was possible her grandmother camouflaged the book from the likes of her parents, knowing they showed no tolerance for unconventional practices. Even when it was only some forgotten custom.

For no other reason than curiosity of why the book appeared special to her grandmother, Sini skimmed through the first chapter. The shaman was a mediator between his world and the otherworld. He'd travel to the otherworld in spirit. He'd have animals as helper spirits, and they'd provide both guidance and protection when travelling through the other realm. To use the abilities of the helper spirits, the shaman would morph into the animal by imitating their behaviour and body postures. Sini didn't believe someone was able to become the spirit of an animal, but the possibility of summoning one got her attention. The shaman entered a trance and summoned his helper spirits by singing and beating his drum.

Apparently, the shaman also had to meditate, as he needed full control of his mind. To be able to focus, he had to learn how to relax and free himself from the reality of his surroundings.

Sini didn't know where her dog's spirit was. She believed it had carried on in some kind of afterlife, just like human souls, but she hadn't given it deeper thought. Was Karo in the otherworld? Was that a place she wished for him? Did it make a difference if the spirit was in heaven or the otherworld when trying to get into contact?

There was an even more important question: would he want to come to her if she called on him? The possibility of getting direct contact with her dog's spirit started to sound a lot more enticing than pretence through lucid dreaming.

Sini shook her head and smiled.

A few years ago, she'd never have imagined she'd one day plan how to get together with the spirit of a dead animal. But the way things were, it didn't matter if she was considered nuts. No one would come knocking on her door and ask what she was up to.

Lying down on the bed, she closed her eyes. Of everything she'd read that day, the teachings in the mystery book appeared most sensible in their simplicity. To calm the mind and take charge of the frenzied horse that was an analogy for runaway thoughts. To sit down and steady the breathing.

Breath by breath, she did her best to sense the flow of air through her nose and into her lungs. Then how the air flowed back up and out. In through the nose and down into the lungs. Out through the nose. The inwards and outwards motion began to slow down.

She observed what it felt like when her body was motionless, except for the slow heaving of her belly. Thoughts on lack of money and unused potential kept entering her mind. She knew they'd come and that she needn't worry. The calmer her body became, the more she witnessed the flow of both essential and mundane reflections enter and leave her consciousness. To make them go away, she forced her breathing to slow down further until it was all she noticed.

A rare but welcomed calm entered her.

Even though she'd soon fallen asleep on the first day of relaxation practice, she regarded it as a success.

Lying down in the afternoon and thinking only of her breathing soon got her hooked. It was the only moment she got respite from thoughts that always circled around the usual subjects. She had permission not to think of how she should fix her life. Every day, she became better at silencing her mind, but as soon as she visualised Karo in front of her, she got emotional. Even the good memories kept her painfully aware of her surroundings. The current situation.

She wasn't any closer to connecting with Karo, but it calmed her mind better than anything else. No medical substances or specialist guidance needed, just slow and deliberate breathing. That was the only reason she continued practicing.

It didn't matter that she eventually fell asleep. What mattered was that she got sleep without messy dreaming. Her mind wasn't as busy as it used to be, but it was still difficult to stop thinking. She visualised putting the thoughts of financial lack and unwanted seclusion on an imaginary boat that floated them away.

Waking up was a bit stirring. Sometimes, she didn't remember whether it was morning or evening. If she parted the curtain, it would be either very grey or pitch-black outside. No streetlamps or light from neighbours pierced the darkness. She loved the peace but still didn't understand why someone would build a house in the middle of nowhere.

Sini snapped back to reality. In her eagerness to get her relax-nap, she'd forgotten to feed the birds. Better do it at once instead of the next morning.

The birds had learnt to rely on her for their energy intake, and she wouldn't forgive herself if they fell ill because of her. Once someone started feeding birds in winter, they were obligated to continue until spring, when natural food was again available. Everyone knew that. Sometimes, she wondered how she'd afford to buy the seeds, but having someone rely on her made her useful. Even if it was only a few birds, she wanted to be needed.

Sini put on warm clothes and stepped into the fresh air. She looked up at the breath-taking night sky. Thousands of stars gleamed against the black background, and her eyes set on the Big Dipper. Looking at the familiar pattern of the seven stars made her feel like she belonged. The constellation of the arctic regions was one constant she could always rely on.

The light seeping through her windows was enough to help her find her way. She took the roof off the bird feeder and poured in the seed mix. The birds would be there when she had breakfast, and she'd watch them dive from a nearby tree, hop along the edge to the best seeds. Push away the others if they were audacious enough. Pick a seed and soar up onto a branch and commence peeling. Some species preferred to feed on the snow-covered ground. Great tits, blue tits, crested tits, willow tits, bullfinches, siskins, greenfinches, the occasional noisy jay. Tuft-eared squirrels as well. Maybe she fed the animals because she was desperate for company. Maybe helping them wasn't as altruistic as she thought.

She put the roof back onto the feeder and looked inside her lit but empty kitchen. When was the last time she spoke to a human being? She'd made a short phone call a couple of weeks ago to ask for the price of firewood and make a small order. She saw people when she went shopping for necessities, but that probably didn't count for meaningful social interactions either. When had she had an actual encounter with a friend?

Not days, weeks, or months ago. When Sini couldn't recall the occasion, she turned to the stars again. In her past life, she never needed to ponder when she'd seen a friend the last time. She saw them every day.

Sini took a deep breath and pushed away the thought. It was so dark. And quiet. And she loved it.

She didn't hate the dark.

She just wished it wasn't dark all the time.

3 REMEMBERED BY NO ONE

"Happy New Year."

Her greeting sounded as flat as she felt inside. She was making up for not answering the phone on Christmas.

Her mother cleared her throat. She didn't pretend to be cheery either.

Sini rolled her eyes.

"How long are you going to stay there?"

Sini sighed in response to the comment she'd learnt to expect.

"Don't get angry. I'm just thinking of your best interests."

Right. "I live here now, remember?" She fought to keep her voice neutral.

"You were only supposed to stay for a while. With the new year, you could make a fresh start, prepare to come back to where you belong. Find a good job and—"

"Well, I'm staying for the moment," Sini stated in a tone of pure matter of fact. Her mother's lack of sensitivity to the occasion was no surprise.

As expected, her mother wouldn't give in. Sini heard her take a deep breath for another round of trying to get the message through.

"Tell Dad Happy New Year from me." Sini wanted to end the call before the rest of the evergreen subjects came up. *You could still fix things… You should try to make an effort to get back in touch with people… Start looking for…*

Her mother might have sounded sincere and well-meaning, but she only wanted for Sini not to cast a shadow over their squeaky-clean, very ordinary life. *Behave like decent people…*

"Bye." She could've hung up on her mother and cut the impending monologue without warning, but it was New Year's Eve.

Jeez, why was the last tie she had left to society an impossible one?

Content at having avoided the depressing rant, Sini embraced the silence. She ignored the fact of how pathetic it was that her only phone call on New Year's Eve had been a couple of minutes long.

Her parents were socially awkward, and they didn't realize it. They had no clue. Nothing had changed. In fact, Sini had noticed it got worse with the years, and she avoided them as much as possible.

Her mother's concern for her current situation wasn't genuine. Her parents had made it clear from the start that heading to her grandmother's house was a mistake. To Sini, the relocation had been a blessing. Her athletic career had crashed, but moving back south was no more enticing than it had been before her life as she knew it ended. To live up north where they had snow throughout winter was a prerequisite for a mogul skier, but just as important was putting distance between them and herself. Having to fight them on her decision had only widened the split.

She hadn't told her mother there was nothing better waiting for her down there. At least in her grandmother's house, she could be awkward on her own.

Yes, she was odd too, but she didn't meddle in other people's lives. Her mother wasn't concerned about her well-being. She feared Sini would end up like her grandmother. They'd never gotten along. Her mother's soul had the depth of a frying pan, and Sini would rather be crazy than cold like her.

She walked to the vestibule and grabbed the bottle of red wine put there to chill. It was a gift from a friend a few years ago, but she'd gotten satisfaction in withstanding opening it and getting drunk by herself.

The truth was, she suspected drinking a bottle of wine now and then could become a habit. She didn't want that for herself. She was messed up enough without it. Besides, there was another way of getting her fix, one that was totally accepted by society.

With a glass of appropriately chilled twelve-year-old Tuscan red wine, Sini sat down in her armchair in front of the fireplace.

To make it more festive, she'd loaded a mix of crackling pine and birch. Midnight was closing in, and she thought she heard faint blasts.

It wasn't like the New Years of the past, though. In her mind's eye, she relived the pompous, expensive fireworks up north where she and her colleagues had trained. It had, for the most part, been winter sports centres with tourists and Finns who could afford spending holidays there with their families. As long as there was snow, she was always surrounded by like-minded people.

She imagined leaning into a friend as they, wide-eyed, watched the sparkling, colourful, brilliant stars exploding into intricate, surprising patterns.

Sini and her colleagues formed a group of their own within the professional institute. They became tight as they spent both working hours and leisure time together. The sense of community made training much more fun and rewarding. She'd belonged there.

It had been paradise, and then there'd been the incident that made the others expel her. Without warning, everything could be lost…changed forever. Although she tried not to think about it anymore, it still hurt. She'd never get over it. Her life had been transformed—but not for the better.

A vision of her hugging everyone around her and wishing them a Happy New Year had her swallow a big sip of the soothing wine.

"Happy New Year." She raised the glass and smiled. "To you, my friends. Wherever you are."

Despite everything, she didn't resent or hate them. She wished them well—just without her in their lives.

Maybe it was all for the good. An athlete's career couldn't last long, anyway.

She laughed out loud. Like she was so much better off as she was now. Alone, jobless, and out of everyone's way.

She had to go where she didn't want to.

The memories of Martin.

The boyfriend with whom she'd planned her entire future.

He came from the neighbouring country. They didn't share a language, but using English had become easy, and it was common in the resorts, anyway.

Martin was a lot more outgoing and extroverted than she was, but his lively character brought out her social side. She'd been in love with him through the years, but what split them apart had made her doubt she knew people at all. One day, he'd changed into a different person. A person she didn't know. Someone she'd forever lost the connection to.

Sini got up and poured another glass in the vestibule. The bottle wouldn't last through the night if she kept recalling the past.

What the heck—it wasn't like she wanted to keep the bottle for long. She never drank. It was New Year's. Another one alone.

And when she said alone, she meant totally alone. No one else there but her. She hadn't heard any distant fireworks. The world could've ended without her knowing.

She opened the door to peek out into the pitch-black, hoping to see something lighting up the sky in the distance. Nothing pierced the dark. Not a flicker.

The thought hit her that Karo might be out there, all alone, just like her.

What if Karo's spirit still roamed the forest? She envisioned the perfect paw prints placed in the middle of the path. If there was a way to connect with his spirit—not just dream it—the best place for it would be the forest.

Sini sat down again and pulled her legs up in the chair. Standing in the doorway had made her chilly, and she wrapped herself in the blanket.

Back to Martin. Dark-brown hair, hazel eyes. Gorgeously cute athlete. Driven, talented, popular. She'd been a catch in his eyes, too. Not the traditional beauty, but exotic. Dark, smooth shoulder-length hair and a face that was the opposite to the soft, fair features typical of the Nordic countries. Dark eyebrows accentuated her ever-thoughtful eyes. Everyone complimented her high cheekbones, but she wished her nose had been shorter. She got that from her father.

Her most stunning feature was her crystal-blue eyes that contrasted against her darkness. People would often get caught in them.

Sini had also been driven in her career. She'd loved training, loved the theoretical side of it, and had loved competing. But she'd left all that behind.

Not one of her friends had wished her a better new year. For all that she knew, she was on nobody's mind.

She'd been erased.

Becoming aware of tears pooling in her eyes, Sini put a stop to the painful memories. Once joyful events had turned into scenes too hard to think of. She got up from her chair, moved on wobbly feet to the computer, and put down the half-empty glass beside it. She did what she always did when things got too difficult to cope with.

She turned on the computer and opened the folder with her escape plan. Eyeing through the thumbnails, she clicked open her favourites. Pictures of white beaches and turquoise water appeared on the screen. Leaning forwards and pressing the wineglass to her lips, she soaked in the details. The alcohol appeared to make the scenery a bit more three-dimensional than usual.

Sini sighed and went for the bottle. A third of the wine left. Better drink it all, since she wasn't going to continue drinking the day after. The soles of her feet were numb as she returned to the computer. The wine had gone to her head.

She had three destinations. The first was the almost affordable one. Same continent, cheaper living, but still kind of close to home. The second one was something she couldn't afford for several years, but if she worked and saved brutally, it was possible, in theory. Then the last one, the fantasy destination. If she made it there, there'd be nothing reminding her of home. No winter season, few tourists, a culture and way of life far from hers.

With her eyes closed, Sini sipped on the last glass and felt the warmth on her skin, the scent of ocean in her nose, and the warm sand between her toes. Goodbye, cold winters and bland summers; goodbye, ex-friends and boyfriends. Goodbye, lousy family. Cutting the ties to her former and current life would be easy. She had no one that relied on her. Her dog was dead, and the birds would learn to manage without her sunflower seeds.

Goodbye, broken dreams.

Sini tried not to get her hopes up as she walked the trail from her house to the forest.

It had been a calm day with a blue sky. It might have been beautiful if the sun had reached over the treetops. She'd wanted to absorb the light that was offered, but it had been too still, too quiet outside. As if everyone apart from herself had accepted the paralysing grip of winter, the all-encompassing snow cover, and stifling cold air.

Sini had wanted to wait until evening before heading to the forest. She thought she'd have a greater chance to succeed if circumstances were as normal as possible. It also seemed logical that a connection to someone in the spirit world would be easier to create in the dark. The drunken inspiration she'd gotten on New Year's Eve had stayed with her, sounding more plausible the more she considered it.

She didn't want complete darkness, as she preferred not to turn on the headlamp. Although she wasn't afraid of the dark, trying to connect with someone from another realm that lurked beyond the light of a simple lamp was a little stirring. But other than that, she felt eager. Hopeful even.

She had to at least try.

The tall snow-covered treetops and the frosted thicket of smaller trees enveloped the forest into a world of its own. In daylight, it still looked inviting. She took comfort in the thought that she'd never experienced anything threatening in the forest, not even when dark.

New snow had fallen since her last walk. Once again, her boot prints had been covered up. Would it ever stop coming? It was only a little into the new year and still the beginning of winter, but there was already enough snow. The more it snowed, the more difficult it would be for her to advance in the terrain.

She crossed the ditch and entered the silent realm of trees. As she ascended onto the path, she went to the left as usual. She dragged her feet a little to scoop away the loose snow. It was all she could do to keep the narrow passage clear.

The woodland looked as uneventful as before. Lifeless. Was that good or bad? She had no idea what she was doing. She'd have to start somewhere.

Her heart started picking up the pace.

Great. She was supposed to be calm. Had her practice been any use? Could she control her mind when not in the safety of her bed? Walking in snow was laborious, and even though her physical condition was above average, she'd never be able to mimic that calm out in the woods.

First, she needed to silence her mind. Looking only at the fuzzy trail in front of her, Sini let her doubting thoughts come to her without analysing or judging. She gave them space and then released them onto the silent imaginary boat that carried them away. She trusted the steady walking and scarce sensory stimuli would calm her.

Five minutes into the forest, Sini felt better. She was careful not to expect too much. It was her first attempt. If her expectations were too high, she could never succeed.

She thought of Karo.

Her beautiful black dog. His slender but powerful figure. More than knee-high with a short but thick fur that was waterproof. He was working breed, created for the purpose of retrieving the prey of the hunter. Jumping ditches and managing the dense underbrush of the forest and the fields posed no challenge to him.

His energy never ran out. Always eager to explore. The scout of the pack. He'd always follow her command—unless more interesting things beckoned his attention. She'd been right. Their forest was the only place she managed to think of him without falling apart.

Loyal. Loving. Accepting.

Looking back at their time together, Sini was comforted by the thought that there'd once been someone who'd loved her unconditionally. The dog didn't care about her accomplishments, her race time, or if she'd made money. Food, shelter, adventures, and a pack were all he wished for, and she could provide that.

Sini forced herself to picture only the happy times, when everything was as it should be. He wouldn't want to come to her if she thought of him as the one who got sick and weak.

She couldn't resist looking around. Would he appear in his earthly shape like in her dream? If she was only able to sense him as spirit—what would it be like?

She needed to be very quiet.

After a quarter of an hour of walking, Sini resented the sound her boots made in the crunching snow. Otherwise, it was silent. Birds didn't sing in winter. Foraging tits would be resting while dark. Furthermore, the snow cover muted sounds.

It was getting darker fast. Trees and bushes turned into indistinct shadows. Looking around again, her eyes caught a dark shape that could've been her dog. She squinted at the static shadow that probably was the upright roots of a fallen tree.

Sini halted.

She breathed in cold air through her nose, kept it in her lungs for a few seconds, and then released it as slowly as she could. She paused and then slowly breathed in again. With her eyes closed, she calmed the beating of her heart and emptied her mind. It got easier.

She listened. She felt. She smelled.

Nothing.

She continued for a while, but nothing happened.

No choice but to resume walking.

A few minutes of standing still allowed the chill to sneak through her clothes. There was no chance she'd be able to stand there long enough—maybe fifteen to thirty minutes? She needed more clothes. Perhaps a warm quilt—or heck, even a sleeping bag. She was no longer able to fathom why she'd once liked the cold.

Sini forced herself not to regress to her life a few years back. She was trying to connect to her dog's spirit, and she wouldn't let disappointment contaminate her peace with memories that only brought her pain. She took a few deep breaths and then began humming a nameless tune in a low voice.

Behind the trees in the distance, the familiar faint light from her house flickered. It looked like someone might be there waiting for her to get home, and at that moment, she wished it were true. The desire for someone to be there with her caught her off guard, but she allowed herself to feel it.

A presence.

Something.

Was there with her.

She slowed down but was afraid to look.

Was it a moving shadow she saw from the corner of her eye? Her forearms knotted. She couldn't decide if it was fear or excitement. Probably both.

Karo? she thought carefully. Something moved in the periphery of her vision—she was sure of it. She wanted to believe.

She demanded her breathing to remain composed, forced her mind not to judge. It didn't feel malevolent—although she was alone, where no one could help her, and in the dark... She'd seen too many horror movies. Her dog was good, and it would be good as a spirit, too. There was no reason for her to fear it.

Sini walked on, afraid to scare the shadow away if she stopped.

Without realizing, she picked up the simple tune again.

She wanted nothing more than to believe she sensed a presence, so she did. As she kept walking, she felt it right behind her, and then more to the left.

Empty mind... Empty mind...

Nearing the end of the path made her uneasy. She knew exactly how many nooks and bends remained. She wanted to stop, to stay with the sensation of the shadow, but it was too cold, too dark.

It was a good thing. She'd sensed something. Finally.

Still, having to leave the forest brought back the anxiety.

Her sensible side told her that staying would force the encounter into something premature. It was so important to her. She'd go home and return the next afternoon. And she'd try again.

The belief that she had—on some level—connected with Karo's spirit form was reinforced when she suddenly stopped sensing it.

Sini grinned as she exited the overwhelming shadow of the forest and walked across the field.

She'd succeeded! She didn't know what would become of it, but she was determined to try again. Even though there'd only been a vague impression of a connection, it brought her comfort.

Like every other evening, Sini shook off snow from her boots and clothes, stepped inside, and placed her coat, mittens, and hat in a warm and airy place. What had changed was the smile on her face. A cup of hot cocoa would feel so good. She wanted to do something fun.

Sini chuckled. Something fun. When was the last time she'd wanted fun?

When she couldn't recall, she thought she might suffer from depression. It was so common, and under her circumstances, it would be a miracle if she wasn't diagnosed with it. But her getting a proper name for her condition didn't matter. She wasn't a burden to society. She didn't have a job to mess up. Although finding one was—now and then—on the agenda.

While waiting for the water to boil, Sini turned on the computer. It was a little outdated already, but it served its purpose. It was sufficient for keeping up with the world. And drawing. Her drawing software was also dated, but it served its purpose as well. She wasn't a real artist anyway.

She put down the huge, ugly mug beside the screen and sat down. The sweet scent of chocolate filled her nose as she brought the mug to her lips and sipped on the hot and satiating liquid.

For the first time in ages, she felt like drawing. She hadn't opened the software since…Karo had gotten ill. Then she'd cared for him and then… After he passed, she hadn't wanted to draw.

Moving the digital pen in lazy circles, she thought of the shadow in the forest and then the onyx shape of her dog. Lines and circles began constructing the contours of an animal. The legs were Karo's, but the hunch of the back suggested a feral form. The round shape of the eyes was his, but she felt compelled to make them a more vibrant colour than walnut.

Sini saved the work and started a new one. Kind but keen eyes, the swirl of fur on the shoulders, the slender but eager tail.

Tears stained her cheeks, but they were tears of appreciation and acknowledgement.

Her heart flooded with emotions she hadn't been able to face since that day he was no longer. The images helped her remember the good times without breaking. She'd done something for him. Remembered him in a positive way.

She sat with that awareness. Drawing made her happy. Drawing what she loved made her happy.

The combination of being outdoors in the fresh air, having the hot cocoa fill her with warmth, and getting back to drawing again was satisfying. A perfect medicine.

She had to admit it had been a good day.

When Sini parted the curtain on her kitchen window the next morning, she felt like the little boy in the beloved animation about the snowman.

Instead of having the chance of another adventure together, he'd found the snowman melted.

Snowflakes weren't falling, but whisked in all directions, as if by an infuriated winter deity. Sini thought she was being punished for playing with spirits and told to stay home. She leaned in closer to get a look at the ground. It was worse than she thought.

There was no time to panic. Or have breakfast. Rushing to the closet to find her clothes, she tried to recall whether there was enough fuel in the tractor. By the thickness of the new snow, it had been coming through the night. If she didn't act at once, it would get thicker by the hour. With such a violent wind, it would be crammed against walls and into things. At least her car stood in the garage.

Wading through the thick snow across the yard was a struggle. The snow on the ground was dense due to near-plus degrees, and she had to shield her eyes from the bombarding flakes. When she got to the old barn with the big hinge door, she was already wet underneath her clothes. It was a huge relief the tractor was clean and dry inside the shelter, but she had to use all her strength and some more to push the door open.

Every minute counted. The little tractor from the sixties didn't start at the first or second attempt. The old technology wasn't always reliable—but easy to fix if needed. Knowing it had always worked before gave her faith. She knew she should've preheated the engine, but she didn't have time.

Please…please… Sini turned the key once more. The engine jumped with a cough into a rough rumble, and she waited for the sound to smoothen before she put it in gear and pressed down the pedal. As the vintage vehicle bravely rolled out from the shelter, Sini braced herself for what lay ahead. Snow already flooded inside, and the wind grabbed at her head as she steered right.

She began at the entrance to the yard, as clearing the way for the car had highest priority. Handling the tractor and the blade demanded full focus, as she didn't want to cause damage to any structures, but she was satisfied at the outcome. Scooping away the snow wasn't as effective as it would be with a modern tractor, of course, but a hundred times better than doing it by hand. As she continued down the driveway, she didn't wish the tractor was equipped with a solid cabin rather than a rollbar to protect her from the weather. Instead, she wished she were in that faraway place where it never snowed.

When Sini got back inside the house, her clothes were soaked. She'd been at it for hours, as she'd taken care of the garden as well with the human-powered snow scoop. It was an impossible mission, but it must be done. She should've been cold, but the physical strain accompanied by teeth-clenching rage had kept her warm. If she'd ever wished she had a partner to do the snow clearing instead of her…

After pulling off the dripping clothes and grabbing a handful of cold meatballs from the fridge, Sini lay down on the bed and covered herself. She swore it was the last time—the last winter—she'd need to spend her whole day fighting the snow. She had no strength left to go to the forest—and even if she did—she wouldn't get through the snow barrier.

Squeezing her eyes shut, she was too tired to think about the possibility that she wouldn't be able to go back until the snow melted in spring.

4 WHO'S THERE?

A week had passed since her first encounter with the presence.

Being back in the forest was a miracle. She'd wasted a day recuperating, waiting for someone to clear out the road, and mourning the forest being closed off from her. She'd phoned the number that her grandmother had pinned to the little notice board in the hall, but no one had answered. She'd always assumed it belonged to a neighbour, and she wanted to know who was responsible for ploughing the roads in the area. They must have known roads were snowed in everywhere and that people needed to at least get to the grocery store. But it was possible no one knew the house was still inhabited.

The second day, when the shoulder pain relented and her hands no longer trembled, she'd taken the snow shovel and gone to the garden. The situation was as bad as she'd feared. The only way she'd get access to the forest was to shovel the snow from every single step she wanted to take. The snow wasn't loose or light, but it could've been worse.

It had taken days. Several hours a day. The more she shovelled, the more tired she got, but the further she got, the less she felt able to give up. She didn't exactly have more important things to do. The further she advanced into the forest, the more it felt like life and death to be able to walk her path again. To her relief, some parts of the wood hadn't been equally affected, and she'd used her feet to clear the way.

If no one cleared the road in a couple of days, she'd have to call the municipality. She'd get by a little longer if she used up the canned soup and meat as well. She needed to buy more and stock up, but the thought of someone invading her private space—even if she had no ownership of the road—had her anxious. The notion that no one could reach her was comforting—which in turn was disturbing.

The laborious and nearly impossible mission of clearing out the snow had produced an unexpected benefit. After hours of fretting over everything wrong with her life, her mind had cleared, and the only thing that was left was her, the shovel, and the snow. She'd learnt what it truly felt like without thoughts.

Returning to the forest without her shovel had been pure freedom. She hadn't missed a day. Knowing how incredibly lucky she was to be back in her safe place, she'd focused on strengthening the connection. There were days when she could clearly feel it, and then there were days when she was more imagining it.

Sini put her gloves back on. The temperature was mild, and there was a looming threat of more snowfall. The white cover was more uniform than before, and the forest would've been beautiful in somebody else's eyes. She walked on.

She'd come to believe that the strength of her perception strongly correlated with her ability to stay focused. Focused meant the lack of strong emotions and staying present. That, in turn, mostly correlated with how well she'd slept, but also with how deep her desire was to connect.

The more she wanted, the weaker the connection seemed.

It was contradictory, and it felt unfair. Her desire to be with her dog again was the driving force. How could she then pretend it wasn't important? Crucial even?

But as the days passed, she more and more accepted what was.

She reminded herself to be thankful for every breadcrumb she was handed. And she felt better, after all.

Walks were no longer lonely. She laughed at her thought. All was well, as she had the company of a shadow!

Sini felt light on her feet when the shadow flickered right beside her.

Her breath caught.

She could feel her heart flip.

That was no dog! Spirit or not, her dog wasn't taller than her and didn't stand upright. Like a bear.

A busy mixture of disappointment, fear, success, and exhilaration filled her at once. Then her mind went blank.

She walked on, pretending not to have seen anything. She should've been afraid of the shadow, but she was more afraid it would vanish.

She could still sense it.

She kept walking.

Her skin was chilly under all the layers of clothes despite dressing warm enough to be able to stand still for a while.

She should've been more cautious. But the goosebumps were born of excitement, not fear.

She noticed it again. Yes, that was not her dog… The sensation was stronger than ever, and she was certain it had never been the dog.

For a reason she couldn't understand, it being something else—not her beloved Karo—thrilled her.

A sound, a quiet monotone but soothing melody, reached her ears.

She was humming to herself again.

Apparently, singing calmed her down.

She felt like she was turning into her grandmother. Stubborn and motivated by unexplainable things.

That night, Sini dreamt nonstop of creatures in the forest grabbing at her. She thought it was her own fault for playing with invisible forces she knew nothing about. Why did she put herself in danger? But she couldn't stay away. As frightening as the violent pull of the strange beings was on her, she was mesmerized, weirdly enchanted by them.

They pleaded with her, and then they threatened her. They tried to drag her into a black hole, darker than the forest itself.

She had no clue what they were or what they wanted from her. On one hand, she wanted to be there with them, but on the other, she wanted to be left in peace.

When morning came, the mood from the vivid dreams stayed with her.

She unwound the forest scene, the one that was the source of her nightmares. What had she really seen? Why had she thought it wasn't her dog? Karo's spirit could've taken another form than of a dog—right?

It was something she'd sensed. She'd just known.

The unease provoked by the nightmarish dreams slowly dissipated as the morning progressed and light again ruled on Earth. But with the clearing day, her experience from the forest became more a thought than a memory. Had she actually seen anything? Had she sensed a sentient presence, or was it pure desperation? Was her need to justify any meaning in her life so strong?

The more she tried to convince herself she *had* sensed something, the more absurd the whole thing sounded.

As the pale yellow of the sky—the only proof the sun still existed—disappeared and the world was turning into a shadow again, Sini felt hope return. She cooked her meat stew with joy, washed the dishes singing an optimistic tune. She put clothes in the washing machine and sorted the laundry. All while glancing at the clock every ten minutes.

If she was in her right mind, she wouldn't continue playing with spirits from another realm. She was on her own and unprotected. She had no idea how to even interact with spirits, let alone on a safe level. The subject had never interested her, and not even as a teenager had she been into ghost stories— and even less, horror. She had the nightmares to prove she was treading forbidden territory.

Sini glanced at the jacket hanging next to the door and the boots neatly placed underneath. A shiver cut through her body at the thought of potential danger lurking in the darkness of the forest. She couldn't wait to go back.

As the perfect moment to go out struck, Sini began dressing. Her hands fumbled with the zipper. She wasn't afraid. She was excited.

And that had her worried.

Although the days were growing longer, Sini spent more and more time in the dusk. Maybe she wouldn't need the gloomy atmosphere for connection, but she still held the belief spirits roamed the night. Would a shadow be visible in light?

The sky was a slate grey again. She feared more snow would start gushing down any minute. She'd worked so hard to keep the forest accessible, and she needed to find out. She needed to get confirmation that the shadow was real and that it wasn't a…bad thing. That the dream had just been a normal reaction to an unfamiliar and unexplainable experience, not a warning or premonition.

It felt different, though. She couldn't relax into it. She tried counting her steps and, little by little, letting her thoughts go. Halfway through her walk, she realized she wasn't thinking about it. The presence.

Sini came to a full stop. It wouldn't do. She looked around, and her eyes fell upon a lump in the snow. It was a smaller boulder covered by snow. She tucked her trousers inside her boots and hoped too much snow wouldn't get in.

Sini had prepared. She wore wool socks she'd knitted herself. Underneath her warmest winter trousers were merino wool leggings. The long-sleeved top was also merino, and underneath the thin down jacket, she wore a wool sweater as a middle layer. It was, in fact, a good idea to pause, as she was getting hot.

The snowy seat looked quite inviting. She plodded through the knee-high snow and sank down on it. If only she had more insulation between her and the freezing snow.

Sini rested her hands in her lap and closed her eyes. No, that didn't work. Her mind was still too busy. She looked around to find something of interest. The forest in its snow clothing was beautiful—she had to admit that. That winter, the first snow that had fallen and every bit after that had remained. There'd been a few warmer days, but the snow hadn't melted away like it normally did.

She noticed the shape of a flower that had dried but nevertheless reached tall above the snow. The brown stem and grey bulb were covered in tiny, white crystals. The longer she studied the different parts, the more she understood it was how it was supposed to be. In its death, the plant was still beautiful, still serving a purpose in keeping the seeds out of reach of the all-covering snow. She thought of nothing else as she focused on its details. Then she stopped analysing. Blurred out the frozen silhouette.

Her breath slowed down as she became more dedicated to the present moment. When she felt ready, she closed her eyes again. She pictured the forest scene and how—if only for a moment—serene and content she was. It was only her and the...

...presence.

Too curious not to, she opened her eyes. Was there something in the periphery of her vision? She was careful not to will it, to only observe.

There was the familiar shadow—a darkness out of the darkness. The height and form matched. It was a lot bigger than her. The ominous atmosphere from her nightmare was about to surface, but she gently refused to colour her experience with fear. She observed it in her mind.

When a moment passed that felt like minutes, she little by little inched her head towards it. Was it moving? Was it alive? She squinted her eyes. It was getting darker by the minute, and the obscure shape got blurrier.

The shape moved! She was certain of it. She couldn't help that her breathing accelerated. She mobilised all her attention to discern what was up with the dark spot that was moving on its own. It seemed to become denser. Was there movement within the shadow? Could that be a shoulder?

For a second, it looked like the shadow was closing in on her. Holy crap! She'd experienced goosebumps before, but in that moment, every inch of her skin felt clammy. She could feel every hair on her head stand.

Then nothing.

Sini got up and looked around. Where did it go?

Oblivious to sensible thought, she plodded through the snow to where she'd seen the shape. There was no trace of it, no evidence of anything alive having been there.

Trying to catch her breath, Sini thought the heavy breathing was more than only physical exertion. She was exhilarated. Then disappointment hit her. She was alone again.

She wanted more.

Sini walked home in a daze.

She came to when she opened the door to her house, as if the handle had the power to break the spell. Thoughts of snowfall, storms, old tractors, or neighbours who didn't answer the phone no longer occupied her mind.

What *was* that?

She stepped inside and did her routine on autopilot. It was not the dog. That was the only clear-cut thought she had. It couldn't be human. She didn't have any passed relatives who could be interested in haunting her. Except her grandmother.

Sini made the black tea brew extra strong, trying to gain clarity on what was going on. The water became opaque as she stood there, forgetting to take out the bags. She grabbed the honey pot and spooned up a big chunk of the natural sweetener. Sugar might aid in sorting her thoughts.

Sini was convinced it wasn't her beloved grandmother. If her grandmother decided to come through as spirit, it wouldn't happen in the forest. Her spirit would come forth in the vicinity of her office desk or the kitchen. Besides, her grandmother had been short, and she couldn't imagine the little woman being able to fill up that much space. The more she examined the event with a rational mind, she decided it was better to stay away, keep a healthy distance.

In the evening, as she picked at her dinner seated at the kitchen table, she knew she wouldn't get any sleep. It would be no use going to the forest exhausted the next day, which probably was for the best. She needed time to recuperate from that mind-blowing encounter.

Three in the morning. Sini had been watching the yellow digits that were the only light source of the bedroom for a while, but she didn't feel the least bit drowsy. She still couldn't conceive of it. She aimed for level-headed denial, but her skin knotting at the thought of it was proof something real had been in the forest with her.

Even though she'd been more intrigued by than afraid of the shadow, there'd been a fleeting moment of fear. Which emotion should she trust? Was it loneliness and lack of human connection that made her susceptible to taking stupid risks? If it wasn't her dog, then what reason did she have to continue opening herself up and becoming vulnerable? To let something in when she had no clue what it was?

On one end was the sensible sense of fear and the corroborating dreams, and on the other end, curiosity and sense of adventure.

Sini's heart was out of control.

A couple of nerve-racking days had passed where she'd forced herself to stay home.

She'd promised herself to pause and let her reckless desire fade. But every passing moment, she'd been dying to go. She'd waited for the sensible Sini to take over, but that version of her didn't show up.

Then she'd told herself that *if* she went back, a pause would be beneficial. She'd find her bearings and make some kind of plan. There was a delicate balance between knowing she was ready and rushing to the forest mentally unprepared, risking losing the connection that had been established.

The air had never felt as fresh, and her feet had never been as unreliable as she walked down the stairs and into the garden. No wind, no snow. Not a sound carried. Only the soft thudding from her feet and the pounding of her heart.

She pondered whether the spirit was of the forest or some other place. Maybe someone had died there and had no place to go? And she was the only one who'd tried to make contact? Could it want something from her? Was she supposed to help it go into the light? Had it vanished before because it had sensed her fear?

If she could only ask someone who might know, like her grandmother.

Getting onto her path, Sini tried again and again to mimic the serene mood from last time. No thoughts, only observing everything in front of her as she progressed.

Would it be in the same spot as before?

She looked at the big boulder to her right. Similar ones were scattered throughout the forest. She'd enjoyed climbing onto them and jumping down as a child. Her grandmother had been worried she'd break her leg in the uneven terrain. The forest floor was mostly boulders of different sizes, clad with mosses and small shrubs.

Wait—was there something beside it? It was as if she always spotted the dark silhouette from the corner of her eye. She looked directly at it.

It was the shadow!

Hello. She felt the urge to greet it.

What to do?

Sini hesitated. Perhaps she should've kept walking, but she froze, stared at it.

There was that internal movement, just like last time. As if it tried to take form. She couldn't know that, but a sense of knowing came over her. The spirit wanted to reveal itself to her.

Oh, God—what would it look like? She prayed it wouldn't be terrifying. Skin-clad wings and big black eyes flashed before her. She desperately tried to wipe away the gargoyle image.

Sini wanted to be polite and wait. There was that shoulder again. Something on the top, but she couldn't make out the shape of a head. It still seemed bigger than a human. What had she gotten herself into?

She'd barely finished the thought when the shadow turned more see-through and then vanished.

No.

That was too short. She waited a while, but nothing happened.

Sini shrugged and started walking.

It was so silent again, unreal. It was just her, the forest, and that thing she couldn't see clearly.

Convinced the ghost show was over for the evening, she started to think about a challenging but constructive way to keep her busy until next time. She should clean the sauna. She hadn't felt like it before, but it would occupy her for a day and take her mind off things. Like her loneliness. As much as it had been forced on her, she'd also willingly chosen it. And as a result, she was there, wanting to socialise with a ghost rather than her own kind.

As clearly as she could see her own breath in the cold air, she felt the ghost right behind her. She turned to look.

Nothing. She walked on.

Back to the sauna. A small wooden building on the backside of the house. The latest layer of paint, the traditional red ochre, had years ago withered into an earthy brown. Like all traditional saunas, it was built with thick logs that insulated well even in winter.

It was very old. Much older than the house. There'd been pride in her grandmother's voice when she'd spoken of it. Sini hadn't cared as a child, but grandmother had been adamant about them having a hot and long bath together. Afterward, she'd felt great. Her body had been soft and her mind sleepy. In fact, she'd always slept well those nights.

Sini felt a sting of regret for constantly choosing the shower instead of the wondrous sauna. It was just that preparing it was so laborious. Cleaning up, carrying wood, heating the stove for hours, carrying water, heating the water, bringing bath towels and refreshments—and all that for one person…

She sensed it. In front of her. She smiled.

It felt good. It was fun. She was having fun.

Crazy…

Sini kept walking. Whatever it was, good or evil, she'd found someone who wanted her company. Someone uncomplicated who didn't demand too much from her.

The light from her windows came into view too soon. She wanted to stay.

Maybe she could do another round?

No, that was a bad idea. First, she didn't bring her headlamp.

Second, if she was going to play with fire, she'd have to get used to the flame little by little.

5 MOONSHINE

Sini stretched her arms and legs, spreading herself across the bed.

She was worn out, but in a good way.

The previous evening was spent preparing the sauna. She'd carried wood and water, cleared snow from the front of the sauna, and carried forgotten gardening tools and chairs to the shed.

She'd continue with sweeping the floors and carrying equipment. Soon.

She wanted to enjoy the beautiful morning a little longer. She'd do the thing, and then she'd reward herself with a relaxing, but invigorating sauna. As she slumbered in the comfort of the warm duvet, she imagined being back in the forest, picking up where they left off the last time. More needed to be revealed.

After breakfast, Sini gathered what she needed; the linen to lie down on, the towel and bathrobe, shampoo, soap, water for drinking… She wished it was summer. Her grandmother had always decorated the sauna with flowers from the meadow or the edge of the field. As she pictured the modest but sweet pastel bouquets, Sini recalled that she'd also put herbs in the water—both for washing and throwing onto the stones. Those had been dried, and Sini wondered if there were any of them left hanging somewhere. She'd seen some, but where?

She'd meant to do the thing after breakfast, but she'd kind of forgotten. There was still time. She might save time if she did it while waiting for the sauna to warm. Walking through the white garden, arms full of items, Sini became aware of how special the moment was. As a child, she hadn't liked when preparing the sauna had taken all day. Sini hadn't understood that the ritual itself was pleasing. It was hard work, but it was a collection of chores that turned into a labour of love. Every effort built up the expectation and then, finally, the reward.

She didn't feel worthy of the reward. Not yet. The labour of love had made her forget about her worries. It was a perfect way to procrastinate. As she walked through the yard the last time, she still hadn't done the thing she'd promised, but she pushed away the nagging thought. She could do it between the sauna and going to the forest.

The sight that met her as she stepped inside the changing room made her more emotional than expected. The gentle darkness, the warmth, and the scents brought old memories to the surface. Tealights on the single shelf and the windowsill provided soft light against the dark walls. A little white porcelain cat sat on the table, another cherished memory from her childhood. She suspected it had been placed there to make her feel more positive about the bath. On the bench, the bathrobe, towel, and linen were neatly folded on top of each other. It was already afternoon, but she mustn't rush it. She took her time undressing, thinking only of the release she'd soon experience.

Sini lay down on her back on the wooden bench and let out a deep, long sigh. A part of her old, worried self, disintegrated. The hot steam rising from the rough, dark-grey stones was perfect. She hadn't realized how stiff and sore she'd been. She rested her head on the little sauna pillow she'd bought last summer at the local fair. Her skin turned moist.

Why hadn't she done it earlier? It was definitely worth the effort. In fact, the extensive work made the reward so much better.

Sini leaned onto her elbow, took a load of water with the little wooden ladle from the bucket, and threw it onto the stove. There was a sharp *tschhh* when the water hit the stones and a loud sizzle as it evaporated. She leaned back and covered her face with her hands as she prepared for the hot vapour to embrace her.

Her skin tingled from the heat. The soothing after effect was exactly what she needed.

Her body relaxed, imbedded in warmth, as she listened to the robust combustion of the wood in the heart of the stove. She turned to watch the orange flames through the little glass window.

Inside, fire and warmth. Outside, cold and dark. Both environments could kill her if she stayed long enough. How strange, though, that she was able to experience both, although the temperature difference was more than a hundred degrees.

She thought of going outside and rolling in the snow.

Nah, not her cup of tea. She'd tried it once, persuaded by her friends. Imagine what lying naked in the snow felt like and multiply that torment by ten.

Sini lost herself in deep relaxation. The hot air enveloped her body, covering every inch of her skin. Her breathing slowed down, and her senses began to numb. The warmth sheltered her from the outside world. All the tension, all nagging thoughts, melted and seeped through the wood and into the ground. She let go of her expectations on life. For that short moment, somewhere between reality and unconsciousness, everything in the world was good.

Sini slowly stirred. She wanted to stay longer, but it would do more harm than good. Her body was heavy as she gave in, sat up, and stepped down the lower benches to the floor. The noise from the fire had lessened, and the heat was slowly fading. She took a bucket and poured boiling hot water from the container integrated into the stove. She put it on the ancient wooden bench and poured some of it into a grey plastic washbowl. Then she took cold water from another bucket and mixed it into a pleasant temperature. She dipped her hair and the top of her head into the soothing water. Washing her hair brought up memories of her grandmother doing it for her as a child. Sini had always insisted on returning the favour.

Scrubbing herself down, she could feel the dirt dissolve. When she was satisfied, she dipped her hair again in clean water and rinsed her body. To wash off the residues, she picked up the bucket with cold water and poured it onto her face and chest. Sini yelped as the fresh water running down her hair and skin became the icing on the cake of the sauna experience.

She'd have no trouble falling asleep that night.

Sini sat down in the cooler changing room and began crunching tresses of her hair into the towel. The sauna had released her from her burdens for a moment. She thought about how she'd almost fallen asleep, even though she'd slept until late in the morning. Mingling with spirits seemed to have an energy-draining effect.

Or maybe *kaamos* time was getting a hold of her. The depressing dark had lasted for a small eternity. Sini thought of the shadowy figure in the forest as she dried her feet and put on her boots. How did it perceive her? Was she a foggy shadow to it as well?

What did it want from her, assuming it was a conscious entity? She'd obviously connected with it by mistake, taken it for something else, but what interest did it have in her? Although it had more than once crossed her mind that it could be an entity that wanted to suck her energy or even possess her, she refused to believe it.

However, if that was the case, she shouldn't return to the forest without some kind of protection.

As Sini walked back to the house, the gnawing sensation in her gut returned. It wasn't hunger.

She needed dinner, though. She still had time to make it to the forest if she ate fast and blow dried her hair. If she could only open the letters fast, do what was required fast, and be on her way.

She shouldn't have done it while eating, because she lost her appetite. The letter was three pages, and simply reading through the text was upsetting. What did it mean? What exactly was she supposed to do? Did it mean she could do it on the computer? She hated applying for unemployment money, as she had to pretend she was actually looking for a job, but the situation had gotten worse.

Sini sat down at the computer desk with her hair half dried and logged onto the Employment and Economic Development Office site. Finding the page to insert her data was more difficult than expected. Couldn't they make it easier to navigate? She'd told herself it would be over in half an hour, but as she began typing, she realised she'd been right all along. It would probably take her hours. It would require blood, sweat, and tears. And some cursing. Maybe even maledictions.

After all the effort to make time pass faster, she wouldn't have time to go to the forest. But if she bailed on her responsibilities and procrastinated another day, it would dominate her thoughts in the forest. It would haunt her. The empty online form would preoccupy her much worse than the dark-shadowed spirit itself. The choice was obvious, but merely the thought of doing the task made her stomach knot. It wasn't solely about filling in information about her current situation and what she aimed to do about it. It was all that it entailed. Everything that had led up to her moving there and turning into an unemployed person with no credible plans for the future. The facts to why she didn't have the funds she needed and why she wasn't working on acquiring them. Things like how her car probably needed fixing, that she needed a car if she got a job, but using the car every day would mean more wear and subsequent fixing. She didn't have money to fix the car, so she needed a job to be able to fix the car...

As if it wasn't disturbing enough that she'd been unemployed for too long, the money she got from the state wasn't enough. Any emergency—as in her car needing repair—would send her begging for welfare money from the municipality.

The never-ending worry chatter was killing her. Her mind was painting one disastrous scenario after the other, and she began spiralling into a very uncomfortable physical reaction. Her chest tightened as she saw nothing good coming out of her future. Determined to sacrifice the evening and save the next day from being ruined as well, Sini loaded herself up with hot and cold drinks and cookies. She forced herself to stay calm as she typed in the answers about what she was doing to find employment or beneficial studies. She had a hard time believing in her words herself and prayed the person reading them wouldn't see through the lies. Call her out for the fraud she was.

What might have been accomplished in an hour turned into several as she did the cursing, doubting, and questioning, mixed with sweet moments of Googling irrelevant things. What words would sound convincing when she couldn't picture herself caring for a job enough to put herself in front of people and act social on coffee breaks? When it was over, Sini leaned back in her chair and sighed. She closed her eyes and rubbed her temples. Her head hurt. It was too late. She'd tried to maintain the belief she could still go out, but she knew it was too late.

She wouldn't see the shadow in the dark, and she didn't believe it would show in the light cone of the headlamp. Her feet were almost numb as she stood and walked over to the window—so much for the relaxing bath. She parted the curtain and squinted at the darkness.

It wasn't pitch-black after all. Cupping her hands to the sides of her face, she leaned into the glass. There was a light source that cast a sheer shimmer onto the snow, and it wasn't one of the garden lights.

She yearned to be there. To get out there. She needed to clear her head.

Without a second thought, Sini began dressing. Her hair had dried, and she needed to get fresh air. Get her blood flowing again.

Lose herself in the darkness.

Sini stepped out into the magical night.

The snow seemed to glow. As her eyes adapted, she discerned more details in the yard. The familiar buildings and structures had turned into elements of a secret world, a place where light was always scarce. If it wasn't for the snow, she might have enjoyed a cup of tea in the garden.

She gazed up at the light in the sky, an almost round silvery disk on a dark-grey background. The moon had reached much higher than the sun did. A veil of white clouds slowly flowed by, creating an illusion of caressing the celestial body. It would be at its largest in a couple of nights. Despite the thin clouds and the moon not being complete, it created dark shadows on the ground. As she'd expected, she didn't need her headlamp.

As Sini crossed the ditch and entered the forest, she became aware of how loud her footsteps were. She stopped at the trail and listened. The humming of her ears. Other than that—nothing.

The forest looked so different. She was able to see everything. The moon made each tree cast its shadow. Here and there, open spaces bathed in the light. Despite being the only human in the area, she wasn't afraid. She'd never seen prints of wolves or other predators. Bears would be tucked into their dens.

She didn't fear wolves—not that she'd ever seen any—but knew that crossing paths with a bear could be life-threatening. She'd heard they were masters of keeping out of sight as long as they sensed the location of humans. Yet every time she dreamt of bears, she was terrified. She didn't know why, but assumed it was a natural reaction to an animal that was a fast runner, a strong climber, and a good swimmer. An animal that could break bones with one blow of the paw.

Once again, she was reminded that if something happened to her, too much time would pass before anyone noticed she'd gone missing and start searching. It didn't matter. She'd rather be out there where she felt alive, instead of safely seated in front of a TV that fed mind-numbing nonsense.

She began following the familiar path that looked frequented by people. Except, no one else walked in that forest in winter—or any other time. She wished for another season, so she could deviate from the path. Or that there at least was a crust that carried her weight. Without it, it was energy consuming and unsafe to walk at random in the bushy and stony terrain.

As she advanced through the slightly ascending landscape, her noisiness irritated her. The swish-swish from her padded trousers and the crunching from her boots. And every time she stopped to listen to the silence, she only perceived the humming in her ears. The magical waxing moon demanded reverence. She'd have to find more silent clothes. Were there boots that didn't make any sound?

Sini came to a halt and breathed in. She refused to have another bad thought and chose to enjoy the moment. Despite the snow and the cold and the dark, the forest was where she felt free, where she could hide. She was the intruder, but all the same, she belonged there.

She looked at the moon. It was just her and Earth's giant satellite. As she let go of her worries, she imagined them floating up and disintegrating in the silvery light. Under the mild, accepting glow of the moon, Sini decided she didn't want to protect herself from the night. She'd rather envelop herself in the subtle darkness than seek safety in the harsh and synthetic light of the human realm. She'd rather open herself to the unknown, take it all in. She was fed up with human nature and wanted no more of it.

It was even quieter than daytime. She'd entered another world. She started walking again, looking at the trees that were more illuminated than in the afternoon. It amazed her how the cold moon made such strong shadows appear.

Moon shadow.

She'd never considered the meaning of the words, that it was an actual phenomenon. Even she cast a sharp silhouette onto the snow.

Sini paused and looked up again. Funny that the sky wasn't black, the moonlight turned it ashy. Only the brightest stars were visible.

"Jeez!"

Her heart stopped.

Nothing could've prepared Sini for what she saw in front of her.

Sini blinked to make sure her eyes were open.

It was a male figure.

She pressed her eyelids shut, again and again, expecting him to disappear at any moment.

A few seconds later, he was still there, next to a boulder. Sini became unsure whether she herself was really there, not in her bed, wiped out and dreaming. No doubt lucid dreaming.

She tried to note as many details as possible before waking up. In fact, she was already kind of weightless.

A big hood covered his head and most of his face, but she noticed strong features. Compared to her, he appeared huge. His clothing was dark, and he reminded her more of a phantom from the past than a modern human.

The cold shivers that ran through her body turned into chills. She had no recollection of having gone to bed. She didn't have any memory gaps between exiting the sauna and arriving in the forest.

That would be the moment to run away, if that was what she opted for.

Self-preservation.

The fact that he was standing off the trail told her he was her shadow.

Her shadow. She'd already put ownership on him. It.

For every shallow breath she took, she expected him to vanish. Why wasn't she afraid? She wished she were, because that would make her normal.

What to do? He didn't move; neither did she.

To prevent herself from fainting from lack of oxygen, she began walking. She put full effort into trying to keep her mind light and send welcoming thoughts.

As she walked at a comfortable pace, she didn't turn to look. Had she made a mistake?

No, he was there. She sensed him again behind her. She smiled.

When she came to an open spot where snow crystals glistened in the moonlight, she stopped.

Magical. So simple, but so extraordinary.

She tilted her face up at the sky again. She loved the moon. And the stars.

Ancient beings.

She had to look. Little by little, she turned her gaze to the path behind her. He was there! She couldn't help but smile. *This is so wrong,* she chuckled.

She turned back and walked forwards, but then she had to check on him again.

Where had he gone? She was about to panic when she noticed the faint shadow. He was a shadow in the shadow of a spruce. She took half a step backwards. Another one.

The shadow moved forwards. She took a few more steps.

As the shadow followed her, the moment it reached the moonlit part, it took form again.

Sini inhaled deep.

It was the moon. Its light somehow revealed what he was. The shadow became real.

She stopped. He stopped. She was reassured he didn't want to harm her. She ached to believe that.

What now?

She could see him more clearly. His eyes were hidden in the shadow of the hood. His clothes seemed thick like the hood. The fabric might have been animal skin. The bulkiness made it hard for her to assess his body type. Did he have a body—like a human being? She couldn't see his feet either.

Quiet. So quiet.

But she didn't dare speak. Never mind try to approach him.

She turned and started walking. It, he, followed.

Sini walked the path in the company of the moon and the shadow. Shadow male. The setting couldn't have been more surreal. She knew she was awake, but it felt like a dream. She gazed at the moon. Then him. The snow reflecting the silvery light in dim but such beautiful crystal twinkles. Moon twinkles.

The moonlight animated the lifeless forest. She was no longer the only sentient being. If it wasn't for the path, she might lose herself wandering deeper into the magical night.

He didn't stick to the path. He was not as bound to the physicality as she was. She could sense him to her right. She'd look, and he'd be there. Either as the shadow, or as the bulky figure. Then he would be in front of her, walking away from her. It was also obvious he was aware of her.

Who are you? She sent out the thought, expecting nothing.

No external thought appeared in her head, but she was convinced the connection strengthened. As if he was listening or trying to convey a thought. Did he have thoughts—like her—or any at all?

She couldn't believe that he'd only be an echo from the past, as it was evident to her that he communicated by the way he moved around her. And always came back. Or waited for her.

The moment she saw the light from her house, she knew it was over. Even if she wanted to stay, she felt exhausted. Sleepy. It had to be enough—it was more than she ever could've expected.

Sini imagined a clear *bye* as she exited the forest. When she got to the field, she tried to get a last glimpse, but she couldn't see the figure anymore.

A heatwave flooded her body. The humming turned into a pulsating buzz in her ears, and she prayed she wouldn't faint before she got to the house. It was like stumbling on that bear. She'd stayed calm not to aggravate the situation, and when the confrontation was over, all the fear and excitement washed over her in a surge of adrenaline.

The exception was the bear hadn't been an enemy.

When Sini woke up the next morning, she found it hard to recall what had happened after she got home.

She probably stumbled straight into bed. When she pulled off the cover, she noticed she was still in her merino underwear.

What time was it?

Four in the afternoon. Wow, she was drained.

Come back.

She didn't remember her dreams, but those words were on her mind.

Her sight was blurry, her mouth dry, and her body ached as if she was hung over. But she felt happy, as if she'd met a nice guy and couldn't wait to see him again. She bounced out of bed and hurried into the kitchen to open the curtains.

Oh, no! A thick, grey matter covered the sky, the kind that gave no hope of clearing up in a while. There'd be no moon lighting up the night, and she wouldn't see his real shape. It was too late in the afternoon to go for a walk in natural light, and she was still convinced he wouldn't show in the light of her headlamp.

Damn.

Sini pulled back the curtains and retreated slowly. Maybe she wasn't fit for another encounter that day, anyway. She'd rest and do something else. What in the world would be worth doing compared to meeting *him?* It.

Whatever…

…was he?

He must be a ghost, a spirit. She didn't know of other entities. Or an alien, perhaps?

He didn't look like an alien. There was nothing futuristic about him. An angel? But why would a celestial being take walks with her in the forest? She didn't see a connection between angels and moonlight.

Come back… Was that him communicating with her?

Again, Sini wished her grandmother was there to give her an answer. Even if she didn't have one, she was the only one Sini imagined telling about it. And her grandmother knew the forest better than anyone, as she'd lived in its vicinity for decades.

Sini thought of the moon. The moon, and specifically the moonlight, was the only clue.

She hurried to the computer and turned it on. Then she hurried to the kitchen and began preparing breakfast. She made it a massive one, as she was starving.

Sini spent the evening by the computer in her underwear, fetching a plate of food now and then.

The Moon was estimated to be four and a half billion years old, only slightly younger than Earth. There was evidence that the phases of the moon had been used for measuring time as far as tens of thousands of years ago. Different cultures had their own deities associated with the moon. Even her own people had imagined creatures that ate or hid the moon and then others that came to save it, free it.

In the old days, it had been common practice to follow the lunar phases when doing certain chores. They'd sow on a waxing moon and weed on a waning moon, since they thought things grew and strengthened as the moon grew bigger, only to dry out and weaken when it grew smaller. One shouldn't shear sheep at a lessening moon if one wanted the wool to grow back soon.

The moon had always been associated with insanity and irrationality, and she pictured how her stories would be received if she shared them. How many times had she doubted her own experiences? Though, according to the article, no significant correlation between lunar phases and lunatic behaviour had been established in the majority of the studies made.

Although Sini had learnt a ton of fun and interesting facts and beliefs about Earth's eternal companion, she was frustrated that nothing had pointed to her friend in the forest. She would've liked to have at least a bit of corroboration that her visions were real. If she could have even one clue to what he might be, it would be easier to strengthen their connection. It would make him less a shadow and more…whatever he was. Was there a clue she'd missed? Was there something in his appearance—the way he moved, *where* he moved—that could steer her onto the right path in her searches? Sini closed her eyes and tried to shed a light on what she'd seen the night before.

What if the info on the internet was too recent? The moon man rather looked like someone from the past.

What about myths? Perhaps the answer lay in the local myths? Where…?

Sini straightened and began tapping in search terms for books in the town library. If she could only find… Yes, there was something…

Finnish folklore and myths, Sami folklore and myths, Mythologica Fennica, A magical travel guide to Northern Finland, The Magic Songs of the Finns…

Sini made reservations for all the available titles. She didn't look forward to picking them up, but she'd do her shopping at the same time. The next day.

Pure strength of will kept her from going back to the forest—despite the absence of moonlight. Besides her being tired, she was afraid of how disappointed she'd be if he wasn't there. She convinced herself that it would be much more beneficial to work on her psychic abilities.

How to communicate with ghosts—she'd have to look that up.

6 THE TOUCH

The full moon had come and gone behind a stubborn thicket of clouds.

She'd had no other choice than to do her walks in daylight again.

To her delight, he'd always been there. Either she was getting better at interpreting the shape of his blurry figure—or he was becoming more visible. Less ghost, and more…*man?*

She'd stopped thinking of him as a ghost. He wasn't human nor had he ever been. He didn't fit the description of a time traveller, either. The more they hung out, the less she understood what he was.

She never saw him try to speak or make a sound. They didn't have a common language. She hadn't discerned any possible facial expressions, either. She made out human features, but nothing else in the face suggested he was human. Did he really look like that, or had he taken on a recognisable form not to frighten her?

She might never know his name, so she'd named him *Kuutamo*. Moonlight had revealed him, and she'd forever remember that night.

Sini cupped the mug of warm cocoa in her hands. Thinking of her new, mysterious friend always put a smile on her face.

The dynamic between them had changed. Instead of him following her as she walked, she went wherever he was. As soon as she stepped onto her path, he'd be there waiting for her. She'd go to him, and he'd start…*walking?*

Sini wondered if Kuutamo would grow tired of waiting for her to arrive at his destinations. She'd see him standing at the big boulder at the top of the little hill, and she could sense the call. Then she'd wade through the thick snow that refused to carry her the tiniest bit. Her boots would plunge through all the way to the ground, and she'd have to take the next step with caution so not to fall headlong into the white stuff. It would take her forever, and when she arrived, she'd be flustered and sweaty instead of poised and lovely.

She'd have to use snowshoes if he kept at it. Skis would've been the natural option.

Sini frowned at the idea. She hadn't skied since that incident. Everyone skied in winter. Not her. Not even with her dog. It had been no use skiing with Karo anyway, because he wouldn't be able to follow her. His paws would've sunk through the snow. And why go out without him? Certainly not because she loved skiing.

Sini had been talented at sports since she was a child. She and her parents had lived in the North then, and she'd had the chance to try out most of the winter sports. Mogul skiing gave her the best kicks. It was understood early that if she combined her natural talent with hard work, she had the potential to go far.

Sini devoted herself to the chosen ambition of heading for the top. She loved the physical exertion, always pushing her limits. She didn't grasp all the psychological elements, but she was good at visualizing results, excellent even, and she'd most often gotten there.

Everything was working out for her. She had Martin, the boyfriend who she pictured herself marrying one day. She was about to try out for the world championships. The other athletes and trainers had become her community. She got their support. They believed in her. She believed in herself. And more than that, she loved going full speed down the slope, upper body level and stiff while legs surged over the bumps and troughs like pistons. The strict downward carving releasing into an explosive splurge of joy. Hitting the jump and executing the *spread eagle* or *helicopter* the exact way she'd envisioned.

Until that dreadful night.

Sini pulled the blanket tighter around her. The dancing flames blurred into a blob of cold yellow as she regressed to the painful memory.

A female athlete from Martin's home country had transferred for a season. It was both natural and expected that Martin would be keen to show her how things worked at the centre. Sini had no reason to think it meant more to Martin than being courteous to a fellow countryman.

Then a couple of friends suggested the opposite. Sini dismissed their message. She trusted Martin and their future together. Besides, Martin wouldn't start messing around when the most important thing was to focus on the big competition.

But they weren't all work and no play, so one night they decided the new girl needed to be inaugurated and threw her a party. They headed for the *Rubout* slope. It wasn't officially in use, and its jumps didn't pass the safety standards. There was something untameable about the site as it didn't comply with the efforts of the slope developers. They called it the Rubout as it, in the blink of an eye, could wipe the skier off course. Sini and her friends loved the unpredictability, and it served as the perfect place to try out crazy things or learn how to read the snow using their intuition. A place for them to test their limits in secret. On that night, some had already had drinks, and everyone was in a good mood. Sini included.

A challenge was presented to the newcomer, and she accepted. The girl had everyone's undivided attention as she performed the jump with ease. They congratulated her, and those who were sober enough joined in. The slopes were lit throughout the night. Some of that light sifted through to their *thrill hill,* making it possible to distinguish its features, but leaving it obscure enough to enhance the excitement.

Sini loved flying through the night air. The new girl headed for another round, and Sini decided to join her. Right before the big jump, Sini caught up with her. What was intended to be a show-off coordinated duo jump turned into catastrophe as the other skier steered right in front of Sini at the last moment. The girl hadn't realised Sini was right beside her.

The warning shout caught in Sini's throat as everything happened too fast. The girl flexed into her twist but then got hit by Sini's left ski. As she tumbled, their skis collided with a terrible clank. Off balance, the girl swirled downwards as Sini only just managed to control her trajectory and land on her feet.

Shocked and incredulous, Sini skidded to a halt and began ascending to where the other skier lay on the ground.

Sini prayed for the girl to sit up, stand up, and start descending. Instead, she just lay there. Sini couldn't discern through the obscurity whether she was moving at all.

Sini was the first to get to the girl, who lay frozen in an awkward position with one ski detached. She kicked off her skis and rushed to the body. The girl's eyes were closed, but she was breathing. For a split second, Sini thought she was pretending, wanting to give Sini the scare she deserved. No movement. She wanted to make the girl more comfortable but didn't dare touch her, afraid of aggravating the damage if bones were broken.

She heard others approaching and perceived that someone was making the emergency call. After that, everything she thought had been her life vanished.

The unlucky skier was placed into a medically induced coma to protect her brain from further damage. After three weeks, they woke her up. It turned out she was severely impaired. In addition to her brain, she also suffered spinal damage. It never got easier to think about the girl whose life she'd destroyed by being just a little too careless.

The nastiest part, though, was the others believed she did it on purpose. That she was jealous of the girl because of Martin's attention and wanted to teach her a lesson. Didn't they know her at all? When had she ever behaved like a vindictive or malicious person?

She hadn't even been jealous. That's how trusting she was. When she told them she hadn't been drunk, they were even more convinced of her crashing with the girl on purpose. It made no sense at all. Why would she put her own career at risk because of such a petty reason, throw away all her hard work?

She hadn't realized it then but looking back at what happened and how fast she became the outcast, she came to think that they must have been jealous of her success. Some of them used to tell her she was so lucky. It wasn't luck. It was hard work. Less partying.

They wanted nothing to do with her. Training became unbearable. The police had cleared her from suspicion, stated it was an accident, but it didn't make things better. Sini tried to ride out the storm, but it never calmed. When she got sick from their treatment and didn't recuperate, she decided to take a break. A long vacation.

After she left, they never wanted her back.

Sini took another sip of the lukewarm cocoa.

All in all, it would take a lot to get her on skis again. Something major.

Like, if someone's life depended on it.

Sini had come to the conclusion there wasn't a strong correlation between Kuutamo's appearance and her ability to stay focused on the present moment. He seemed to be able to stay in her vicinity even when she didn't focus on him.

That day, for example, he walked closer to her than before. It was new moon and the coldest day of the winter so far. Below minus ten. The many layers of clothes made her movements clumsy. It was important to stay warm as long as possible.

Something was different. Sini was raw from recalling her past.

It was nearing dusk. She had her *companion* with her, so she wasn't technically alone, but she yearned for someone to hold her just for once. For someone to tell her things would get better. Even though she desperately wanted to believe she didn't need anybody, she, deep down, knew she did. To only for a moment get a connection to someone who wouldn't judge.

Kuutamo had come to a halt on the path in front of her. Out of habit, Sini stopped as well. He turned towards her, and she responded by taking a few more steps.

The dark shape towered on the path, unmoving.

Sini stepped closer again. Then the only thing on her mind was him. Despite being a tall woman, he was almost a head taller than her. About two metres, perhaps. She had to tilt her head to look at him. Although the immense hood kept his eyes in shadow, she distinguished them. They were dark, and she guessed a dark blue. As he regarded her, still emotionless, she saw he looked rather handsome. He had somewhat rough and very masculine features.

Although she found his emotionlessness a bit intimidating, the reveal made her smile. When his lips parted and broke into an appealing smile, Sini had to swallow. If there'd ever been a moment when she genuinely thought she'd imagined everything, that would be it. Maybe she'd died that day in the snow, frozen beyond saving, and then she, too, was destined to walk the path as a ghost.

She felt more alive than ever, though.

Kuutamo's hand rose towards her. Sini raised her hand as well, greeting him. His hand, that looked like a perfect human hand no longer hiding in his long sleeve, stayed upright in front of her.

What did he mean? She tried to convey a question by focusing on his eyes. He lowered and extended the hand towards her as if he wanted her to touch it.

Sini answered by ungloving and extending her own, and when he stayed motionless, she took one last step so she could reach him.

At that moment, she was sure her heart was racing, but all she comprehended was they were going to touch.

Just as she'd expected, though, she couldn't feel him. His hand was like a hologram that her fingers went through. He didn't seem surprised, either.

He closed his eyes.

Sini steadied her feet and closed her eyes as well.

She felt nothing. She peeked to look if her hand was still on his or if her hand was grasping at the air. Still there.

Sini pressed her eyelids shut and focused. Emptied her mind of expectation, envisioned her skin against his. A soft tingling at the tip of her fingers shifted into something solid caressing her hand. Then the sensation of cold, immense cold. So immense it felt like burning. Either freezing or burning— she didn't know which. But it didn't hurt. Instead, she felt a rush of energy from his hand go through her, filling every cell of her body with an extreme sensation of pleasure. It was like a fresh autumn breeze, like liquid sunlight, like…something long lost returning to her. She didn't know whether her legs were sagging or she was soaring through the air. Too soon, the sensation dimmed, leaving her with her blissful emotion.

An emotion so strong she was embarrassed to open her eyes.

But he wasn't there to witness her rapture. She was alone. What on earth…?

She couldn't move. She looked at her hand. Then she looked all around her. He was gone.

Afraid the spell would be broken, Sini stood there recalling the sensation over and over. She'd never experienced anything like that before, not even close, but in it, she found something familiar her conscious mind didn't comprehend.

She realised he wasn't coming back, and she was getting cold.

In a daze, she walked on unsteady feet to her exit out of the forest and crossed the border to her mundane life.

⌘ ⌘ ⌘

Sini lay on her bed on top of the cover.

Her eyes were open, but unfocused. She guessed she felt amazing. With such a strange experience, she wasn't sure what she felt. In hindsight, it might have been dangerous to touch an unknown entity like she had. But she'd never truly been afraid of Kuutamo—it was only her adulting mind that wanted her to be careful, suspicious, self-preserving.

She tingled as she recalled how the energy from Kuutamo's hand had entered her and rushed through her whole body. She didn't have words to describe how it felt. How was that even possible? Although he wasn't solid like her, he seemed to have a lot of energy.

Her body felt warm, energized. It was past dinnertime, but she didn't feel hunger. So otherworldly. Why had Kuutamo done that; what was the intention behind it? And what was that impression of familiarity in the middle of something so incomprehensible?

Sini eased the cover from under her and pulled it over herself. She closed her eyes and tried to remember what he'd looked like under the secretive hood. Why did he cover up like that? He'd appeared good-looking in her eyes, so he had no reason to hide.

It was too good to be true.

Sini sighed. If only the night and the day would pass rapidly so she could get back to the forest and be with him. The sensation was already fading, and it became harder to focus.

Once again, Sini woke disoriented by the near dark. She prayed she hadn't slept through the day. It was eight o'clock in the morning. Thank goodness.

She felt like she'd been dreaming all night. She was sure she had, but she didn't remember anything. Dreaming all night usually left her tired, but she welcomed the cool shock to her feet as she got up without hesitation.

Her stomach ached from hunger. If only she had something more filling than the usual oatmeal porridge.

Sini dressed her portion with as much protein as she managed to find; ham, cottage cheese, and slices of Swiss cheese and put it in the microwave. When the bell sounded and she took out the steaming meal, she put as much butter on it as possible without it turning disgusting.

Although the kitchen was a bit chilly, she felt comfortable in her short nightgown. It was as if her senses were messed up. The curtains were still shut, but her eyes stared right through them as she spooned the porridge into her mouth.

Half-past eight. How to speed up the passing of time? There were tasks to do in the house, but she couldn't recall any.

What kind of energy cocktail had Kuutamo served her? She still had no clue to what the purpose was. She knew nothing at all except that she sensed he was good. His energy had been good. Evil couldn't feel that good—right? Or look that good?

As daylight got more intense, she remembered less how it had felt. The more time passed, the less real it seemed. She was certain she hadn't dreamt it, though. She needed more. Would he be there the next time, even if he'd disappeared on her?

A silly thought struck her, and she tried to push it away. What if he didn't like how she felt?

Sini spent the day cleaning the house. Cleaning the toilet, scrubbing the tiles, putting things back to where they belonged. Washing clothes—even pillowcases of the sofa cushions. It was madness, but she needed to do something tangible. She wasn't capable of doing any brain work. Not even drawing.

She should draw him. She would—one day—when she got a clearer visual of what he looked like. His clothes were so bulky, and that hood always covered most of his features. She didn't even know the colour of his hair.

Sini giggled.

Sini couldn't believe how much she had been able to accomplish in a day.

She brimmed with energy, and her body was already hot in her warm underwear, middle layer, and top layer. Her hands trembled. Going to the forest had always been exciting when trying to connect with her dog, then the shadow, and then Kuutamo, but she'd reached a new level. She prayed he'd be there.

Sini took the old backcountry skis that had belonged to her grandmother and tossed them on the snow. She'd found the boots that matched the ski closure and was thankful the size fit. The old skis differed from the ones she'd used as an athlete, and putting them on wasn't as painful as she'd expected. Sini grabbed the ski poles and pushed herself forwards.

It was amazing how interacting with Kuutamo had surfaced the single thing she didn't want to think about. She wanted to better follow him on his odd routes through the forest, but why did it require the one thing she didn't want to do? She'd spent the day considering where her grandmother had kept her skis and then finally yielded.

Awkward.

Sini bent down and released her feet from the skis. She'd get there faster if she walked and carried the skis. If she needed them, if Kuutamo wanted her to follow him into the terrain, she'd use them.

Maybe.

Her heart was beating fast as she got to the path, but not solely from carrying the skis. Would he be waiting for her?

What would he act like? She couldn't ask about last time, but would they behave differently? Would…

Further down the path stood the familiar shadow.

It started moving, and it was her cue to follow. She put one ski and one pole in the other hand for balance as she began walking along the narrow groove in the snow.

A few minutes in, the shadow stopped. It waited for her but then disappeared before she got halfway. Sini walked on and noted how moisture formed on her back. The balance between being too hot or too cold was difficult to achieve, especially as it got colder. Why couldn't it be summer instead? She wondered what kind of clothing Kuutamo would wear on a warm and sunny day. Would he reveal more of himself?

Sini began looking around as she approached the spot where she saw him last. As she'd guessed, he was further up the slope that reached deeper into the forest. She took one look at the stretch of snowy terrain between them and repressed a sigh.

Afraid of her emotions, she turned them off. She bent down and fastened the skis.

Cold chills cut through her body as putting her hands through the loops of the poles stirred a familiar emotion. She was breaking the unspoken vow she made the day she left her old life behind.

Sini looked up towards Kuutamo, who stood at one of the bigger boulders. If she stayed focused on him waiting for her, she might close the distance between them without falling apart.

With her eyes fixed on the shadow, she steadied herself on the poles and stepped into the snow. The skis cut through the top layer but carried her better than expected. She pushed herself forwards as she coordinated her feet. Her right ski slipped backwards and her left ski followed suit. Sini lost her balance and hung on to her poles for dear life.

Sini cut the emerging curse in half. She would not lose her chance of spending time with Kuutamo to a pair of stupid skis.

She stood upright, took a deep breath, and began carefully ascending the slope. Leaning a little backwards and pushing forwards with the poles, she got the old skis to hold on the loose snow. She smirked at the thought that Kuutamo must have been wondering what the commotion was all about. Was he laughing at her? Did he have a sense of humour?

As she approached him, she forgot about her awkwardness. That was where she wanted to be. Kuutamo was facing her, his feet disappearing into the snow and his almost opaque right hand resting on the bare wall of the rough stone.

Curious to get a glimpse of his eyes, Sini couldn't resist bending her knees and leaning forwards a little. The scarce light source emanated from behind him, and Sini only saw a shadow. She hunched and loosened the bindings and stepped away from the skis with relief.

Sini's breath caught as she straightened herself and looked at Kuutamo. The hood was pulled back from his face.

His face wasn't as rough as she'd perceived.

Those eyes.

His features were prominent, with full lips and a masculine nose, high cheekbones, but she focused on the eyes. Their perfect sapphire took the attention off everything else.

Sini took half a step forward. She wanted to get closer, but hesitated.

Kuutamo extended his left hand like he'd done the day before. She was unable to let go of his eyes. They were friendly, compassionate, but without a trace of pity. Blue, a deep blue. And they never left hers.

Sini stepped closer to within touching distance. It was as if his eyes could see everything. As if he knew everything. He was definitively not human—or at least not one from her world. Human eyes didn't have that depth, knowledge of the universe. Yet he was there, playing with a human nobody. Except, having his attention like that made her feel special.

When he reached out his hand further, Sini had to release herself from his gaze.

His palm faced upwards in an invitation to put hers on it. Easing herself a little closer still, she ungloved her right hand and extended it. She braced herself for the tornado of tingles that would shoot through her.

Sini gasped as her hand touched Kuutamo's. He felt solid, smooth, and cold. Before she could reflect on the sensation, the energy flowed between them. Kuutamo's eyes remained open, and she didn't close hers either. She was prepared. Relaxed, and anticipating.

It was different.

A pale light appeared and gradually got brighter. A fog rose between them, and it became harder to discern him or the landscape. When the light became blinding, she had to blink.

As her vision accustomed to the white on white, she thought it looked familiar. She was looking at a snowy landscape, not like the one surrounding them, but the one from her dream.

She saw nothing but snow and subtle shadows from the gently rising and falling terrain. No trees, no life, but the serenity made it beautiful.

For a reason unknown other than it being familiar, she felt safe. The sun was there, and she sensed its soothing light upon her face. There was something far in the background. Based on its shape, it was an animal.

Then there was the other familiar sensation. She was suddenly hot, and she found it hard to breathe. It was like a slow burning inside her.

Oh, no. She didn't want to suffer that horrible nausea again. A moaning came from what she believed was her own mouth. When it intensified, she sensed the others. Like a choir of tortured beings, the sound increased, and she perceived herself part of it. A hundred animals screaming in agony. The death scream of an entire world.

Her world as she knew it disintegrated. Disappeared. A reality that existed no longer. No trace left.

No!

Why?

She could no longer breathe, and it became silent.

The silence terrified her more than the screams.

Sini fought to wake up from the nightmare. Her eyes were upon those blue ones that were familiar.

Kuutamo.

She was still there. She was alive. The world was intact.

A flicker of agony in his eyes. Their immense beauty was magnified by the pain. She couldn't be sure it was pain, as he was so different, but that's what she felt.

Sini retrieved her hand as if his touch had burnt her.

Why did he do that? What was that? She didn't understand.

Sini's eyes saw that his shape once again melted into the background. Her emptiness was complete as she stood there alone.

Her feet gave in, and she let herself sag onto the snow. A wave of nausea washed over her, but she didn't know whether it was more physical or emotional.

She took a deep breath, relieved she was able to breathe like she'd always done and always taken for granted. She had no idea whose souls that agony belonged to.

The forest appeared as quiet and monochrome as before. It had nothing in common with the horror she'd experienced a few minutes ago. She welcomed the cool air in her lungs. When she'd calmed down a bit, she didn't want to stay any longer. He wasn't there with her, after all.

Her eyes fell upon the indentation in the snow where he'd stood. Had he been as solid as he'd felt?

Why didn't he stay?

Why did he leave her there all alone without an explanation for what he'd done?

She wanted to cry. Her expectation of a lovely reunion with some more light energy bonding had turned into the worst thing imaginable. If she had to imagine the worst kind of suffering, that would be it.

Sini looked at her skis. She hated the idea of putting them on again.

She'd backed down on her vow for him, and that was the result. Abused and abandoned by the one she'd trusted wouldn't hurt her.

Sini got up and lazily fumbled her boots into the closures.

The only thing more humiliating than skiing back home was wading in the thick snow until she cried from frustration.

7 CONFUSION

Sini fell asleep within minutes of arriving at the house.

Sleeping through the evening, Sini got up only to change clothes and turn off the lights. She tossed and turned. She was hot and then cold. Her body was still out of sync, but she no longer found it endearing. She'd begin dreaming of the ice landscape and then mercifully wake up. But that meant no coherent sleep, as the dream returned every time she relaxed into oblivion.

As morning came, her skin was sticky, and her head felt like a punching bag. Her muscles were limp. Touching Kuutamo had short-circuited her system.

Grossed out by her dingy state but too tired to get up, Sini stared at the ceiling. If the first time had been delightful and amazing, the second was the opposite. Why did Kuutamo want to make her see that, feel that? It didn't seem like him at all. On the other hand, she'd been wrong about people before. Totally. And about so many.

Those eyes.

She'd trusted in what they reflected. Something good. Something she wanted to be part of. She'd assumed she'd be part of it when she took his hand.

Still shocked by the result, Sini tried to think of a reason. What if she hadn't been able to receive his energy, and her body had misinterpreted the situation. Her body had hurt, and her mind had then responded by showing her the memory of her worst nightmare in years. Why else would she have the same vision as in her dream?

Would she ever get an explanation?

She forced herself out of bed and to have breakfast but returned halfway through.

The nausea wouldn't yield. She'd have to postpone all her wonderful plans for the day and stay in bed. Better yet, if she watched TV, her visions of the end of it all would pause.

Sini tried to concentrate on the TV shows to keep out her own thoughts. She laughed. Nothing on it came close to what she'd experienced lately. Her encounters with Kuutamo were too strange. The thought that she probably was hallucinating and making him up stung.

Perhaps extreme loneliness with time did that to a person. She'd invented her own complicated relationship with an imaginary friend. Someone so different from her former friendships that she wouldn't fear him leaving her. But why would he turn on her, too? She'd done nothing bad. She'd been living in seclusion so she wouldn't mess up other people's lives.

Sini noticed the daylight come and vanish. Her exhausted body wasn't up to another encounter, and although not seeing him again made her sad, she welcomed the excuse.

Her physical state was proof that mingling with spirits—or aliens—was demanding and not something to go about foolishly. She *should* be more careful instead of rushing in, accepting his invitations to who-knows what kind of energy transfers.

Her body began protesting about lying down, and she tried to shift positions on the little sofa to get the blood flowing. Despite everything, she wanted to be back with him.

She wanted to be better prepared.

She needed to find out what he was.

The second night, as Sini lay in bed, she doubted sleep would have mercy on her.

Her head was still a mess, and she feared what old traumas would be amped up by the new ones. She prayed the dreams would subside, but as she dove into unconsciousness, they were only replaced by others, just as sinister. The accident happened again and again, and every time, she saw a new face telling her she was bad, self-serving, or even evil. She couldn't take any more of their false accusations and shouted at them to leave her alone. *Leave me alone.*

"Leave me alone!"

Sini was woken by her own scream. Violent but merciful, it snapped her out of the disturbing state. She rubbed her forehead with the bases of her palms and moaned. As the last scene continued to play out, she punched her fists into the bedsheets.

It was the skiing. She shouldn't have taken out her grandmother's skis and used them. As a result, she'd have to start processing her past again. She mustn't think of skiing, because then she dreamt about it. It didn't matter that she'd once loved skiing—and still did in her dreams—as the dreams would always end in that horrid clashing sound.

To detach from the nightmares, she summoned up her escape plan. The one she'd set in motion as soon as she got the extra money. The plan wasn't that detailed, but enough to get her mind off her circumstances, even if the relief didn't last long. She couldn't save any of her income at the moment. There was only one additional income source she'd managed to come up with: berry picking. Some people picked enough wild berries in the summer to earn thousands of euros. Berry picking was exempt from taxation and didn't affect the unemployment benefit. It wasn't like she had other obligations, so next summer she might motivate herself to try.

Even if she didn't earn thousands of euros, or even one, she'd be delighted to take the cheapest flight to the cheapest destination. As long as it got her mind off the cold, unlucky relationships, and her life going nowhere. She had to stop bringing back those moments from the past. She'd just about reached some kind of peace—with flashbacks on rare occasions—and she mustn't bring them to the surface again. The sad truth was she was alone, and she wouldn't survive dreaming of the accident at night and spending the day driving out grim memories.

She was so done with winter.

By midday, Sini felt her energy return.

Her first thought was to go to him, but her sensible side implored her to be careful. She knew nothing about that being who infused her with awesome feel-good energy one moment, only to whisk her into a lucid nightmare the next. She needed to do something. Another day of recuperating would only make her more restless.

Sini remembered the books she'd reserved at the library. She felt better and could drive to town in the afternoon. As much as the books gave her hope, a knot tightened in her stomach at having to pick them up. She always went to the same supermarket for food, but she'd never been to the library.

Hoping for a miracle, Sini would give the internet another chance. There must have been others who'd had similar encounters. There must have been others like Kuutamo. Either others that looked like him or took on forms like that. The thought made her head spin. She had her notions about his character, but she had to admit there was no evidence of whether he was good or bad. She didn't know whether he held positive or negative intentions towards her.

Typing in the search terms, she appreciated having more facts to go on. Blue eyes, able to solidify, able to manage energy exchange—and—undeniably good-looking.

Sini struck gold when she found a list of alleged extra-terrestrial beings that people claimed to have met in close encounters with UFOs. She couldn't picture him as a Grey or a Reptilian as he didn't resemble one in the least. Look-wise he could be a Nordic alien, but she just didn't buy the alien theory. Then, if he came from Earth, could he be one of those beings that some people claimed they saw?

Elves were supposed to be beautiful and possess magical powers. They could be dangerous to humans, especially women, and they could cause illnesses. It seemed the belief in the existence of elf people occurred across the world. Then again, elves were popular in fiction even in modern times. Kuutamo might well be of elf origin. He possessed supernatural abilities, and the forest would be a natural element for an elf.

Did he have pointy ears? Had she seen his ears? She'd only once seen his face, and the hood covered up most of his head. Some of it added up. Still, he didn't appear elflike to her. On the other hand, maybe the reason she couldn't resist him was that he was inherently seductive? Though, she couldn't recall getting the impression of him trying to lure her in.

Sini glanced at the clock. It might be good to get out of the house, refresh the brain, get new impressions. Less fairy tale and more real world.

Driving through stretches of woods and fields, Sini felt upbeat, but as soon as she stepped inside the grocery store, she knew she'd made a mistake. She fished out the long list of things to buy and used it like a protective shield against the world. She told herself she was nervous because she so seldom came to town.

Walking her cart along the too-narrow aisles, she put into her cart the usual cheap cans and boxes of food that wouldn't expire in the near future. To soften the appearance of someone stocking up a private doomsday bunker, she picked up fresh food as well, just not the expensive meats. Except, she craved fish.

Halfway through her list, the familiar anxiety creeped up on her. To fill up her cart was cost-effective but spending all that money on food made her chest tighten. Picking up the pace, Sini stepped through the familiar route and threw in the usual choices. Why did she think she'd enjoy the shopping trip? She never did.

After stalling at the magazine shelves, she walked up to the cashier, feeling her heartbeat. When had she become like that? How could she have turned into someone who was afraid of people in the grocery store? Someone who suspected everyone was looking at her because she was a freak. She'd never had those tendencies before, but on the other hand, she'd never been alone. A little private maybe, but never a loner. She chose the cashier with the shortest line and made the mistake of looking them in the eyes. Sini imagined the blue-eyed, blonde woman recognizing her as the quirky, always alone, no-one-knows-who-she-is girl. Or worse, she knew who Sini was and therefore knew why she was strange. Because it ran in the family.

Sini answered the woman's greeting as she began stacking the products onto the belt, but she made sure not to look at her again. The food cost way too much, but she forged her agony into gratitude. After all, she had the money to buy all that food. Packing the bags with care, Sini was also grateful she'd soon be back in her car and on her way. The worst part was behind her.

Stepping into the low, white, and once modern building that housed the library, Sini knew she wouldn't stay and rummage through the shelves as she'd planned. She was relieved her books would be waiting for her, stacked together in the corner of some easily accessed shelf. She'd appear poised and resolute, do her thing, and then get out. The moment she asked the librarian where the reserved books might be, she saw that wasn't going to happen.

The grey-haired woman in the knitted shirt in abstract patterns of bright colours looked at her briefly, only to turn back and let her gaze linger on Sini's face. Sini hurried in the direction she'd pointed and felt her face heat up. Wow, she didn't remember choosing that many books. She glanced back at the desk where the librarian had sat down. Change of plans.

Sini read the signs at the end of the shelves until she found what she was looking for. Maybe she'd find books on old fairy tales. Domestic and foreign. She didn't recall elves being that popular in her culture. Reading the book titles one by one, Sini didn't know which ones to pick, but it gave her respite from her surroundings. Now and then, she peeked at the desk, but the woman never left.

Sini checked the clock on the wall. She wanted to go home, and her arms were getting tired from carrying the books.

Quietly walking up to the lending machine next to the nosy librarian, she was careful not to look at her. She kept her eyes on the machine, stacked the books on the table, and took out her library card. Halfway through scanning the books, she saw movement in the corner of her eye. She faced the other direction.

The woman said something, but Sini focused on flipping the books in and out of the laser beam.

"You look so familiar…"

The soft, nosy voice was directed at her—she knew without looking. Four books left. She leaned forwards and grabbed hold of her backpack.

"Now I know…"

Sini could no longer pretend she didn't hear her and glanced at the woman.

"…you must be Satu's grandchild. Yes. You came with your grandmother when you were little. When the library was in that old place—the old wooden house that got mould." The librarian sounded pleased with her discovery.

Sini had no idea if she'd seen the woman before, but she vaguely recalled being in a place with crammed bookshelves in small rooms with creaky floors and a distinctive smell. She pretended to consider the statement.

"No."

"No? I've seen so many children visiting the library and watched them grow into adults. I can imagine Satu's granddaughter growing up to be as pretty as you." The woman was scrutinizing her face now. "You resemble her, you know?"

The voice began to doubt itself as Sini made no effort to corroborate. She'd known right away the woman was a snoop. Perhaps Sini had remembered her after all.

"No, not me. Excuse me, I'm in a hurry." Sini forced a smile but directed it at the zipper of her backpack. "Thanks, and bye." She passed the woman, pretending to look at her wrist-watch. She couldn't get through the door fast enough. Thank heavens for self-service. If the librarian had seen her library card, she would've recognised the name.

Sitting in the car with the engine running, waiting for the window to clear of condensation, Sini wondered why her reaction had been so strong. Why had she panicked when the quite harmless elderly woman recognized her? She'd most likely been friendly with her grandmother and hadn't sounded the slightest bit judgemental. Well, that was because she didn't know Sini actually believed in elves.

She cringed at the realisation that someone who knew who she was knew about her exceptional interest in myths and fairy tales.

It was dark when Sini arrived at home with her backpack full of library books and three bags of groceries. Her gaze turned to the black forest as she unloaded the car. She wouldn't go back until she was better prepared. He must know much more about her than she knew about him. He was the intruder, after all.

Turning on the light and smelling the familiar scent of old house and countryside, Sini had never been happier to be exactly where she was. The quiet that sometimes bothered her had never been more welcoming. The outdated furniture and the décor didn't match, but never had she been happier to sit on the creaky yellow kitchen chair or light the unadorned fireplace.

Carrying the heavy grocery bags into the kitchen, Sini appreciated the extensive purchases. While stashing away the groceries, she contemplated how to go about researching all the books. The food would last at least two weeks—three if she used up the existing canned food. She looked forward to treating herself with rainbow trout.

When her last bag was empty, she realized the cupboard was filled with purchases except for the spot reserved for sweets and chips. That was a first. Maybe something good would come of the mystery. Even if sugar cravings hit, she'd resist driving back to town. She'd have to be pretty desperate.

Her reaction to the kind woman who looked the same age as her grandmother still surprised her. Why was it a catastrophe that someone from what should've been her community had shown her interest? Would she judge like the others if she found out Sini had been alone in the little house for years and wasn't making an effort to return to a decent, more practical existence? Would she start meddling if she knew Sini was more into spirits than real people? That she sometimes wanted to die before moving on?

She might dream of getting her life back together and returning to civilisation, but it was clear she wasn't ready. She wasn't ready to face relatives and old acquaintances and explain where she'd been the past years or why she wasn't in pursuit of a family or a career like normal people.

If she could only save some money for that ticket far away, where she wouldn't need to explain herself. If someone asked, she'd choose better-sounding words like *widening her horizon, searching for a different path, being tired of the Finnish way of life.*

The more she thought about it, the more logical moving abroad and starting fresh sounded.

Sini had the first book open in front of her as she prepared dinner.

She took care not to splatter fat from the sizzling frying pan on the dictionary of Finnish folk religion. It burst with nature deities, rites, and superstition she'd never heard about. If she read through the over four hundred pages, she'd very likely stumble upon things considered significant.

She checked the other books loaded onto the kitchen table. The book on Finnish mythology had almost five hundred pages, and the one on Sami mythology even more. Even if she spent her entire day reading, it would take days, most likely weeks, to get through them.

Trying to find knowledge about Kuutamo would be like looking for a needle in a haystack, but those books were her best chance. Would she recognize the corresponding facts when she found them? Would she approve of them? Would he turn out to be one of the good guys? Based on what she'd read so far, people of the past had a strange way of perceiving things.

Would she have the perseverance to go through the books before she went back for him?

Oh well. Reading about the cultural history of her ancestors and their beliefs couldn't be a waste of time. Based on her first impression, the stories were a lot more exciting than the ones on her grandmother's bookshelf.

Even though Sini was eager to rummage through the ample knowledge planted into the books, she ate at a leisurely pace. The salmon with a crusty skin fried in butter and seasoned with sea salt melted in her mouth. The potatoes and vegetables tasted OK. She'd have to grow her own next summer. Her grandmother's garden contained plenty of space to grow whatever—she just hadn't been inspired to care for it before. It required lots of work. In fact, the main reason was she'd never intended to stay for long. But even though the status of her escape plan was active, she found only good aspects in growing her own food. For one, she wouldn't have to go buy it from other people.

As Sini at last got to relax on the old sofa with a cup of mint tea and honey and the selected book in her hand, she recalled how she, as a teenager in school, had read from the *Kalevala*. The Finnish national epic had been constructed from sung poems compiled around the country a long time ago. There'd been a vast effort in collecting the knowledge passed on via oral traditions from generation to generation before it was forgotten. The national epic had been used as a way of developing the identity and boosting the self-image of the Finnish people in a time when independence was but a dream. She remembered reading it, and it'd contained some interesting plots, but she'd thought nothing more of it. She didn't remember learning about all the other creatures that her library books brimmed with.

To her, it had been only a bunch of fairy tales—not a source of information. But people had told those stories for ages—had they themselves believed in them? She didn't remember that any of the characters, may it be the hero or the villain, resembled Kuutamo.

She remembered Väinämöinen, the old sage who was as old as Earth, and his enemy, the powerful witch of Pohjola. Väinämöinen was wise and resourceful, but according to the story, he'd mess up when it came to women. Louhi was the old and evil female character that ruled over a difficult to access dark and cold land. They'd fight each other over things, and it would most often be Väinämöinen who wanted things that Louhi had, like her beautiful daughters or source of wealth.

Reading up on the main events in the epic, Sini recalled other characters. Väinämöinen had two partners in crime: Ilmarinen and Lemminkäinen. Ilmarinen was a blacksmith who forged wondrous things like the dome of the sky and a magic mill that produced grains and gold. Handsome Lemminkäinen was into women and loved going to war. It was a bit ridiculous how all three of them were in desperate pursuit of the beautiful daughters of Pohjola. The *Kalevala* was for the most part based on the old poems, but its creator, a national hero, had edited and rearranged them to construct a comprehensive story.

It annoyed Sini that Louhi, the only female with great power, was portrayed as old, scarce-toothed and greedy, while the most important heroes were appealing and talented men. That the old story lacked gender equality was no surprise, but they didn't have to make the matriarch of Pohjola ugly and one-dimensionally foul. Though, it was kind of cool that the great antagonist was a strong and independent female.

The hero protagonist, Väinämöinen, was a powerful sha-man, depicted as older and bearded. His greatest strength was the song, and he played the traditional stringed instrument, the kantele. He'd get into a trance and go on journeys to the underworld in search of knowledge.

She couldn't help wondering who those characters had been. The people and events of the epic were based on myths, the old songs, but had there once been a famous person who was the original Väinämöinen? A real person whose bravados through time had been exaggerated by storytellers until the original story became unrecognisable.

It was early morning when Sini found the most meaningful clue in one of the dictionaries. Linked to a story about burglars was the belief that the full moon illuminated everything and nothing could hide, as it showed the true character of every being whether it was good or bad, camouflaged or hiding. Was that the connection between a visible Kuutamo and the light of the moon?

But that was it. She'd learnt that people and their animals could be captured and hidden by the forest. A spell was put on the person by gnomes who lived underground, the *maahinens*, or a jealous neighbour so that they couldn't find their way back home. Another reason to be cut off from the normal world was misbehaving in the forest. People who went searching for the missing couldn't find them as they were camouflaged as a stone or tree stump. If the person realised they'd been hidden, they had to perform a series of backwards rituals or movements to break the spell—like turning their clothes inside out. In one region, they used a cat to find out who was guilty of casting the spell. If the cat ran to the forest after throwing it over one's shoulder, the forest spirit had done it.

She also knew that cattle could be protected by circling them twice clockwise and once counter clockwise.

Still nothing that pointed to Kuutamo. Not even close. The only thing she considered a fact was him being from another dimension. Or time.

What did he want from her? He wasn't there just to hang out. How could she trust him when she knew nothing about him? She'd been open-minded about getting to know him, but was he worth her faith—had he earned it? Why was it more important to her to get a connection than be safe? Whatever creature he might be, he sure was alluring. She should demand answers, or at least try to ask for an explanation. She shouldn't keep meeting him in the dark forest without knowing where they were heading.

She needed to stop using her rational mind when she got preoccupied with the idea he was some kind of monster or demon who would reveal his true character once he'd lured her in. Despite the uncertainty and need for caution, she couldn't wait to get back.

She needed to breathe freely in the guaranteed absence of humans. She needed the grounding energy of untouched nature.

Going to that forest every day had become crucial to her— even before Kuutamo.

Sini woke up with a book next to her face.

She'd slept like a rock. Eight o'clock. Perfect! She had time for more studies before heading out.

The old skis were left standing upright against the wall of the shed as Sini headed for the forest. Skiing had proven to still be too difficult. She'd taken other measures to ensure a comfortable afternoon. The backpack carried an insulated sitting pad and extra pairs of gloves and socks. To be on the safe side, she'd packed an extra pullover. She was prepared to stay longer than usual. That was her intention until she got to the edge of the field and a chilly wind smacked her face.

Sini grimaced. She hadn't realised it was windy and that she should've worn her extra clothing instead of carrying it. She'd taken three steps when a gush of wind grabbed hold of her and the backpack and tried to push her into the nearest snowdrift. Determined not to have another dark moment headlong in the snow, Sini managed to keep her balance. She pulled up her hood with faux fur trimming and kept walking. The hood was the best of inventions. It shielded her face from the icy wind, it was no wonder Kuutamo found it useful.

Would he be there?

Yes.

That was the answer that came to her. She wanted to believe that she could sense him waiting for her.

As she reached the open part of the field, she understood the evil gust wasn't an anomaly. The wind attacked her with full force, making her stop and wait for it to relent. She contemplated turning back to safety, but the vision of her sitting with her books in front of the fire didn't feel appealing at all. She'd rather get answers straight from the source instead of spending another day deliberating old long-bearded men and how superstition had filled the lives of people in the past. Determined to get answers to what Kuutamo was and what on earth he was all about, Sini pulled the hood tighter and trudged on.

The weather could've been worse, though. It could've been more freezing or pouring down snow.

Sunny weather would've been nice. It would make the day longer, help her discern more details of Kuutamo—his clothes, his face. But she hadn't seen the sun in weeks. Was it really weeks already? The sun would still not crown the treetops, but it might get a few rays in between the trees.

There he was!

She saw him the moment she reached the beginning of her path.

How did he know when she'd come? Was he waiting for her? Or did he sense her arrival? Could he see her house, or was there a visual barrier around the forest? She harboured so many questions, but she didn't know how to ask them.

She'd never tried to speak to him, except for that one time in the beginning. He'd never uttered a sound, and she didn't know if he was able to. In her world, that was. He had a mouth, didn't he? A well-shaped one.

Sini smiled at the figure, whose movements indicated impatience. As much as she resented the horrid vision from the time before, it pleased her to see him. She obliged by following him, but it would be more on her terms the way they'd communicate next time.

Kuutamo walked in front of her for the longest time so far. Where was he heading?

When he eventually paused to wait for her, Sini stopped at a safe distance. She waited for him to advance deeper into the forest before following. He was moving towards a denser area, and she had to be careful not to lose him among the trees.

He stopped in a space surrounded by an incomplete circle of spruces. Inside it were a few boulders, and with him standing there in his dark cloak, it looked magical. Like a sacred grove, where worship or secret rites had been carried out in a forgotten time.

Sini stopped at the edge of the magical circle. She watched Kuutamo reach one of the boulders and swipe his hand at the snow. Sini's jaw dropped when he managed to scoop off the snow from the stone surface. He turned to her and did another swiping motion of the hand.

Sini looked at his face. He wanted her to sit down on the stone? She approached him but stopped a few steps short. Kuutamo took a step backwards, and then another. He must have sensed her hesitation. Sini showed her appreciation for the space provided by taking the sitting pad and placing it on the snow-free layer of moss and lichen. She sat down on the soft seat that was at a perfect height. The wind didn't reach through the thick, snow-clad spruce branches.

Was something up?

She sensed Kuutamo's gaze on her. He appeared to always be looking at her, and she wished she could return the gesture. His tall figure stood in the middle at a stone that looked like an altar. He was touching the stone again. She wanted to know what purpose the stones had. To her, they were ordinary, boring boulders of common granite that could be found anywhere.

When he'd finished whatever he was doing, he turned to her and pushed the hood down onto his shoulders.

…wow…

Sini thought her jaw actually dropped as his face had her wordless. The blue of his eyes was a shade lighter than before—probably due to the light—and every feature of his face was perfect. He was not a contemporary beauty, but a model of ancient times. His hair was ash blond, and the gently curling wisps that framed his ears and almost reached his shoulder looked thick and strong. Cave warrior. That strong mouth that she'd referred to so many times got a more sumptuous curve when it was accentuated by those eyes.

He must have known the effect his revealing had on her. Perhaps he tried to make up for last time.

She felt the urge to touch him. She wasn't going to. But she wanted to get closer. She had to get a closer look. Before he did his disappearing act on her.

Sini slowly leaned forwards, got up, and stepped towards him. As otherworldly as he was, he definitely looked human. A very, very appealing human. But scrutinizing him wasn't embarrassing. He wanted her to, and she wanted to learn what he was. From a scientific aspect. To get more details to help her in her search for recorded information.

Kuutamo reached his hand towards her, and she flinched. He sensed her fear and lowered it. Sini was sorry for her reaction, but she couldn't let him touch her. No matter how gorgeous he might be, she didn't want another lucid nightmare.

Kuutamo turned his face up at the sky. Before she could check what had caught his attention, something came flapping down and landed on his shoulder.

A little feathery ball.

It was the owl!

"Oh!" Sini's mouth opened round. She looked to Kuutamo, who smiled at her reaction.

The little creature looked comfortable perched on his huge shoulder. She didn't understand anything, but she'd forgotten about her fear. The round, yellow eyes fixated on her, and Sini felt the urge to touch it. Was it real? Or was it like Kuutamo, sometimes solid and other times not?

Sini reached her hand towards the owl. She didn't want to dishonour it with her request, but…

Light as feather and with two wing flaps, the owl jumped onto her mitten-clad hand.

She was unable to repress a giggle, but her sound left the bird unaffected.

She didn't touch it, though, but inspected its features.

Its body was as tall as the length of her hand. The wings were a dark chocolate brown with round, white feathers that looked like big translucent pearls cascading down its back. The front was striped with chocolate and those pearls. Its face was framed with two half-moons with tiny white pearls scattered on their dark edges. If the bird hadn't been so small, she would've been worried about the feather-clad talons gripping her fingers through the mitten.

She barely felt its weight.

Sini recognized the species. It was the second smallest of the owls nesting in the country. *Pearl owl.* The name in her language was spot-on. She would call it *Helmi.* Was it she or a he? There was nothing translucent or fairylike about it. She wanted to know what the relationship between Kuutamo and the living being from her realm was.

Sini looked at Kuutamo, who'd been watching their interaction with apparent contentment. Was he perhaps one of those animal whisperers?

Careful not to touch him, Sini extended her hand towards his shoulder. Helmi hopped over onto the massive frame, settled into a comfortable position, and closed her eyes.

Last time she'd left Kuutamo, she'd been confused and hurt. As she walked away from him and the lovely creature that rested on his shoulder, she felt her body wrench for another reason.

Leaving them behind made her heart ache.

8 QUESTIONS

Sini smiled as she crossed the threshold to her home.

Although she was getting a feel for winter again, the warmth was welcoming. Winter had started to mean Kuutamo, but it wasn't her natural element. She envisioned sitting opposite to Kuutamo on their respective stones surrounded by green leaves and flowering wild rosemary. The sun high enough to bring warmth. She didn't have to hurry home before getting chilly.

Sini lit the fireplace and stripped to her underwear. It was freedom not to wear layer upon layer of clothing. She felt bouncy. Happy. What happened in the forest was huge.

She'd forgotten about the awful incident from the time before. Kuutamo was forgiven. He'd brought her to a sheltered place and showed her something special. He'd revealed so much about himself. That he had an owl companion. He'd been able to remove the snow from the stone, and the owl had been able to perch on his shoulder. With the hood completely off, she'd been able to see his features so clearly. There was nothing evil about him. He didn't have pointy ears, either.

Bouncing over to the kitchen table, Sini decided to open the new white envelopes she had stuck under the stack of junk mail and free newspapers. She picked one up, took a deep breath, and ripped it open with her finger. She eyed it quickly, an ad for a roof repair company. She picked up another one, the one she dreaded the most.

Oh, no!

Sini read the text twice to be sure she'd understood. In a few months she would stop receiving unemployment money. After that, she'd either have to get a job or rely entirely on welfare. Sini raised her hand, ready to squash the letter, but used all her willpower not to do it. Instead, she smashed the papers on the table and began pacing the living room.

Why couldn't they understand she was incapable of having a job? Being isolated for years hadn't made her condition any easier. Besides, there weren't any jobs close to home. She'd have to spend at least a couple of hours driving to and from work. Which meant she needed to do full days not to lose too much money on fuel. And what about her unreliable car?

Sini realized she was speaking out loud. She couldn't stop pacing. What was she to do? To have to live on welfare was the last straw. She'd be at the mercy of social services, having to report everything she needed money for, and they weren't guaranteed to give her enough to survive. She felt dizzy, as if blood had stopped flowing through her brain. What if it was the onset of a panic attack? She should sit down, but she didn't know how.

She should go to the doctor to have herself checked. They'd see she wasn't capable of taking on a job. But what if they did diagnose her with something mental? Depression or something else? Then she'd have to go to therapy or pop pills or much worse... No, she'd rather take a job than be diagnosed unfit.

Then again, she had no one else to help her. Not even her parents. She envisioned her mother going on a rant about selling the house and moving back to civilization, where suitable jobs were found. For a start, she could work as a ski instructor, teaching what she was most talented at.

That would never happen. Ever.

She had to lie down. She couldn't feel her hands.

Sini collapsed onto the bed. She rested her forearm on her face in an attempt to close out gloomy reality.

Sini had put all her eggs in one basket when she'd decided to study economics. Her plan had been to, together with Martin and a couple of friends, combine their sports careers with a business. That way, they might use their know-how and connections to start up a winter sports resort or the like after their active athlete careers had ended. As she'd left all that behind, she had nothing to build upon. She hadn't been that interested in the business aspect, but it was the logical thing to do.

Art classes she'd truly enjoyed, but there was no money in art unless one were highly talented. However, talent didn't guarantee making a living as an artist. And she wasn't that talented. She remembered drawing all the time as a child, but the love of drawing had dissipated as she'd gone to school and started doing sports. Her grandmother had always encouraged her to draw and paint. She remembered painting with water-colours at the kitchen table or being allowed to sit at the desk when her grandmother wasn't using it.

Sini sighed and let go of the vision from her carefree childhood. If there existed a decent job that didn't require being with people and going far from home, she'd give it a try. Earning her own money doing a job she didn't like was still better than depending on welfare. But what about her new friend? If she got a job, she couldn't go to the forest in daylight more than a couple of days a week. She might lose Kuutamo if she worked all day, but not having money might mean losing her house.

She couldn't imagine herself staying away anymore.

Her body finally relaxing, Sini regressed to the day when the owl had saved her from perishing in the snow. Not that she would've let herself freeze to death but seeing that lovely creature had brought her spirit back to life. She wondered if Kuutamo had also been there.

Sini stirred when she remembered the fire. It needed more wood. She eased herself up from the comfort of the bed and headed to where a cosy warmth was arising.

As always, when she was home alone surrounded by warmth and light, she told herself she might have lost her mind that day and had invented them both, so she'd have something to live for. Nonhuman creatures that liked her. Because they knew nothing about who she really was. An outcast. A nobody outcast.

They didn't ask her questions like … *what do you do for a living?* … *are you married?* … *what are your plans for the future?*

Is there a future for you?

She meant to look for work.

Honestly. She'd visited the site with job announcements for people like her. People who lacked specific experience for the jobs they applied for. She had no business going on sites aimed at professionals or go-getters. She needed something simple and close to home but with a salary she could manage on.

Sini had given it half an hour and then, discouraged, turned to her books.

She had a new clue to the Kuutamo mystery. The owl, Helmi. She'd decided it was a female.

The pearl owl, *Aegolius funereus*, was the most common owl in her country, though rarely spotted. It was active by night and, when threatened, ruffled up to appear bigger or made itself tall and thin to resemble a branch. Sini smiled as she imagined how Helmi ruffling up wouldn't make her at all intimidating. They could migrate long distances in autumn. The owls nested in March and laid three to six eggs in tree holes or nest boxes. The pair would usually not stay together from one breeding season to another. Unfortunately, the species had been categorized near-threatened, as the population had begun declining in the recent decades. It didn't surprise her that the main reason was decreasing coniferous forest habitats.

Owls were as mystical in literature as in their natural habitat. She didn't find anything about owls in the books of Finnish mythology. Well, apart from some people considering the hooting of the owl a bad omen. That meant nothing, since the Finns had considered the appearance of many bird species a bad omen.

Turning to the trusty internet again, Sini found a lot of mentions of owls in mythology. It amazed her how the owl had been associated with death and bad omens in all parts of the world. The scientific name of Kuutamo's owl verified her findings as it signified bad luck and funerals. What made the birds unpopular was their nocturnal way of life. She understood that hearing hooting sounds in the dark might be eerie to anyone. The only nice thing she could find among owl myths was the Greek goddess Athene, whose favourite bird had been the *little owl*. To the ancient Greeks, the owl was a protector. The little owl was of the same size as Kuutamo's owl. She found an image of a painting where the tiny owl was about to land on the shoulder of the goddess. It had been dated to two and a half millennia ago.

Athene held a spear in one hand and a helmet in the other. She was said to be associated with wisdom, handicraft, and warfare. As exhilarating as discovering the image of the tiny owl and the mighty goddess was, Sini knew Kuutamo was neither Greek nor a god. Neither would reside in her forest, wanting to connect with her.

Frustration was a mild word for what Sini felt late in the evening.

The connection to the Greek goddess was remote, but she and Kuutamo had the symbiotic relationship with the owl in common. She could see Kuutamo also having wisdom—he must know so many things Sini didn't. He didn't give the impression of a soldier, but she could see him defending what was valuable to him. He appeared gentle and patient, yet he was able to infuse a person with strange energies and visions.

The clothes he wore were odd—plain and stripped of any hints to his origins. No symbols or markings that would refer to a language. He always wore an all-covering bulky cloak like garment, and even that she couldn't picture clearly. Should she be alarmed that she saw his perfect face in her mind's eye when other details were a blur? Although, she couldn't have made him up. She'd never been one for living in a fantasy world, not since she was a child.

She had to find a way to ask him.

As Sini entered the forest the next day, she spotted Helmi perched on a young arching pine.

She looked around, searching for Kuutamo. He was never late, and she sensed he was there somewhere. She really did. Did he have trouble getting solid?

Just as Sini began to worry, she perceived his shadow in the corner of her eye to the left. She turned her head but saw nothing.

What?

She took a few timid steps and then picked up the pace, willing to wait for him to materialise. The sky was a light grey, and the white landscape was easy on the eye. She should have no problem distinguishing him. The warmer weather felt rather comfortable. A squirrel had left a trail of leaps in the soft snow. She sensed him behind her, as a delicate nudge in her back. She turned around, but again, nothing. Sini squinted her eyes. Was he playing with her?

She started walking again. This time, she turned fast as lightning when she spotted the shadow in her right corner.

Damn, he was fast. Sini laughed.

"OK, then!" Sini closed her eyes and waited.

Behind her. She turned.

On the left. She turned to her left with eyes still closed.

In front of her. She took a few tentative steps forwards until she couldn't feel him there.

She got really good at it. He turned her around in random directions. Then he made her wait so she wouldn't cheat by guessing. It was so much fun, but she suspected recreation wasn't the reason for his playfulness.

Behind her.

Sini whirled around and felt a silky touch on her cheek.

She opened her eyes and saw Kuutamo standing in front of her. His eyes were a bright shade of blue, like hers. Then he flickered before he vanished.

Come on!

She hated his dramatic exits. Especially after a precious moment. Sini continued walking. Alone or not, she'd get her walk. Maybe he'd come back, maybe not.

When Helmi dashed by and continued in the direction of the trail, she knew he was still there. If touching her had made him weak, she had a notion where he might be heading. Playing the energy game had her a little tired, too, but she was pretty sure she sensed him walking in front of her. At a distance.

When she approached the part where she'd have to get off the trail to reach the sacred grove, Helmi soared down from the top of a tall spruce. The owl dove in between the trees, and Sini followed.

Kuutamo stood with his back to her, holding his hands just above the snow-covered stone. He appeared his normal solid.

Sini approached him on light feet. She was not as flustered from treading through the snow as she'd been in the beginning. Having caught up with him, keeping a polite distance, she waited for him to turn to her.

Sini was still exhilarated from their playing, but Kuutamo's expression—or what she discerned from inside the hood—was earnest. Sini mimed the gesture of pulling back a hood.

She smiled as Kuutamo raised his hands to the hem of his hood, but he only pushed it back enough for her to see his face. She supposed he also needed to protect his head.

He should've worn a hat instead.

The way his eyes wandered from her eyes to the features of her face and then along her body made her heart go faster. She was suddenly apprehensive of how she appeared in his eyes. What was his preference? Would he favour blondes like himself? Or did he like that she was different?

Sini took her hat off, pulled up her hair from underneath the collar, and shook it loose. He looked at her as if he was making scientific observations. What was she to him?

As he studied her, she took the chance to stare at his face. The blue in his eyes was darker again. Perhaps the colour of his eyes reflected his mood? Though she hadn't seen much emotion in his face—and she had no idea what he was thinking—she was convinced he felt things.

Still, he came across very different.

Kuutamo raised his right hand towards her, and she wasn't fast enough to evade. With his hand only a hand's length away from her chest, she wanted nothing more than to be touched by him. She closed her eyes and took a deep breath.

Sini looked at him again and nodded. His eyes were questioning, so she announced her approval by saying. "Go ahead." He probably didn't understand, but she may as well try to teach him some basic phrases.

As his gloved hand slowly closed in on her left shoulder, she steeled herself against the impact. She didn't know whether she was afraid it would hurt or whether she was afraid she wouldn't feel him. The moment his fingers reached the fabric of her jacket, her breathing stopped.

She *was* a little afraid.

Her eyes stopped focusing as she concentrated. She wanted him to succeed.

Sini felt his soft touch as the sensation of fabric being compressed against her skin. Sweet chills ran through her body. Thrilled and embarrassed, she gazed up at his face. His eyes were fixed on the hand as if he needed all his energy gathered there.

There was a faint flickering.

"No, don't go!" Sini's hand dashed towards his retracting body and nudged his arm. She felt him!

Kuutamo swayed backwards and reached his left hand towards the boulder. Sini watched with anticipation as

Kuutamo seemed to draw energy from the lifeless rock. She crossed her fingers. Waited. His body stopped flickering.

Kuutamo turned towards her. A faint smile appeared on his lips. Her eyes lingered on their shape.

She had to stop herself. Kuutamo was *not* a human. Not a man.

She took a step forward. It was her turn. She took advantage of her momentum, while she still had the courage.

Standing close to the stone, with one hand still on it, Kuutamo nodded slightly.

She detected his approval, like a knowing. She rolled her shoulders, took a deep breath. It was as much about her abilities as it was about his.

Slowly, very slowly, she raised her hand and pushed it through the air towards his chest.

She felt a slight resistance where he began, but her emerging joy was premature. Her hand appeared to go through instead of pushing on the fabric of his cloak.

OK, not that bad. She'd almost succeeded. She tried again, mimicking the expression he'd done. She imagined the fibres of his garment, the cells of the fibres, firm as her own gloved hand.

No. She couldn't feel it.

Sini retracted her hand and slouched her shoulders. She just stood there, waiting for his reaction. She knew he wouldn't judge her, but she wanted him to know it was important to her, too. His chest looked perfectly solid to her.

Kuutamo's hand appeared in front of her face. The waving motion of his fingers snapped her out of her disappointment. He pointed at her hand. She was still holding her hat, and she noticed the cold tugging at her ears. Kuutamo's full attention was on her as she took off her gloves, tucked her hair behind her neck, and put the hat back on.

She looked at her bare hands. Maybe she needed to touch him without gloves? He had worn his, but he was also more skilled. She raised her free hand and looked at him. Kuutamo motioned for her to put the gloves back on. It was either sweet of him to care for her comfort, or…he didn't want direct contact. She chose to believe the first option.

His shoulder heaved upwards, and his eyes told her to do the same. She took the fullest breath she could manage without the cold air hurting her lungs.

He closed his eyes.

She closed her eyes.

Sini looked for calm inside her. The kind of calm that had brought them together in the beginning. She loaded her expectations and disappointment onto the capable, sturdy deck of her boat and let it float away on satiny, dark water. She had all the time in the world. She wasn't doing it for herself only. It was for him, too. He wanted to connect with her.

When Sini only felt the fresh air in her face, and all she heard was the silence of the forest, she opened her eyes. His eyes were upon her. Soft, his whole expression soft.

He nodded, but it was more like a slow closing and opening of his eyelids.

Once again, Sini carefully raised her hand. When she focused on his chest, he motioned with his hand to look him in the eyes.

When he had her attention, Kuutamo's entire face broke into a smile that jolted her heart. She felt the energy of pure joy flush through her body. Her own face turned into a big smile without asking for her permission.

Bewildered, she watched the beauty that radiated from his face and felt his power over her. Sini's hand stopped at something solid.

As if she'd forgotten what she was trying to do, Sini looked at her palm resting on his chest. She didn't dare push, but rather moved her fingers inside her glove and felt the resistance. Encouraged by her success, she let her hand slide in slow motion over the fabric, upwards, to the side...

She tried so hard not to let any thoughts arise, but she couldn't help wondering what he'd feel like underneath that enormously thick cloth.

Despite the cold air, her cheeks heated. With great reluctance, she lowered her hand.

Afraid she'd made him spend too much energy on her, she backed away.

Her face probably already blushed from the cold, and her reaction wouldn't show. She was more concerned that he'd sense her emotions. If he were a human male, she needn't worry about it, but how would he react if he knew she had inappropriate feelings?

She tried a casual smile, waved for him to follow, and started heading back. The day had been intense. She needed the calming effect of walking her path.

Only walking.

With the monotone winter scenery before her, Sini was relieved by the return of coherent thoughts. For once, she could appreciate the muffling effect of the all-encompassing white on her mind. The path, despite being a reminder of their restricted freedom, provided respite in offering her simple direction. Knee-high pine saplings bending into submission by thick lumps of snow. Wild rosemary and bilberries portrayed as mere dull bumps in the terrain. She took inspiration in their acceptance of things that were and couldn't be changed.

She still didn't know his intentions, why he showed such strong interest in her. A being who looked and felt like him was probably not desperate for company, but was it safe for her to want a deeper connection?

More than fear for her own safety, she feared that he'd be repelled by her weakness. That she might want something that wasn't being offered.

She shouldn't have thoughts about him that made her blush. Falling for Kuutamo was crazy. The more she tried to push her embarrassing thoughts away, the stronger they got. She was grateful he couldn't see her face. He only needed to smile at her to get complete control of her energy.

Sini pressed her gloves to her cheeks, as if they'd be any more efficient at cooling her flaring skin than the cold air.

As they closed in on the end of the path, Sini switched her thoughts onto the thing that was always on her mind. It might be pushing her luck to do it, but she was dying to know.

Sini looked around for a stick of some sort, but everything was covered up by the snow. She didn't want to break a branch of a tree and used her hand instead. She bent down and drew a big circle in the snow and then a small shape that resembled a dog's bone in the top hemisphere. She took a few steps down the path, took off the glove, and drew an enlarged shape of her country beside the circle that was supposed to be the globe. She made a small indent within the country outline to mark their current position. Then a few more steps to the right, where she drew the shape of a spruce and then a house.

When she was finished, she quickly covered the aching finger with the glove and hoped he'd understand her clumsy art.

Kuutamo stood at a distance from her. He looked at the shapes and then at her. He wore the hood again, but she could make out the slightly raised eyebrows and hint of a smile.

Sini pointed at the big sphere and gestured in a wide as possible circle as if to enclose everything beneath their feet. She pointed at the shape of her country in the sphere, then the bigger shape beside it, and then the smaller one again. She took a few steps back and checked whether Kuutamo was with her.

He didn't approach but gave a short nod.

A slight shiver moved through her. It could work.

She pointed at the spot on the country shape, at the shapes of the tree and the house. She pointed from the tree to the nearest spruce, and from the house to her house across the open landscape. It was the first time she'd *mentioned* her house, and another shiver cut through her when he looked directly at the building in the distance. To be even clearer, she pointed at the spot on the country and then at the ground.

Sini felt nervous as she approached the big question.

She pointed at herself and then at the ground, and all the figures in the snow. She raised her eyebrows as she pointed at him.

If she'd half expected a blank stare for an answer, she'd been wrong. He motioned with his hand for her to come closer, so she did. But when he raised his ungloved left hand in that specific way, Sini took two quick steps backwards. She was so not ready.

Either he didn't know how to draw, or his home was difficult to explain.

Sini looked carefully at Kuutamo, but he just smiled. His kind reaction didn't surprise her, as Kuutamo never seemed to get upset about anything.

Sini returned the smile and looked at her house. It was getting dark, and she was both tired and hungry. She didn't want to leave, but she couldn't stay. The afternoon had been lovely, but she was always left wanting more.

At least he was still there with her.

Sini closed her eyes. She tried to become still by taking long and even breaths. Would he take her cue despite her rejection a moment ago?

She waited.

A featherlight pressure travelled along the arch of her brow, ended up at her temple, and faded away. Her soul wanted to follow his energy, but there was nothing to trace.

Even though Sini had known he'd be gone when she opened her eyes, her heart stung as she started walking towards her home.

Where would he go?

9 THE COLD

Sini felt cold.

Walking home didn't help her body heat up again. In her eagerness to get back to Kuutamo and the owl, she'd forgotten to bring her backpack. By the time she reached the doorstep, her body shuddered.

Sini frowned and fumbled with the key. To get the flu would be devastating when she wanted to spend more and more time in the forest. It was a blessing she hadn't already caught it.

The shaking got worse, and she kicked off her boots and threw her clothes onto the floor. She couldn't get under the hot shower fast enough. At first, the warm water made her sigh with relief, but then it began to sting. Every drop of water was like a needle pricking her skin. She turned the knob upwards, but the cooler water hurt as well. She prayed it was nothing serious.

Sini forced herself to stay in the warm water until the shaking turned into shivers and then into a semi-comfortable feeling. She needed to take precautions.

Sini dried with care and wrapped her hair in a big towel. She walked over to her closet and put on warm leggings and a soft angora shirt. To be on the safe side, she draped herself in her light-green fleece robe with pink flowers, put two sets of wool socks on, and wrapped a scarf around her neck. Better hot than cold.

Burrowed between the sheets, Sini did her best to pour a mixture of garlic cloves soaked in hot water and honey down her throat. She'd also prepared currant juice to keep hydrated. It might have some vitamin C left despite being frozen. No TV—she wanted to stay positive. A book, perhaps?

Sini pulled the covers off and heaved herself out of bed. The camouflage book, as she called it, lay on grandmother's writing desk. Although the desk belonged to her, she'd always consider it her grandmother's. She picked up the book and returned to her place between the sheets.

The robe might be a bit excessive, as she was getting quite hot. She pulled it off with some struggle but kept it close.

Sini opened the book roughly where she'd stopped reading the last time. The calling and the authorisation of the shaman were done by spirits. He also needed to be chosen by his community. The calling of a shaman was rare and demanding, and it often manifested through dreams and visions or a difficult disease that brought on a coma and subsequent visions. Sometimes, the disposition to be called on by spirits ran in the family. To become a shaman was a great responsibility, and many fought the calling. There were stories of how exhausting resisting the calling was and how doing it had, in some cases, resulted in death. In practice, the shaman learnt from another, older shaman in a master-apprentice relationship. Being called and accepting the call wasn't enough, though. The shaman apprentice was required to go through an initiation ritual where he experienced his death and dismemberment on a spiritual level. The shaman needed to become a better version of himself so that he could help others.

When hunter-gatherers began settling down and became farmers, the role of the shamans changed. They were replaced by *knowers*, a kind of sage whose tasks were a bit different and more varied. Of course, the new religion that accepted only one god played an important part in eradicating the practice of all kinds of paganism.

Sini didn't know what to think about shamanism, whether it had a place in modern society. It was a shame, though, that instead of being proud of their unique tradition, they'd eradicated it. She recalled hearing that a kind of new age shamanism was practiced around the world and that there were courses, but she couldn't see how they'd actually access the otherworld.

Sini woke, soaked in sweat. Still half propped up and with an aching neck. The wet clothes needed to go before she got cold. To her relief, the robe lay within arm's reach.

As soon as she'd changed into dry clothes, a shiver sliced through her body. It didn't look good. Sini pulled the duvet and daybed cover up to her ear as she turned to her side and huddled her legs and hands to keep warm. She'd try to sleep again. Sleep might help her get well faster.

The entire night turned into a mix of shivering, sweating, and bizarre dreams. She was walking in the forest—she thought it was hers—but instead of providing shelter, it felt menacing. In the darkness were creatures—half animal and half human—that called out to her. She carried her headlamp, and pointing the light at the creatures was the only way she could keep them at a distance.

Although feeling threatened, she tried to listen. They didn't make any sense. She looked everywhere for Kuutamo, but he wasn't there. She wanted him to protect her from the insistent chanting. There was no way out, no exit. She just walked, and walked, and walked, caught in a loop.

Sini opened her eyes to the dim light with great relief. She reached for the light switch to make the distinction between night and day clearer.

Ouch. Sini squinted her eyes at the stinging light.

She felt better, though. No more switching between the temperature extremes. She needed another shower. Better later. She didn't want to jinx it.

Before her feet hit the floor, Sini knew she wouldn't get to see Kuutamo in the afternoon. She'd have to force herself to stay indoors until she felt safe stepping out in the cold again. Besides, who'd care for her if she got really sick?

She'd stay in bed; read, drink garlic and honey, watch TV, drink some more, have some soup from a bag… Staying away from Kuutamo was hard, but her patience would be rewarded. She turned off the light and resisted the urge to go right back to bed. She didn't want to risk falling asleep and getting lost in more dreams.

Walking to the kitchen, the soles of her feet hurt. The light from the kitchen window had her squinting again. Strange. It wasn't like the sun was shining from a clear sky or anything.

Although it wasn't advisable to have coffee when fighting a flu, she couldn't resist making one. She wouldn't swallow another sip of the garlicky stuff until she had the taste of coffee in her mouth.

Damn! Even the coffee stung. Sini put the mug on the counter and waited for it to cool. She wouldn't put cream in it. She never did.

Sini took the mug, pulled the curtains closed, and sat down on the sofa. She pulled the old-fashioned quilt with the crocheted squares on top of her. Her fingers smoothed across the simple flowers surrounded by layers upon layers of yarn in all the colours of the rainbow. She didn't know who'd made it. She'd never seen her grandmother do any crocheting.

Kuutamo. She'd touched him! And he'd touched her. A shiver tingled through her body. That one felt different, it didn't concern her. She recalled him gently brushing her face. Another shiver.

As it had been established—unless she *was* crazy—that he indeed was solid, he couldn't be a ghost. She'd abandoned the angel theory long ago, so she'd been right. She didn't believe in the time travel theory either. If he came from the future, he'd got the clothing wrong if he was trying to fit in.

He'd be solid all the time, though, if he came from the future. Of course, something might have gone wrong. But…then he'd surely have some device that helped him communicate with her in case in the future they had developed a different language. Or evolved into nonspeaking beings.

He seemed human, yet he didn't. He looked like a human, but one with superpowers. She'd created many theories of what he was or where he came from, but she couldn't grasp what he could be doing in the forest. Was he trapped there? He didn't act like it.

Kuutamo wanted to answer her question. She understood why her instinct had been to refuse being served another vision, but she regretted not taking the chance. She might know already, instead of sitting there turning her brain inside out. Why had she thought she'd find information about beings like him from the *Kalevala*? He didn't resemble any of its characters. He was so calm and benevolent. He might have looked a little menacing in his cover-all cloak and hood that hid his face, but she'd never feared him. Or believed that she ought to.

Sini stacked a couple of pillows against the arm of the sofa and lay down. She was so tired.

Maybe she could go to the forest later if she got a good rest.

Sini's violent turn bumped her into something solid.

Where was she? The familiar smell of the quilt. Still on the sofa but with her back crammed against the backrest. Fumbling at the lining of the quilt, closing her eyes and trying to pull it all the way to her neck, she finally registered what woke her. The phone was ringing.

She wouldn't answer. She wasn't fit to talk to anyone, it would either be a sales call or the employment office. Sini turned around and pulled the quilt tighter. The second the annoying ringing stopped she'd fall asleep.

Sini twitched on the verge of unconsciousness. The damn phone was still ringing. Only one person had the audacity to let it ring that long. If she didn't answer, the harassment would get worse.

"Hello." Sini struggled to clear her head. She wanted to sound normal so she wouldn't have to answer any additional questions.

"I've been talking with your father."

What was going on? Sini tried to recall any recent concerns that might be unsolved. "Uh-uh?"

"We know you have been struggling with not having enough money as you haven't had a job."

Sini was too tired to reply with something sharp to make the rant stop before they escalated into an argument. She returned to the sofa and lay down, ready to stay calm until it was over with.

"Since you're alone there, we thought, well, *I* thought, that we should help you out."

"I could really use some help at the moment." She blurted it out, surprised at her candidness and how tired she sounded.

"Yes?" The voice turned lighter. "I could send you some money, to help you manage a few months."

"Until I sold the house and moved back there?" She resented the fact that the support offer would come at too high a price and that the subject was so flammable.

"No, it's nothing like that. I'm worried about you. We want you to be safe."

Sini wanted to believe the offer was sincere. "I am safe." She felt safe in the warmth of her old quilt, but she knew it wasn't true. "Thank you. I'll think about it." Her calm reply amazed her mother as much as herself, as there was a brief silence at the other end.

Sini took a deep breath as the conversation ended. That was so unexpected. She longed for someone to help her, but she never expected her mother to be the first to offer it. Without conditions. She longed for motherly love, but she couldn't accept the help. She'd never have the money to pay back, and that meant she'd always feel indebted and would have to oblige her parent's future requests. Besides, her mother might have meant it for the moment, but surely, she'd try to persuade her daughter to make radical changes. If Sini accepted the financial help, it meant admitting she didn't manage living on her own in her grandmother's house. Near the forest.

Sini abandoned the analysing and turned to her favourite subject. She put the phone on silent and stared mindlessly at the window with its curtains drawn, trying to find a comfortable position.

She'd dreamt of Kuutamo. That even when she wasn't with him, he'd be waiting for her return. She felt so much better, but it was already getting dark. A curse escaped her lips. She was sick of the dark that invaded every corner of her life.

She'd go to him the next day.

He didn't belong in the forest. Although his appearance might indicate a Robin Hood-like character, his presence didn't match the environment. She thought of the manlike maahinens, the beings that lived beneath the earth. Like humans, but opposite, as everything underground was upside down. Or the Gufihtars of the Sami folklore, who were wealthy and owned large herds of beautiful reindeer. They were a bit smaller than humans, and the women possessed extraordinary beauty. Sami men were known to marry Gufihtars, and if specific rituals were performed, the female gnome could turn into a human.

Apart from wanting to live a normal life on the other side of the human world, they had a dark side. Sini giggled at the idea of Kuutamo wanting to kidnap her and take her to his underground world. He had the looks, and it wasn't hard to imagine someone wanting to marry him, despite his shady background. He was too tall, but maybe he'd chosen to take on a shape bigger than her.

Then there were the Jatulis, the giant people that inhabited the country before humans arrived. The Jatulis were tall and robust and skilled at using magic. They disliked humans and lived in the ground. Stories told that remnants of their housings had been found in the form of stone arches and walls.

Kuutamo didn't have a house that she knew of. He didn't eat; she didn't know if he slept; he simply didn't *do* anything. He just *was*.

Waiting for her…

Sini checked the clock on the wall. Already late afternoon. Had he been waiting for her? In her mind's eye, she saw him standing close to where she always entered the forest. He was looking at her house.

I can't come today. I'm sorry. She pictured his intense eyes veiled in patience.

It is all right. Be well. The tall, dark figure at the edge of the forest remained where he was.

As she didn't fall asleep again, Sini got up, turned on the TV, and headed into the kitchen. She was nauseous from hunger. Once again, she'd make dinner for one. She wished Kuutamo could keep her company. Why couldn't he be a normal human, a regular guy? Of course, if he'd been a regular guy, Sini wouldn't have met him, nor would she have been interested. To find an impossible friendship was her fate. He obviously didn't know she was no one special. Though, she wouldn't help him understand he'd made a mistake in choosing her to play with.

The chicken noodle powdered soup tasted awful. Unnatural. The onion-and-herbs seasoned chicken had been fine before. Maybe it was spoilt. Sini picked up the bag from the garbage. The best before date was OK. Maybe it was a bad batch. A couple of slices of wholegrain bread helped get the soup down. She didn't have a choice—wasting food by pouring it down the drain wasn't an option. She convinced herself finishing it would make her better.

Sini gave up when the next spoonful made her heave. In an attempt to rinse out the horrid taste, she filled a glass with tap water. The cool liquid felt amazing in her mouth. She emptied the glass and filled it up again. The water was soothing, fresh, life-giving.

Sini parted the curtains that had been shut all day. The bird feeder was vacant, as the birds only fed in daylight. The birds!

She put the glass down and hurried to the door. Despite the short distance to the other side of the house, she dressed in outdoor clothes. She avoided looking to the forest as she exited the house and wrapped a scarf over her mouth. Lifting the lid of the bird feeder, she saw the seed level was alarming. She guessed it was a positive thing the birds had a good appetite. She poured in seeds to the brim—in case she forgot again— and scattered some on the ground.

Sini had done her best at resting and doing nothing, watching movies, but she gave up. She wasn't capable of watching them. The violence came across so vividly she imagined how it felt being hit or kicked or stabbed. The sad scenes made her cry as if her own heart was ripped out by grief. She'd cry sometimes, but only when one of her own memories was triggered, not like that, when she felt for those strangers. What was happening to her?

Sini turned off the TV. She'd succeeded in quietening her thoughts and numbing her longing, but enough was enough. She got up and went to bed. The only thing she'd eaten after the soup were fruits, but she wasn't hungry. Just awfully tired. And afraid.

As her head hit the pillow, she prayed her night would be peaceful and that she'd wake as her old self.

⌘ ⌘ ⌘

Sini stirred in the bright light.

She knew where she was. The fact that she stood on the snow-covered plain without warm clothes on—still perfectly comfortable—told her she was in that mystical place that was Earth—or not.

A soft breeze played with her hair. The same gust picked up snowflakes and whirled them off to a spot farther away.

She could smell the snow. The air was so pure that it had no scent, yet it felt wonderful as she breathed it. It didn't hurt her lungs. It didn't make her nose dry up and itch.

She began walking. She wore some kind of thin boots adorned with a simple, pretty pattern. They resembled suede. Her steps were so soft it rather felt like floating.

Sini tilted her head up and spread her arms. The sky was a perfect blue. No vapour trails from airplanes, no orange hues of pollution. The horizon was so far away that her eyes couldn't make it out. She was alone, but she felt powerful, free, whole. It was so new, but still so old.

She sat down. She shoved her hand into the soft layer of snow and grabbed a handful. It didn't melt in her palm. She blew at it and watched it scatter into glistening sprinkles. She laughed out loud. She missed laughing like that. Then she sensed a presence. Her heart started beating so hard it bounced against her chest.

The light turned into darkness. Another, much softer, light enticed her to open her eyes, and she found herself in the familiar, closed space of her bedroom.

When Sini realised that she'd woken from her new recurring dream, she was sorry it ended. Turning onto her back, she wished she could fall back asleep and return. The snowy plain was the place she'd seen when touching Kuutamo. She'd have to ask him. She needed to know if it was only her or if Kuutamo had something to do with it. Had being with him in winter created the dreams, or was there a direct connection between the dreams and him?

Sini closed her eyes and relished in the peace the dream had imbued her with.

The next time Sini came to her senses was in the echoes of a violent shudder. She was freezing. She pulled everything that caught her hand over her, but it didn't help. The fabrics were heavy on her, but she could've just as well been in her underwear. Waiting had no effect. The fast-increasing number of shudders that shook her indicated rocketing body temperature. She had no choice but to ride it out and wish for a fast recovery. But even if the fever subsided by the next day, she'd have to wait another day before going out again.

Why, oh why couldn't it already be spring with sun and warm air and flowers…

As the shivering slowly dissipated, Sini fell into a shallow sleep.

Even when she thought she was conscious, odd images told her she was somewhere between the two states. Her dreams became a mix of rapidly changing scenes and unfamiliar faces. She woke, cold from the moist clothes against her skin.

The fever went down a notch, and Sini grabbed the opportunity to fetch several sets of dry clothes, a jug of water, and some fruits. She couldn't find any medication to take in case the fever climbed too high for her to manage. As she closed the last drawer, she prayed she wouldn't need them. She reprimanded herself for being careless and complacent. Living alone in the middle of nowhere, she should've been more adamant about preparing for potential challenges.

The chills returned as she headed back to bed.

The following night, her body temperature seesawed. She only got deeper sleep between the highs and the lows. She counted the time between the highs, expecting them to ebb, but they only got more frequent.

By the third night, Sini had gotten used to the ups and downs. When she was cold, she imagined lying on warm sand on a serene beach, and when she got hot, she went to the place of snow and ice.

By the fourth night, she wanted to cry. The fever no longer relented at all, but she preferred the heat as she at least stayed dry. Her whole body ached, and she hadn't gotten enough to eat. She was weak from hunger but didn't have the willpower to get up and make food. Hunger and weakness became a vicious circle. She couldn't get up, as her body would start convulsing, and she had to wrap herself in the warm blanket. Getting to the toilet or to the kitchen turned into a perilous journey, and she always waited until the last moment. She felt absent and unmotivated to care for herself. The fever had weakened both body and mind.

The fifth night she cried. It was a still sobbing because the tears stung her sore eyes. She feared she wouldn't make it through. If she got worse, she wouldn't be able to call for help. The constant lying down left her muscles in unceasing pain.

Sini was sorry. That wasn't what she'd had in mind when she wished she was dead and that they wouldn't find her body. She didn't want to die—not anymore. The thought of people finding her rotting in her bed was disgusting, terrifying. Yet, there was nothing she could do. She was also sorry that she'd declined her mother's offer to help. If things had been only a little different, her mother might have been there with her, bringing food and helping her walk.

She called her mother, and they talked through everything. Sini forgave her mother for being overbearing, and her mother forgave Sini for abandoning her parents. Sini would move close to them, and she would never again have to fear dying alone. Instead, Sini would have the support of her family when going through difficult times.

She woke up, barely aware of what was dream and what was reality. The phone had died, as she didn't have the energy to move to put it on charge. Rocking herself on her side, she hummed a lullaby that her mother used to sing to her as a child.

She cried for Kuutamo, who'd been waiting for her. He was the only one who'd understand her choices. He wouldn't ask why she lived the way she did. He was the one she wanted to be with, but he wasn't able to help her either. He couldn't come to her house, but she didn't know why. She, in turn, couldn't fight the cold. It kept her from getting back to him; it had made her sick. The cold was an enemy she couldn't defeat. Winter was a barrier, beautiful but deadly, that she could never penetrate.

As the fever once again peaked, Sini dreamt that she'd caught something from Kuutamo, and the thought haunted her through the night. He'd reach his hand towards her, and she'd flinch, afraid of what he'd infuse her with. Kuutamo's piercing stare alternated with the chanting. At first, she was the one chanting, but when she stopped, the lamenting sound echoed, recorded in a continuous loop. She was like a listless dummy floating on the vibrations of the beat, whisked into nothingness and then caught by the soundwaves again. Tossed around by the will of someone else, too weak to defend herself.

If only the singing would stop for a minute so she could sleep. For brief moments, she managed to escape to the light, quiet world of her own, where no one could touch her. Then, too soon, she was in the forest again, trying to fend off the creatures with her dimming headlamp.

What if her last moment had come. She'd die in her bed before she'd gotten her chance to live.

Grandmother, help me! Unable to open her mouth, she screamed inside her mind. She was choking on her hot breath.

Sini moaned. She wanted her grandmother so badly. Her grandmother was the only one able to help her. She needed her to come with healing food, to sit with her and hold her hand. To stroke her cheek and tell her she was going to live through it. Between the slits of her swollen eyelids, she could see her walking about in the kitchen. When her grandmother hummed, it was the most beautiful sound in the world. She could smell the strengthening aroma of soup—not the crappy stuff, but the genuine kind with fresh ingredients.

Grandmother?

Yes, my dear?

I'm so happy you're here with me.

Shhh… Sleep, my little one.

Sini felt a warm hand caress her hair and face. A familiar touch from her childhood.

Someone else had stroked her cheek. That shadow in the forest. With crystal blue eyes. Like hers…

She wanted him, too…

Sini opened her eyes to a light bedroom.

Her eyes didn't hurt anymore. She distinguished all the details of the simple room, and the flower pattern of the old wallpaper was the most beautiful thing she'd seen. The effortless flow of air in her nostrils felt too fresh, considering she hadn't aired the room in days.

Her body didn't react to her pushing off the duvet or placing the soles of her feet on the cold floor. The floor was scattered with plates of half-eaten food and dried-up remnants of fruit. Empty glasses covered the nightstand. Her mouth was dry, and her stomach told her she was starving, but at least she'd managed to get something inside her.

Standing up, Sini no longer felt dizzy or weak. If it hadn't been for the numerous glasses and plates, a house that had cooled, and the subtle aches all over her body, she'd have considered the illness nothing but a dream.

She remembered thinking on several occasions that she was going to perish, but those moments were already distant. Nothing had changed in her life, but she'd never been more grateful for another chance.

Sini put on a fresh robe for good measure and headed for the fridge. She picked anything she could put straight into her mouth and regarded herself blessed for being able to eat. Chewing on a slice of smoked sausage, cheese, and a bite of cucumber all at once, Sini looked out the window. The birds flocked at the feeder. Like a miracle, the seeds had lasted through her days of fever. Instead of the cool light stinging her eyes, she saw the details of the plumage of the little tits. Their quick flights to and from the feeder was a sign of change in temperature.

What a strange disease. Fever and pain were her only symptoms, and she feared it wasn't an ordinary flu. But apart from the remaining soreness that could be explained by lying in bed five days in a row, she felt perfectly fine. Since she'd stopped doing sports and lived on her own, she hadn't suffered any serious ailments. Staying out in the cold too often and too long were clearly the cause of the fever, and it was such a relief it hadn't affected her airways. Sini grabbed the phone that had fallen to the floor and put it to charge. She wasn't completely sure it had been five days. It was so strange, though. At times, she'd felt a little cold spending so much time in the forest, but she'd never been worried. Picking up the plates, the decaying chicken and sour apple core made her nose tingle.

She was dying to get outside. Out in the fresh air.

She walked over to the living room window and opened the curtains. Gazing at the forest that was too dense and far away to distinguish any living creatures, she imagined seeing his shadow. Oblivious of the freezing snow and biting winds, she felt a pull so strong her stomach knotted.

She remembered her grandmother kept binoculars somewhere and checked the cabinet. Yep, she found the bordering-on-antique binoculars that were heavy but usable, got back to the window, and focused on the spot she'd imagined him. Although he wouldn't be visible through the binoculars, she could picture him clearly as a painting.

I can see you… She grinned. She couldn't wait to see him. *I'll be there tomorrow. I missed you.*

Good… Be well…

She was convinced she could discern him thinking of her.

Sini stroked the leathery surface of the binoculars and recalled the image of her grandmother. The only thing that had saved her from going mad from fever was sensing her presence. Among the hundreds of dreams and nightmares that had kept her company, the one with her grandmother caring for her had been the only one that ended well. It had been so real.

As if the spirit of her grandmother was still a part of the house.

10 ANOTHER WORLD

What Sini hadn't known as she'd been lying in bed for days was how the weather had changed.

It was minus fifteen, one of the coldest days so far, and it seemed to be getting worse. She'd been on the verge the whole day, trying to decide whether it was safe to go outdoors. She'd promised. On the other hand, it would benefit neither of them if she got sick again.

Her latest decision had been to stay inside, but as soon as the best moment to leave the house struck, she hurried to the vestibule and began dressing. She'd have to wear warmer clothes.

She found the faux fur hat in the closet. She'd had it for years, a relic from her glory days. It was too big and white. The beige and grey fur of the front brim and ear flaps was pretty, but apart from the red sports logo, it reminded her of the Winter War. She never used it, but it was the perfect thing for roaming the winter forest. Rummaging through the drawer, she picked the biggest mittens and thin gloves to wear underneath.

The cold on her face shocked her, and she feared for her lungs. Standing in the doorway, she took a careful, short breath. Inhaling a bit deeper, she still seemed fine. She pulled the wool scarf over her mouth and the hat tighter onto her head. It would be OK—she didn't have to stay for hours.

With clumsy but eager steps, Sini walked towards what was waiting for her. She'd sensed him the moment she stepped outside. As if he was standing next to her. She'd had that same feeling inside the house—in fact, the moment she'd woken up. If she could've, she would've run.

She didn't spot him. Had she lost the ability to see him? She began following the path, but when she didn't catch sight of him in the distance either, she stopped. Time to adjust her focus.

Sini closed her eyes and steadied her breath. She didn't know if she was breathing heavier because she was recuperating or because of walking in bulky clothes.

He was there, stronger than ever. She waited.

A touch on her nose so sweet it sent a shiver through her body. Her muscles didn't like the reminder of those tremors. She repressed a frown and slowly opened her eyes.

Dear Kuutamo.

How splendid he looked. Those eyes clearer than ever before. His face more nobly defined than she remembered. The way he looked at her. As if he thought she'd stayed away too long.

Sini understood why she'd called for him in the middle of her feverish haze. She had to avert her gaze from his. Did he sense what was on her mind?

He wasn't wearing the hood, yet he didn't seem to suffer from the cold. His hair looked longer, and the shade appeared lighter. The cloak was parted almost all the way to his chest. She got a better look at the garment that seemed to be some kind of wrap jacket, perhaps tied with a belt at the waist. His collar was looser against his throat. Looking at him made her chilly. She wondered if he could catch the flu like humans, but she couldn't picture him suffering any ailment.

I think we should walk. To stay warm. She motioned with her hand in the direction of the path.

He turned around and began walking. Sini followed. She couldn't keep her eyes off his hair. It was shoulder-length. What would it feel like against her fingers?

She looked down at the path to stop her thoughts. She was afraid they weren't entirely her own anymore.

As her gaze returned to his shape like a magnet, she tried to focus on the scenery before them. She hadn't noticed how light from the low sun turned everything into a perfect, luminescent white, awakening the beauty of the snow burdened trees. Although frozen and inanimate, there was movement. A breeze not strong enough to make the branches sway pushed powdered snow into translucent cascades slowly descending to the ground. As the light hit the tiny swivelling flakes, it made them glitter like fairy dust. Peach clouds and streaks of mauve stretched across the pale baby-blue sky. She tried to catch every cascade, thinking they were wishes granted.

Enough of the walking. *Wait.*

Kuutamo slowed to a halt. Sini's heart ached when he turned towards her. How she'd missed that face. She couldn't help but smile. She couldn't hide what she felt. Her candidness paid off as he returned her smile.

I want to know. Although their connection seemed to have developed to a higher level, she didn't know how much he understood of the human language. Or maybe he just understood her language? She tried to recall what she'd thought of. Maybe it wasn't so much the words, but the emotion, or intention.

He took a step closer. His face was questioning. Had he become better at showing emotion, or had she become better at interpreting his facial expressions? Sini had to clear her throat to keep focused. She'd waited for so long to know, and she felt ready at last for what he wanted to show her.

Sini took a step backwards. She pointed at herself and then at the ground, and then at him. Did he get it? She pointed again, and after pointing at him, she scanned the surroundings as if searching for his home.

There was that patient smile again. Wait, that one looked different. There was a hint of purpose. Perhaps he'd waited for the chance to tell her.

When Kuutamo stepped up to her, she forced herself to stay put. She tried, but she couldn't keep her heart rate going from casual to charging. There were so many reasons to fear what might happen, but she really, really wanted to know where he came from. Knowing would reveal so much about him and his purpose.

Kuutamo obviously sensed her fear. He only needed to look at her.

Sini startled when Kuutamo's arm suddenly lifted to the side. Alarm transformed into bewilderment when she saw he'd done it to welcome Helmi, who descended from nearby.

Kuutamo held the little piece of art in front of her, and the little head with its big, yellow eyes turned to her. Sini laughed at its astonished expression. Helmi looked exactly like she felt in Kuutamo's presence.

Kuutamo regarded her reaction. Sini looked into his assuring eyes and smiled. To think of something good was the best way to push away fear, and Kuutamo knew what worked for her. She'd give it a chance. Although it seemed over-dramatic afterwards, there was a moment during her worst fever assault when she'd thought she wouldn't make it. To be there with him and feel joy was precious.

Sini closed her eyes and took a slow, deep breath. She was ready.

As she opened her eyes, she saw Helmi had taken a comfortable seat on his shoulder. Helmi looked at her with her eyes half shut, as if she also wanted Sini to be assured. To show Kuutamo she was ready, she took another step closer.

She was so close she could almost smell him. Was it her imagination, or did he have a scent? She drew in a careful semi-deep breath. He *did* have a scent, but she couldn't place it.

She was steeling herself again. When he looked more real than ever, and even had a scent, Sini was no longer sure she'd pull it off. The fear came creeping back. It wasn't easy to forget the feeling of the cells of one's body disintegrating. *I don't know…*

You are safe. Kuutamo slowly raised his right hand and placed it on her chest. She couldn't feel his touch through the thickness of her jacket.

She didn't feel ready…

Sini looked at his hand right above her heart. A sensation of calm radiated through her body. The soothing effect was so complete she had to close her eyes. Her shoulders came down, and her knees loosened. While she experienced complete calmness, her body was infused with an invigorating force. Something that felt that good couldn't be evil. Or dangerous. Only a threat to her sanity.

She thought she'd been cured from the terrible ailment, but when Kuutamo's current streamed through her body, she felt it clear away the residues of stale energy and pain. It might have been the lightest she'd ever felt. Her next breath felt like the first in a decade.

I am safe. Careful not to disturb the perfect harmony, she kept her eyes closed as she raised her right hand. Maybe she wasn't required to take off her glove, with the freezing cold and all, but she wanted to feel his hand.

The air was as cold as expected on her bare skin. She gasped as she felt his palm. His hand was bigger than hers. After that, the only thing she noticed was how cold he felt. He was colder than the freezing air.

Like the first time, her skin was freezing, then burning. She knew he wouldn't physically hurt her…

Then the vision took over her senses.

As soon as the bright light blinded her, she knew where she was. It was her dream. She was in her ice world dream with Kuutamo.

The landscape looked the same, but with more details. A bird flying in the distance. Farther away, something that first looked like mountains appeared to be built structures.

It was different, though. She wasn't her—it was as if she saw through Kuutamo's eyes. She sensed his love for his home world, but also something else. Restlessness. Concern.

Knowing Kuutamo's calm and composed character, she thought it might be serious. *What is it?*

No.

Sini searched the connection between them. She sensed he didn't want to frighten her, like last time.

The sun was low in the sky. It might have been sunset. The rays reflected on the snow cover and revealed soft hues in beautiful colours; warm yellow, rose, light green. In her own dreams, she'd never felt cold, but now she felt relief, as if the cold was comfortable, the natural element… Of his people?

She didn't see others like him, but she sensed he wasn't alone. That place was his home, where his family lived. A thousand questions came to her. But the most important one…

Where is this?

Here.

It's here on Earth? Is it the North Pole? She pictured the northernmost place of the globe.

No.

Antarctica? The South Pole…

No.

I don't understand… It didn't matter. She wanted to stay. With him. There. In a world of their own. Her hand hurt. Why was her hand hurting?

As Sini remembered it was a vision, not a real place where they could be together, the beautiful light began dimming and turned into grey. *No…*

With her eyes still closed, she became aware of the flickering energy.

Please… No.

It was no use. When she opened her eyes, he was already gone. Five seconds ago, they'd been closer than ever, and then she was lonelier than ever. Was he there now? She couldn't feel him.

Sini remembered her aching hand. She lifted it before her face and inspected both the palm and the back. Nothing. No harm had come to it; it was just a little cold. She cupped her hand with her other hand, put it against her mouth and blew warm air on it. His hand had felt ice cold, and it surprised her that hers hadn't been at all damaged.

Sini began walking. She opened and closed her fist inside the glove to get the blood flowing. She should've been happy—satisfied—that she at long last had the answer to where he came from.

Instead, she was torn between the joy of being with him where he was at home and the confusion of why touching him hadn't felt good.

Dusk began to settle. The shadows grew bigger as she walked on. None of them was Kuutamo, and they looked rather menacing. She wanted to pick up the pace to get home faster, but she needed to be careful not to strain herself. As she thought of her illness, a wave of nausea washed over her. She swallowed. It dawned on her that she'd fallen ill immediately after the previous time they'd touched.

She just couldn't take another round of that fever.

As Sini crossed the ditch that cut off the forest from the real world, she saw the vision of her and Kuutamo sitting on pillows of soft moss in green foliage crumble.

It had become more apparent than ever he didn't belong in her world. His world turned out to be a place she'd never survive in. She had trouble staying healthy in winter, even if it involved only part of the year. He was so cold. She could still feel his icy palm against hers. He was meant to feel cold. He thrived in cold.

At least she got the biggest clue so far. Knowing what his home looked like didn't make her any clearer on what he was, though. What kind of creature other than polar bears would thrive in harsh cold? And why did she feel so positive about the icy world? She hated winters. Had she sensed his love for his home world and interpreted it as her own?

Her mind oscillated between contentment and horror. She was thrilled to finally have the answer to one of her biggest questions. His home was a beautiful and serene place that she herself had loved in her dreams—but it felt so wrong, impossible. She'd have to wait another twenty-four hours to ask—as long as she was still well the next day.

At least she was able to ask. Something had opened a telepathic passageway between them. He hadn't said much, but his answers had been clear in her mind. It must've been the way he'd touched her. Maybe he possessed the power to change the way her body worked. Thoughts were energy, after all.

Then there was the other explanation—the one where she'd lost her mind for good. The fever had scorched the last traces of normal human thought in her. Why else would she think the home world of Kuutamo was the one from her dreams? Or that there was someone in the forest who communicated with her.

Back at home, she realised how cold it had gotten inside the house. She had to make sure she stayed warm. She kept her outdoor clothes on as she prepared the fireplace, and she didn't dare change into her comfy clothes before the temperature rose.

In front of the sparkling fire with a big mug of hot cinnamon spiced tea, Sini calmed down. There was nothing physically wrong with her. She felt great. In fact, she wished she was back with Kuutamo, together exploring the other world.

The other world.

What kind of place was that? She'd sensed agreement from him when she'd wondered if it was on Earth, but he'd claimed it wasn't any ice-covered place she knew about.

Sini jerked as the fire gave off a deafening crackle. She shouldn't have loaded so much spruce, as the noise it produced could be a little over the top. More firecracker than comfy popping.

She recalled how her highly superstitious forefathers believed the thoughts one had when a fire made a loud snap would come true.

Could it be Greenland? Or the Arctic tundra?

With her second big mug of fragrant warmth in her hand, Sini went to her desk and turned on the computer. She wouldn't get her answers from the books of myths. The only place she'd read of in them that might be considered a cold place was the village of Pohjola.

Sini wrapped herself in a soft fleece quilt and sat down. Time to work. What other places had vast plains of snow and ice?

She typed in the words *snow and ice places on earth* in the search engine and pressed enter.

Glaciers. She chose the *Wikipedia* article. Sini skimmed through the lengthy material she expected to be tedious. Types, formation, structure, motion… When learning glaciers existed on Mars, of all places, she decided to read the whole thing.

Glaciers covered ten percent of Earth's surface, and they were scattered all over. For instance, Pakistan had seven thousand two hundred and fifty glaciers. She hadn't expected them to have any. Glacial ice was the biggest reservoir of fresh water on Earth, and they'd all be in deep trouble if the ice melted.

Antarctica, one of her guesses, had an ice cover with an average thickness of more than two kilometres. It would be impossible to live in a place like that. A shiver sliced through her body at the thought of always having to be in a cold environment.

Was there a chance she'd gotten it all wrong? Had she seen the wrong vision? Had she once again seen her own dream instead of what he intended to show her?

Sini leaned back and laced her fingers behind her neck. What if she hadn't been able to grasp what he tried to show her, and one of her latest dreams, a vivid one stuck in her mind, had shown up instead? But she felt sure he'd been there *with* her.

She leaned forwards, put her elbow on the table and rested her head in her palm. It was beyond her ability to grasp. Everything about Kuutamo was unheard of, and she doubted she'd find anything about him and his world on the internet. As long as she couldn't find anything that corroborated her experiences, there was a chance she'd been hallucinating. Made him up to ease her loneliness. Someone she didn't need to tell anyone about, someone who conveniently showed up when she wanted and wouldn't come bother her in her home.

Trying to get a grip on reality, she continued with the research. Wasn't it interesting that glaciers flowed downhill by the force of gravity, and that there were phenomena like glacial earthquakes? Those things she could grasp, though it was new to her.

She also learnt there were up to two hundred thousand glaciers on Earth. How was she supposed to know which one she was looking for when her only clues were snow and ice? There were no glaciers in Finland. The only glaciers they'd had were during the ice age.

That was at least eleven thousand years ago. His raw masculine appearance and clothing could match that era, but she doubted it was possible to time travel from that far in the past. Time travellers came from places of advanced technology. Unless Kuutamo was a type of sorcerer. A very powerful sorcerer. Even though the characters in her people's myths did wondrous things, she hadn't stumbled upon time travel. A shaman would be able to travel between worlds—but from the ice age?

And what for?

Surely a shaman from the ice age, possibly tens of thousands of years ago, wouldn't cross that time only to see her? She was fairly sure he was interested in her. He hadn't asked her to take him to her *leader*.

As Sini contemplated how to express to Kuutamo her myriad of questions, new ones welled forth.

Sini abandoned hope on finding anything remotely sensible about Kuutamo.

To ease her mind, she opened the drawing program and began sketching. First the clothing. Although his outfit included nothing that gave anything away—no specific style, no colours, no symbols—she drew what he wore as accurately as she could. Perhaps the lack of details was the best clue.

One of her questions might be about the uninspiring clothing, but she wasn't going to ask. It was most likely effective camouflage. Having no distinguishable colours or shape came in handy when hiding in the shadows. He must've been aware no one else wandered into those woods except her.

What tied him to her wood?

The eyes.

The blue of his eyes had several shades, so she chose her favourite.

Sapphire blue.

His eyes were set a bit deep. She wouldn't be able to convey the depth of his gaze. It was a depth that came from having secrets. Thick eyebrows that framed the eyes. Straight above the eyes and arching down the temples. There was no doubt he could look fierce if he wanted to, but she chose her favourite expression—the smile—when the blue would sparkle.

Sini sat with the drawing until late in the night. She wanted to perfect it, but she'd be satisfied if she came close. Drawing him from memory proved challenging because she'd seen different versions of him. She couldn't quite pinpoint it, but she thought he'd looked more edgy, rough, in the beginning.

Last time, he'd looked more refined. It could be the resolution. When he turned more solid, she was able to see his features clearer.

But then there was the other thing. On some level, he was familiar. Not that she'd seen someone like him before. But his features weren't that big of a revelation to her. Did she see herself in his eyes?

Sini looked at the face looking back at her. She'd managed to catch a good part of his essence, and she felt a warmth pouring into her body. She smirked at the realisation that he couldn't disappear on her until she turned off the computer.

Maybe that was why she had trouble quitting and going to bed. She'd been staring at the screen for almost ten hours. If she wanted to see that face again and get some answers, she'd need her sleep.

Sini was about to turn off the whole thing when her eyes fell upon the drawings of her Karo. She felt out of breath. The sadness overwhelmed her in a second. Was it true she hadn't thought of Karo in days, maybe weeks? Was that how strong her love was for the one who'd been her loyal companion for years?

She'd so easily traded him for Kuutamo. She wiped away the wet that was forming in the corners of her eyes and took a deep breath. Extreme loneliness drove her to it. She'd have to forgive herself. It was clear that the reason she'd let Kuutamo come close to her was she believed the shadow was her dog's spirit. She fought to believe that her dog would be happy for her that she'd found a friend.

But still…

I'm sorry, forgive me…

She yearned to smooth Karo's shiny, strong coat. His eyes gazing back at her as light-hearted as always. The judgement she suffered couldn't be found in them. Sini forced herself to turn it off. Staying up all night crying wouldn't benefit anyone.

She headed straight for bed and turned off the light.

Instead of getting up, Sini grabbed the book that had lain on the shelf above her bed since she got sick.

Her sleep had been shallow. Unable to silence her already busy mind, she decided to combine resting and prepping. She wanted to know more about how the shaman travelled between dimensions.

In mythology, the cosmos consisted of many layers. There were at least three, but there could also be nine or even more. Humans lived in the middle layer. In the middle world, the shaman's free soul was able to travel in the form of any helper spirit, but especially as a bird. The bird was also an important messenger.

The mythological character Ilmarinen was considered a shaman since he journeyed *over the moon, under the day, and on the shoulder of the Big Dipper.* The shaman needed to have knowledge of the structure and routes of the cosmos to travel from one place to another. They might travel to the otherworld along a river or paths lined with dangerous spirits. The land of the dead lay far away in the otherworld. Only a powerful shaman with exceptional mental and physical strength was able to make the demanding trip to the land of the dead and return unharmed. After having tricked the keeper of the otherworld to let him in,

Väinämöinen only just escaped the place by turning into his helper spirit, the snake, and wriggling through the fence.

Journeying to the other dimensions was risky and wasn't done for fun. The shaman was in search of knowledge, the answers to a disease, or a solution to a problem in the community. One of the shaman's most important duties was to heal the sick. Disease was thought to be a consequence of the free soul having escaped from the body. To cure the sick person, the shaman must fetch their soul from the land of the dead.

The gateway to the otherworld lay in the interface between the earth and the sky. When heading for the underworld, the shaman would choose the guidance and shape of a fish or a snake, and a bird when heading to the upper world.

The author said there were numerous, endless even, levels and realities, each one with their own world or universe. Despite being invisible to each other with different density and different timelines, they were all somehow united. There was no mention of an ice world in the books. Sini recalled that the village of Pohjola at times was described as cold and dangerous, but also as the land of the dead that was situated far in the north beneath a vast area of water. It was the place where the hunting tribes sent the dreaded souls of their departed. She couldn't imagine Kuutamo living in such a place.

The fact that Kuutamo was almost as solid as her didn't work for the soul journey. He did have an animal with him, though.

In addition to learning head spinning facts of realities she'd never heard of, Sini managed to come up with specific questions that hopefully revealed whether Kuutamo had shamanic abilities.

Are you here in your body, or is it behind in the other world and only your spirit is here?

Do you have a connection to Helmi?

11 ASK ME

If it wasn't for Kuutamo, Sini would never have gone out in that weather.

When she had the dog, she'd been forced to, but if there was one good thing about not having a dog, it was not having to spend time outdoors in close to minus-twenty degrees.

She'd have to be meticulous about clothing. She couldn't simply stack more shirts or leggings on herself, as she wouldn't be able to move. The solution was to choose the warmest pieces and her warmest jacket. She wished she owned warmer clothes. As a winter sports athlete, she'd spent a lot of time outdoors, but she mostly wore technical clothing optimised for movement. The challenge back then was to stay dry and warm while wearing quite thin layers of clothes that allowed physical freedom.

Sini wished she had money to buy new clothes. A puffy, warm down jacket that reached to her thighs. Thicker and waterproof trousers. And new boots. Hers were great, but the lining had flattened with use and no longer insulated well. Wool socks could only do so much.

Another challenge was getting hot when walking in the snow—and then cold when she stayed put for a while. She wanted to do more things than always trying to keep warm...

Sini pushed her thoughts away. Communicating with a stranger from another world ought to be interesting enough. She needed to find out more about him and if there was a reason behind all the strangeness. Not pretend he was her boyfriend. Or that he might want to be.

She had to make do with the clothes available. She shouldn't stay long, anyway.

The cold tugged on her face the moment she stepped outside. It would've been sensible to use a ski mask to protect her face, but she'd be too embarrassed to do that in front of Kuutamo.

Quiet, grey, and dull. The snow was hard under her clumsy feet, and the steam from her mouth filled the air. The surroundings gave no clue to the time of day. Walking through the field, she realised it was a blessing the path hadn't been crammed with snow since that dreaded storm. A pair of jays exited the forest and headed for her house, without doubt in hunt of nuts and sunflower seeds.

Upon entering the forest, she picked up on a different vibration. An atmosphere of expectancy, or even joy.

He walked towards her, a bright expression on his face. Sini's cheeks hurt as she returned the smile. Was he happy to see her, or was there something going on?

Sini observed Kuutamo. The more she bulked up, the less he wore of his outfit. The hood was down again, and his cloak was wide open at the chest. Watching him walk up to her with such ease, that hair flowing, and those eyes fixed on hers, she felt utterly unattractive. Sausage like in her clothes and probably red-faced. She might even have frost in her eyebrows.

Hello…

Well, hello there… She had to compliment him on his appearance. Then he was before her, and she could only stare. Take it in. His hair wavy and bouncy in contrast to hers—squashed under clothing. His complexion flawless—very unlike her blotchy face. Her breath looked like steam from an old locomotive, but nothing came out of his mouth.

Had she never noticed that before? Did he breathe? Should she ask him?

Sini shook off the unsettling discovery.

She lowered her gaze to his chest. The lapels of his cloak framed a bluish garment. At last, some colour. The fabric looked weaved and had a matte sheen. It resembled silk. On an impulse, she raised her hand in an attempt to touch it. Almost there, she stopped herself. She didn't want to be rude.

Kuutamo raised his hand and touched the garment that shimmered cobalt under his fingers. She noticed he wore something around his neck underneath the cloak. She pointed at it.

Kuutamo touched the simple piece of string and looked at her. Sini nodded.

He pulled at the string and revealed the piece of stone tied to it.

It looked like an ordinary rugged piece of stone to her. It was dark grey and the size of an egg. She leaned closer. Still looked like an ordinary piece of stone. As if he'd picked it up in the forest.

Sini pointed at the stone and then at the ground beside the path. Kuutamo nodded.

Oh, how she wanted to know why he had a worthless stone tied to his neck. Could it be for research reasons, or simply a souvenir? She must have looked clueless. How to ask? And what about all the questions she'd formulated at home? The bigger ones?

Sini thought Kuutamo had caught her frustration when he stowed away the stone and fired a smile that wasn't lost on her. He seemed to be in an exceptionally good mood. She watched as he fished out a pair of plain gloves and put them on. Next, he held his left hand in front of her and slowly pressed his palm to her chest.

As the energy began flowing, she closed her eyes to centre herself. It felt cool, but not cold. Strong, but soft. Wonderful. She couldn't resist opening her eyes.

She didn't want to find him gone when he was done. Kuutamo just kept smiling. Was he enjoying it?

Does it feel good?

Yes. He had no idea how much.

Kuutamo's smile widened.

Oops, he caught that too.

Their communication always improved after he touched her. Somehow, it opened up something inside her. They were synchronizing. A revelation hit her.

The stone. She visualized it. *Does it help you...* How should she form the question? *...to be more here?*

She sensed the *yes* clearly. It was her chance to ask more.

Kuutamo retrieved his hand. She was too enthused to feel disappointment. Then, he took off the gloves, and her heart fell. Didn't he want to touch her?

She turned her gaze, pretending to look at the nearest trees, as if she was perhaps wondering where Helmi was. From the corner of her eye, she saw his hand coming up to her face. She looked at him again the moment his fingers gently stroked her cheek. As she thought his hand wasn't that cold on her already chilled skin, she saw him flicker.

Sini felt equally shy and happy. And then afraid he'd leave.

Please, stay.

I am here. Ask me.

Sini fought to organise her scrambled mind. She visualized the icy plains.

Your home. The ice world. Did you mean it's here?

Yes.

Sini shook her head and pointed in a half circle around them. *You really mean here, where I live?*

Yes.

I don't understand. There's no world like it here. Hasn't been for a very long time.

Yes.

OK… Do you come from the past? From another time? How to formulate her question so he'd understand? She visualized herself becoming younger and then a child, her mother getting younger and then her becoming a child, and then the same for her grandmother and great-grandmother.

She gathered he understood, somehow.

Yes. No.

Yes, from another time?

Yes.

No?

Now. Here.

Either he didn't understand, or she wasn't able to. It must be her. She'd have to try something else.

Your body. Are you here now? Is this you? She was struggling with that one. *Your home… is your body there?* There was no way she'd be able to convey the question to him.

My body is here. With you.

Sini felt something. And she knew he sensed what she'd felt.

Helmi. She imagined the owl sitting on his shoulder. *Where is she?*

Kuutamo raised his hand and turned to his left. He pointed to a tall spruce behind him.

Sini searched the length of the tree but didn't see the bird. She believed he'd pointed at it, but it would be hidden by the long snow-covered branches.

She was struggling with the next one, too. Several ideas for a question popped into her mind, but none of them sounded right. She should just go with it and trust that he might, in fact, understand. He'd done something to her, because it was obvious they were communicating significant things.

Are you connected to Helmi?

Yes. She sees—I see. She hears—I hear.

Wow. It was so shaman. *Is she like you? Is she from your world?*

She is better than me.

Why, what do you mean?

She is real, like you. I am not.

She sensed something that resembled sadness. *You want to be like me?* Sini was sure she'd misunderstood.

Yes. Sometimes.

Their *talk* was going in an unexpected direction. Her joy of having caught onto an intriguing subject was deflated by a shudder. She'd been so immersed in their communication that she hadn't realised she was getting cold. Shivering cold. Standing still would make her cold no matter how much clothing she wore.

I am sorry. I have to go home. There was no chance that plain walking would make her warm again. If there was a chance, she would've grabbed it. But as always, no matter how incredible spending time together was, she couldn't risk getting sick again.

Sini looked at Kuutamo's relaxed figure. *Aren't you cold?*

Yes.

Sini laughed. *I mean, the cold doesn't feel bad?*

No. Kuutamo smiled.

Does it feel good?

Yes.

A painful shiver sliced through her body. Oh God. What was he? She was dying to know, but if she stayed, she wouldn't be able to come back for a while. She pointed at her house and then motioned towards it.

Can you walk with me to my house?

His smile was gone. *No.*

Disappointed at the obvious answer, she deliberated on how to say goodbye. He hadn't disappeared on her yet. Hugging was probably out of the question, and shaking hands would be weird. A kiss on the cheek would be too much.

Kuutamo straightened as if he'd had a revelation.

Oh no...

I want to try.

Sini felt as awkward as a girl getting her first kiss from the guy she liked. How should she stand—what if she leaned a little forwards so that he could reach the small surface of her face exposed between the fur brim and the scarf? Her thought process came to a halt as he stepped closer than he'd ever been. Her eyes were at the height of his neck. There was no question he was there in his physical form.

She tilted her face upwards and to the side to offer him her cheek. When his upper body bent towards her, she shut her eyes. Touching had always been nerve-racking and even scary, but the situation had her heart racing for another reason.

She felt his hands gently grip her by the shoulders and then a pressure on her cheekbone from something cool and soft. His lips lingered on her skin, and although it wasn't an ordinary kiss, maybe not even pleasant, it was the most special kiss of her life.

Sini didn't open her eyes when she perceived him fading. The kiss had been a miracle in itself, but what she was left wanting was for him to pull her into his embrace.

She stood there until the last sensation of him on her body disappeared.

Sini sighed. For that very special moment, she'd forgotten about the feeling of entering a deep freeze.

Although it obliterated the sacredness of what happened between them, she began hopping and flapping her arms. She needed to get warm at once—even brisk walking wasn't enough to get warm blood pumping through her body in that weather.

As she did her aerobic routine, she saw the little bird descend from a tree. It landed on a short pine sapling, where it sat regarding her. Sini smiled at the sweet gesture.

Back at the house, Sini took her traditional warm-up shower and lit the fireplace. The day was a success in many ways. She recalled the kiss and sighed. When the smile on her lips wouldn't fade, she knew she was infatuated with a strange male from an ice world.

Ice world. He'd confirmed he came from her place. The only ice world that had existed there was when glaciers covered land a very long time ago. During the ice age.

Here... Then... And *now...*

So, if he did come from the ice age, but not entirely from the past, it meant that either there was no time difference, or the ice age existed in another dimension. A parallel universe. Or maybe those were the same thing.

Sini sat down in her chair with some baked sandwiches. She'd decided to celebrate by having something delicious.

She tried to wrap her brain around the mystery of Kuutamo's origins, and every time she thought she understood, her mind went blank. And then the memory of Kuutamo's hands on her invaded that space.

Did he have any feelings for her? She still didn't know who she was to him. At least next time she could try to use their telepathic connection and ask *why her*? He must have a family in that world. So why was he in the forest alone? It was possible the others didn't have his ability to cross worlds.

She must remember to ask what was special with her forest—why had he chosen to come there?

Sini took a bite from the bread covered in melted cheese. She spit it onto the plate. The pineapple had burnt her tongue, and she tried to ease the pain with a mouthful of cold mineral water.

Touching Kuutamo's fingers had kind of hurt her, too. And his kiss had been cold. The difference in temperature became too great. The memory evoked a painful wave of shudders. He'd put his gloves on before touching her, and he'd seemed to be fine. But then, always when he touched her skin, he'd flicker and often disappear, as if touching her was too much for his system. It dawned on her what it meant when Kuutamo liked the cold, thrived in it.

He didn't like warmth. Touching her hurt him.

Sini felt hollow inside. Her body numbed as she sat with the insight.

The pineapple had cooled, and she took a bite. The mix of bread, the saltiness of the tuna and cheese, and the sweet of the fruit felt awesome in her mouth, consoling.

Was he hungry? Didn't he need to eat? There was no end to the questions queuing up.

He was so incredible, like an alien on Earth, yet she'd felt the male standing so close to her. He'd been like any other gorgeous guy in front of her, but much more intriguing.

She'd have to write all her questions down. Putting her plate and quilt away, she got up and walked over to her grandmother's desk. She opened the top drawer to look for a notepad. There was a stack of note-its, but she needed something with larger sheets. She pulled at the solid wooden pulls to the other drawers, but as always, they wouldn't budge.

She really wanted that notepad, though.

Sini sat on her knees to try to solve the mystery of the uncooperating drawers.

Her grandmother wouldn't have been senseless and keep a desk with that much unusable storage space. She pulled the desk out to peek behind but saw no hidden locks or mechanisms. It didn't have signs of swelling due to water damage, either. She bent down to look under the drawers. Nothing. She ran her hand along the surfaces as if there might be an invisible switch of some sort.

Sini laughed at the idea. She was already giving mundane things magical properties. But who knew what kind of hidden things existed if someone only knew to look for them?

Grabbing the little rectangular pull of the middle drawer with all her fingers, she pulled as hard as she could. The drawer didn't budge in the slightest. Pushing the pull upwards, she tried to edge the drawer loose from whatever it had attached to. Still no change, not even a millimetre. Only her fingers whitening from the pressure.

Sini changed into a hunching position, trying to use her weight as she pulled one last time. The drawer must have been glued shut. The thought was illogical, but never had she been more interested in looking at her grandmother's belongings. Her emotions oscillated from amused to frustrated as she repeated the procedures and got the same result from the other drawer.

"Open Sesame," Sini uttered with a deep voice, leaning one hand onto the drawer and waving the other in a circle like a magician would.

When she pulled at the middle drawer, it slid towards her with very little friction. Sini lost her balance and tumbled onto her behind.

A shiver ran through her body and made every hair on her neck raise.

What the…?

Her mind wanted to check what lay inside the mystery desk, but her body didn't obey.

She slid closer and tried the other drawer. It would've opened just as effortlessly if she'd had the courage to pull.

Sini got up and began pacing the small space of the living room. She hadn't imagined it.

Some spell had been broken by her.

She had to do it.

Sini eyed the gaping drawer from across the room. The contents of those drawers belonged to her. She needed to find out what was so important that it needed to be protected like that.

Her nerves erupted in tight laughter. *Protection spell.* She'd read about the magic songs of the Finns. How the ancestors used singing for putting spells on things and living beings. They said that singing the spells made them more powerful, but it also helped in memorising them. In summers, the cattle used to roam free on the meadows and in the forest, and it needed protection against bears and getting lost. Luck and wealth were considered limited assets and possessing them led to jealousy in others. Neighbours especially would resort to using harming spells to even out the distribution of fortune. Also, people such as brides and grooms, needed protection in delicate situations, as well as little children.

It had also stuck in her mind that iron, salt, and quicksilver, as well as dead people's body parts, were potent ingredients in protection spells. And symbols of different kinds carved into buildings, belongings, and even cattle hooves.

Protection spells and symbols were important ingredients of fantasy fiction and common amongst the old Finns, but it was still make-believe.

Then again, that was all she knew and the only theory she had. Compared to spending time with a being from an ice world who'd crossed over to her world, a spell that sealed the contents of a drawer from unauthorised eyes wasn't any more dramatic.

What could the drawers contain? Poison? More books about shamanism? Dirty fantasies?

Finding courage in the thought that there wouldn't be anything dangerous in an old desk that belonged to her beloved grandmother, Sini drew a deep breath and walked over to the scary thing. Without breathing, she pulled the middle drawer out further and peeked inside.

In three rows were tens of book spines in different colours side by side. Black, red, white, blue, brown. They had no titles. They must be the notebooks.

Sini was dying to know what was in them, but she felt depleted. The exciting day began to have its toll on her. If she picked up one, she'd start reading it, and then look at another, and she'd stay up forever.

She yawned as she welcomed the prospect of rest. The notebooks were probably diaries filled with observations of weather and nature events. Most likely spiced up with philosophical notions inspired by all those books. Maybe she'd get to learn more about her grandmother's peculiar side after all, get to know her better. Feel closer to her.

Sini closed the drawer and stood. She had to choose the bed. Besides, the earlier she went to sleep, the earlier the next day came.

Amazing how her life had all of a sudden changed. It was years since she'd been excited with a new day and new possibilities.

Adventures. Could life even be more exciting?

12 GOING NOWHERE

What time was it?

Sini scrambled into a sitting position and squinted at the brightness. It looked like midday already. Twelve? Her head didn't like the sudden change in consciousness, and a throb emanated at the back.

Sini whisked the duvet and cover to the side and jumped out of bed. She'd have to hurry if she wanted anything done before going out. The cold floor and leaving the warmth of the bed had her shivering. The light seeping through the kitchen curtains seemed a bit excessive.

With her arm wrapped around herself, she pulled the curtain open to a very bright day. The sun must have reached over the treetops, because the light reflecting from the snow was blinding. She'd gotten used to the dark, the dusk, and the monochrome tones of the landscape.

Sini gasped as her eyes hit the thermometer in the window. She blinked hard a few times and focused on which number the blue column had halted at. Minus thirty degrees! Jesus Christ! It was probably correct, since the sun was blasting from a clear sky and the temperature had fallen inside the house.

"Shit!"

She'd be lucky to reach the forest before having to head back home.

No one spent time outside in that freeze if it wasn't absolutely necessary.

If she'd complained before about the lack of warm clothes and the bulkiness, the situation had just turned impossible. She'd get cold in that weather no matter what she wore. Just breathing would be difficult enough. She couldn't go.

Sini forced back the tears. She'd have to wait for it to pass. The positive aspect was that managing the cold would feel less difficult when the temperature rose again. The positive aspect wasn't consoling, though.

Not able to shake the bad news, she walked over to the closet and pulled out warmer clothes. To think she needed to bulk up inside, too.

With her coffee running and bread in the toaster, she walked over to the fireplace and lit it. She'd have to keep the house warm with a fire. Turning up the electrical heating didn't tempt her, since it would show in the bill.

Expecting it to be stuck again, Sini pulled at the drawer she'd opened last night. No problem. As smoothly as an old drawer could slide open, it revealed the neatly packed notebooks. She picked a random book with a red cover and pulled it out. The notebook had a plain cardboard cover and a black satin ribbon hanging out at the bottom.

Sini flipped the front cover. On the first page the initials S. K. were written. She assumed they stood for Satu Kataja, her grandmother. On the next page, there was a date followed by script in black. The script wasn't elaborate, diarylike, but looked like it was done in a hurry or a state of excitement. At a first glance, she couldn't grasp what it was about. She read slowly, but she was more guessing than understanding. After a while, she had to admit she had no idea what it said.

She turned a few pages and the script looked the same. Sini looked up and sighed. She'd expected something different. Eyeing random pages in the book, the rest of the notes turned out to be as unreadable. They felt so unfamiliar, as if she didn't sense her grandmother in them. The notes ranged over a year's time about fifteen years ago.

Sini laid the notebook on the desk and pulled out another one. It was black with a more worn cover, as if it had been used as reference. She opened the notebook and did a fast flip through.

Wait! There were some illustrations. Sini searched for the one she'd glimpsed. It was quite a good sketch of the upper body of an owl.

Helmi.

Sini checked the date. It was from twenty years ago. Owls didn't live that long, and it didn't have to be Helmi, but the drawn details were clear. It was the same species. Maybe the notes were just about owls, or birds, in general. Sini flipped through the pages again, and she found a couple more drawings of the bird from a distance. There were no other illustrations. Sini felt the chills again. It could be excitement or the cold.

The notes must be her grandmother's. The handwriting was the same, and the initials matched. Like the other book, she didn't grasp if it was a diary about Helmi, or about the species, or what?

It was clear her grandmother also had been interested in the owl.

Sini tried to read the scribble again. It was like a foreign language, or the order of the words was random.

Her stomach churned. She'd forgotten her breakfast. Sini got up from the floor, went to the kitchen, poured a big cup of coffee to clear her head, and put a thick layer of cheese, ham, and tomato on the cold toast. She brought her brunch to the desk, put more wood in the fireplace, and sat down.

After a few mouthfuls of coffee, Sini pulled up a third book, and then a fourth. They contained the same script that made no sense and were from the same time period. The seventh one, on the other hand, shed light on things.

The brown notebook with a cover that appeared to be leather was from forty-five years ago. Its pages were more yellowed, and the handwriting looked different. The initials said S. K., nonetheless. Could it be her great-grandfather? His name had been Simo Kataja. She'd never met him as he'd passed away at the fairly young age of 60. He'd lived in that house, and her grandmother had been born there. To Sini's knowledge, the family had been people living ordinary lives and having ordinary dreams. Living in the middle of nowhere, their main ambition must've been to lead independent lives, not relying on society. She didn't know how many generations had lived there before her, but she'd gotten the impression they'd been many.

What she saw were illustrations of symbols, and they looked familiar. She went to the sofa table with three stacks of library books and picked up the dictionary of Finnish folk religion.

There it was—the symbol used for marking historic sites of interest on maps, the Saint Hannes cross. According to the book, people painted or carved the square with outward-pointing loops at its corners on objects, such as buildings and jewellery, to bring luck and protect from evil. It had been used inside cheese moulds to both decorate the cheese and protect the making process, as well as in embroidery. The oldest Finnish Saint Hannes cross had been found carved into a piece of a ski from a thousand years ago.

On another page of the notebook were drawings of spheres and circular objects. She had no clue what they might depict. She checked the vocabulary for orbs, spheres, circles. There was an insert on hoops. All kinds of objects in the shape of a hoop were considered possible passageways to the otherworld. A branch grown into a hoop was especially powerful and had been used for making medicine by pouring a liquid through it.

Sini got immersed in the dictionary. Suddenly, the symbols that people had used in their traditions before became much more interesting. Her relatives might have had a natural interest in history and nature, but with all the things happening to her, she suspected it could be more than that. It was such a shame that her mother had steered things so that she hadn't learnt about her heritage from her father's side.

She held all those books written by her grandmother, but she was still no closer to learning about her. She couldn't read them. As if she were a child that didn't know how to read or write. She didn't recognise any foreign languages in the words, and she couldn't imagine her relatives knowing a language or dialect she'd never encountered.

Tracing the indented words of a passage from her grandmother, Sini felt the frustration of not being able to go out and not getting anything out of her discovery. It was just like with Kuutamo; heaps of questions and a couple of answers. If the contents of the notebooks were gibberish, why the protective measures? There were a few possible explanations: either her grandmother was nuts or illiterate; she wrote in code, or the meaning of the writings was protected from the wrong reader.

Was she the wrong reader?

⌘ ⌘ ⌘

Sini leaned back in her chair and closed her straining eyes. Why did her grandmother have to leave her? Satu could've been at her side and told her how the scribbles had meaning and that she did right when trying to read them. The books didn't seem to be personal diaries, but there had to be other reasons why they mustn't be read by just anyone.

If they were written in code, there was nothing she could do about it. She doubted she'd find helpful decoding information on the internet, and it wasn't like she intended to show them to anyone. She didn't believe she'd find the key anywhere in the house, either, and she couldn't ask her parents. Her mother obviously had something against her father's relatives, but she'd never explained why. Her father never mentioned them, as if he'd forgotten about them. Sini knew her grandmother's parents had lived in the house, and her grandparents before that, but the rest of her relatives were distant.

She closed the notebook and put it on top of the pile. She turned to look out the window that faced the forest. How she wished she was able to go. Thinking about the kiss, her stomach filled with little butterflies. She lingered in the sensation.

He'd be there, waiting, but he'd understand why she couldn't come. She could tell him she'd found something interesting, and that she'd seen a drawing of Helmi or perhaps the owl's ancestors. Although, no reason would be more important than simply going to him.

Sini thought of other things she could do as she was taking the day *off*. There was laundry, and it was important to keep her outdoor clothes clean, so they'd insulate well. She could look for jobs—not that she harboured any hope of finding a suitable one.

She shuddered at the thought of being forced to go by car somewhere in that weather. The engine would have to be preheated a long time for it to start. An even bigger challenge was whether the car would start once she was heading back. Being stuck in town and having to ask a random stranger for help would be much worse than having the cashier and librarian look at her funny. Worse than having to rely on the good-will of strangers was suffering a malfunction in the middle of nowhere and risking freezing to death before someone reached her.

What frightened her the most was that she had no one to call in case of emergency. She knew nobody and hadn't been interested in reaching out to anyone. Did her grandmother have someone she'd call? She belonged to the older generation, when people could always count on help from one another. People would volunteer; they'd work together cleaning up a place, building something, or just helping a family in need. They'd trade services with each other. In present times, things and services had to be bought, and all was well as long as they got the money.

She pictured herself calling the road service from the wilderness and how much it would cost for them to come and fix the problem or tow the car away for repair. Without doubt, much more than she imagined. While she stayed there, it would—after all—be sensible to get in touch with the nearest neighbours.

Sini sighed. She was so stuck. With no answers to anything.

She got up, stretched, and looked at the open drawer and the heap of books on the desk. Although she doubted anyone else would be able to decipher them, she felt they needed to be protected. She carefully inserted them between the others and closed the drawer. She hoped it wouldn't play any tricks on her and not open the next day.

Leaning into the old desk, she looked at the simple living room and the little kitchen. The house was old and ordinary, but it was hers. She might be alone and at risk, but at that moment, she didn't want to be anywhere else. She was warm and comfortable. No one there to tell her what to do and who to be. She was trying to decipher something that was possibly very interesting and that could shed light on the lives of her ancestors.

Plus, a beautiful, secret stranger was waiting in the forest for her return so that they could continue figuring each other out.

Sini sighed and sat down at the computer.

All she'd accomplished was a round of laundry. Knowing Kuutamo was out there, all splendid and able to communicate, she hadn't been able to do anything intellectual. Only when the dark set in and it was too late to go out, she managed to focus on the tasks.

Even though she hated the thought of having to drive to work in winter and having to face strangers, losing her house because of lack of funds was the worst option. Her getting a new career needed to happen eventually.

She opened the browser and typed in the site for job ads. What appeared to be plenty of opportunities soon turned into disappointment. There were jobs, even good ones, but for professionals such as builders, carpenters, electricians, cleaners, salespersons. Accountants. In theory, she could be one of those. The thing was, she hadn't studied economics so that she could work for someone else. She hadn't chosen economics because she liked it—obviously—but because of her plan to become a winter sports entrepreneur. She needed to steer her thoughts in another direction. Thinking of her wasted education or business opportunities was not what she needed at that moment.

Knowing that reading any further would throw her into a whirlwind of discouragement, she typed in the word *illustrator*. If she had talent and experience, what would be available?

Several years of practice, use of designing programs, concept design, communications skills, flexibility… She didn't even understand what half of the requirements meant. She wasn't familiar with the gaming industry, either.

Studies to become a graphic designer would take a minimum of three years. Years of studying subjects that didn't interest her. She just wanted to draw. Even if she managed to work while studying, she wouldn't earn enough to support herself. Besides, studying in another location would require for her to move or pay for accommodation, anyway.

She hated her degree, but she couldn't get a new one. What about people who were talented artists despite lacking specific education? It was a shame she wasn't one of those either. She hadn't spent years developing her drawing skills. She didn't even know if she might be talented enough. Others had years, even decades more experience than her. She'd never be able to catch up with them.

She wanted to cry.

Thinking of what kind of portfolio she could create for an application; Sini opened the drawing software. She might have a few things completed, but would they be enough? Of course not. She hadn't practised for years, which meant a career as an artist was but a dream. But she might be able to work from home, which was a huge plus.

What if she just started practising? No one would come and offer her money because they pitied her. She wasn't a productive member of society, and after a while, they'd stop caring. If she wanted to stay in her grandmother's house, she'd have to start doing something. Anything.

A pair of blue eyes appeared, and she wanted to catch them before they disappeared.

I'm drawing you.

Did he know what it meant? Maybe she could show him one of her works one day. Did he know what he looked like?

Oh, no, those questions popping into her mind again. If he came from the ice age, he wouldn't have knowledge of technology. Would he be horrified if he came inside her house? She couldn't wait to ask him about everything. He didn't seem savage or ignorant, though. It was rather she who was the wide-eyed one, who didn't know what was going on. He'd come from a faraway place and managed to solidify, like a magician. He didn't seem the least disoriented despite being far from home. Contrary to his sophisticated conduct, there had been almost nothing but snow and sky in the visions of his world. No signs of cultural development other than what might have been buildings. How were they able to survive in that environment? It didn't add up.

Sini grinned at the eyes gazing back at her. Her ability to describe his features was improving. She tried out plenty of shades before finding the exact blue for the clothing that peeked from under his cloak. What she'd glimpsed didn't look like the clothing of a caveman.

Then she drew Kuutamo with Helmi perched on his hand. An image of herself with Karo by her side appeared next to him. She tweaked her stupid outfit so that it matched his better. She also had a big hood that was pulled onto her shoulders.

Watching them standing together soothed her. Her cheeks heated as she drew another one with them standing closer, with their faces turned towards each other. It reminded her of when she sketched secret images of the guy she was in love with at school.

Sini rubbed her face. Another day had passed, and she had done little to solve her money problems or make her less forgotten by the world, and instead spent it focusing on him and everything surrounding him. She glanced at the writing desk and remembered she still didn't have a notepad for her questions.

She'd have to check if all the notebooks were used up.

Sini kicked off the duvet and hurried to the kitchen window.

She'd made sure to wake up on time.

The thermometer must have broken, because it had stuck at yesterday's temperature.

She put on her robe, opened the door, and stepped outside. At first, the first seconds, it didn't feel that bad. But when the effect kicked in, the cold made her skin shrink.

Sini cursed and slammed the door shut. She was safe inside again, but the cold lingered on her body and clothing like an entity. Rubbing and tapping on herself, she tried to snuff it out.

She stood at the living room window, looking at the forest. There was such a contrast between the killer cold and the inviting dawning light. She cursed again. Who knew how long the extreme conditions would last?

But what to do about it? The sleeping bag she'd thought of when it all began, before she'd gotten accustomed to the cold… It had been more of a joke that day, but she actually owned one that she'd won in a competition years ago. She'd never used the winter sleeping bag that was too warm for summer. Not that she'd been camping during summers either. The bag should be somewhere in the house. Somewhere in the attic.

Sini ascended the narrow and steep stairs to the second floor. The upstairs was suitable for living but hadn't been used by her grandmother. It was a simple room with a couple of small windows, and with only one resident in the house, it was used for storage rather than spending time in. Sini had now and then stayed there as a child when she wanted to be alone. She'd be drawing or reading a book, sitting in an old rocking chair.

There were a couple of big closets. She'd emptied one and moved the old stuff to the other one when she moved in. Perhaps her grandmother had clothes she could wear outdoors.

Sini rummaged through her stuff and found the sleeping bag in a corner. According to the label on the sack, it would provide comfort at zero and protection at minus ten. Perfect. It would buy her more time.

Sini hadn't been able to go through her grandmother's things more thoroughly in the beginning. They reminded her of her loneliness and grief, and then she'd forgotten about them. Looking through the clothes on the shelves, she imagined them still imbued with her grandmother's signature scent. She used to smell of forest and fresh air instead of cinnamon buns.

Sini let her hand slide over the folded stacks of clothes and stopped at a thick-looking knitted shirt. She pulled it out and let it hang from her hands. Brown bears and red lingonberries in alternating rows on a warm yellow background jumped at her. She vaguely remembered her grandmother wearing it outside. The funny design was the opposite of sentimental. It defied the boundaries of good taste, but there in the middle of nowhere, it was perfect. The shirt screamed of autumn, her favourite season if she disregarded the cold weather.

Sini gathered her findings on the grey-painted wooden floor. She walked up to the black rocking chair that had been huge when she was a little girl. It still had the woven black, white, and red cloth tied to it. Sini seated herself with care, not wanting to impose on the delicate snippets of memories coming to her. It wasn't because of boredom or lack of her grandmother's attention she'd come there. A flash of her sitting with a paper pad in her lap, absorbed in drawing things she'd seen…

The rocking came to a sharp halt as Sini wondered if her drawings still existed. She was sure her grandmother would've kept them. Her eyes fell on the sideboard beneath the window. It was painted in the same dull tint as the floor and matched the humble room.

The little door opened without effort. Sini sat down on her knees and peeked inside the dim shelf. A few old children's magazines. A box of crayons. Sini picked them out and flipped through the magazine with the yellow bear in trousers and a blue hat. The world's strongest bear. She remembered reading those. The crayons had turned into stubs with frayed paper wrappings. Underneath the magazines lay a stack of papers.

The slightly creased sheets with shapes in different colours trembled in her hands as she looked through them. Animals, trees, a little house that probably was the one she was in. They must've been made by her, but she had no recollection whatsoever of drawing them.

Her head spun as she got to the last drawing. A little girl sat on a stone. In a forest. Someone stood in front of her, holding a big object in their left hand and a smaller one in their right hand. She had no clue what was going on, but the air of the event was solemn. The girl wasn't detailed enough to convey her facial expression, but Sini sensed her enthusiasm. It looked like the whole forest had gathered around them. Bears, squirrels, hares, foxes, birds…and last, the unmistakable shape of a little owl.

Why did she get the impression the little girl had known…things…

⌘ ⌘ ⌘

Sini snapped out of the weird energy.

She descended the creaky steps to her familiar reality with three objects heavy in her hands. All of them contained memories that on their own could have her spiralling. She put the sleeping bag next to the door. Martin had won a tent in the same competition, and they'd joked about going on a camping trip once they got holidays. They'd laughed it off then, believing they had time. In retrospect, camping with Martin would've been awesome. Just the two of them for once.

Sini pressed the knitted shirt to her face and inhaled. The only thing she smelled was the wool, and she was kind of relieved. She wouldn't have been able to use it if it smelled of her grandmother. She tried it on. Apart from being a tad short on the sleeves, it was perfect. She laughed at the colourful apparition in the hall mirror. It would be loose enough to insulate well even after she fit a couple of layers under. She couldn't be better prepared. A thermos of hot blackcurrant juice would top her keeping-warm kit.

She looked at the painting placed on the chest of drawers. It was made by a child, but it looked crammed with symbolic elements. It hadn't been signed by a young Sini, but she recognised her style of drawing. She couldn't for her life remember if it depicted a game she'd played with her grandmother or if she perhaps had been inspired by a story from a book. She was certain she'd never seen most of those animals in the forest. Squirrels and birds for sure, maybe even hares leaping across the field.

She'd have remembered if she'd seen a little owl. It was natural to forget childhood art, but that wasn't a scene of a fairy-tale princess in her garden, or a pretty horse. The painting was just another reminder of her not having anyone to talk to about it. The drawing would look perfect on the wall. She could put it in a frame if she bought one. Together with the unfashionable shirt, they'd bring her closer to her grand-mother. Next to her grandmother's painting was free space, where she could see it every time she walked by.

Holding the drawing against the wall, Sini thought its earthy colours and enchanting scene would match the cryptic atmo-sphere of her grandmother's art. No one would come to the house and look at it, never mind ask her what it depicted, but the thought of hanging it on the wall had her feeling exposed. She walked over to the old desk, pulled out the middle drawer, and put the drawing on top of the notebooks.

Sini straightened and took off the shirt. She was about to go out and face the horrors of winter weather, and she needed to be mentally sound. She'd done enough feeling sorry for herself for a lifetime already. Bittersweet memories and unfulfilled dreams would only weigh her down.

The sleeping bag would come in useful after all, and wearing her grandmother's shirt would keep her warm in more than one way. And even if she had no recollection of the drawing, it had brought some light to things forgotten.

She'd loved drawing the mysterious beings of the forest from the beginning.

As Sini began her routine of getting dressed, the butterflies returned.

She'd packed the thermos with steaming hot liquid and the empty notebook she'd found in the drawer. The ski mask was also packed, in case it became necessary. With a bit of luck, the thick layer of protective cream on her face would suffice. She wore both thin and thick wool socks, and she was trying to tuck and secure her padded trousers into the boot shafts. Extra pairs of gloves—she'd also need to bring those. It was like going to a survival camp. She chuckled at the thought of going through all that trouble for a short moment with a guy.

It also felt like she was risking her health for him. On the other hand, staying away from Kuutamo any longer would disturb her mental well-being.

She tried to be swift as she was getting hot under all the layers of clothing. She wrapped the scarf tight around her neck and pulled it over half her face, and then finished the Michelin Man look with the fur hat that she fastened under her chin.

And off we go to new adventures! She tried not to make a face at the cold that was trying its hardest to turn her back home.

At first, she'd felt hot, but then the cold started penetrating the thick armour of fabric, wool, and air pockets. She'd be OK as long as she kept moving. The sleeping bag felt slippery under her arm. The sun had dived under the treetops, but they'd have a couple of hours of sufficient light. The snow snapped and popped under her feet.

Huffing and puffing, Sini ascended through the opening to the forest. She grabbed hold of a little willow to pull herself up. She got to the beginning of the path and grimaced. Although relieved to be back, it was a horrific experience breathing in the air that desired to choke her. But it would be worth it.

She began following the path anti-clockwise. The entire landscape was covered in frost. Nothing had been left exposed, no branch, and no trunk. The largest ice crystals she'd seen covered the thin willow stems. They were nature's vision of the world's most exclusive strings of never-ending diamonds in all shapes and sizes. It was a real winter wonderland. Beautiful beyond description, but deadly.

Still trying to catch her breath, Sini progressed at a slow pace. She was just about to wonder if Kuutamo wasn't there when she saw movement further down the path. She ducked.

Who was that? There was a stranger in her forest.

She straightened herself again and walked a little closer. The figure seemed to be heading in her direction.

Shit…

13 PAINFUL YEARNING

Sini's immediate reaction was to hide.

She'd never met another human in her forest. That fact alone had her scrambled. Second, a stranger in her forest could mean nothing good.

There was no time to waste. She needed to find a place to hide before they saw her. Before they came out from behind the trees. Sini spotted a pair of spruces to the left. They didn't look sufficient, but they were better than nothing.

Sini almost fell as she lifted her foot high in the air, trying to get as long a step as possible. Her foot sank into the deep snow, and she grasped at the nearest branch to steady herself. The sleeping bag and her backpack didn't cooperate with her. Their weight made keeping her balance a struggle, but she couldn't leave them either. Risking that the swaying branches would give her away, Sini pulled herself past the trees and towards the nearest boulder. Thank the forest god for the boulders. With her pulse pounding in her ears, Sini hunched down in the snow. The bulk of her clothes shielded her from immediate cold.

What the hell were they doing in her forest? Was there more than one? Had they gotten lost? It made no sense for strangers to be in the forest in that horrible weather. She doubted anyone would be out on an excursion, and she'd never seen local people wandering about. A researcher might roam the forest, a field biologist, but in such harsh conditions? There was nothing to see, as all living things were covered up.

For the first time, Sini genuinely appreciated her white-and-grey fur hat. It gave her a chance to check the intruder out without being spotted. Remembering the red logo, she cursed at not taking the time to detach it. She also cursed at the holes in the snow that would reveal her hiding place. She tried to breathe slower as the cloud of air coming out of her mouth would expose her. Being out of breath and trying to deposit the icy dry air in her lungs was a bad combination. It was not the time or place to have a coughing fit. Pressing her hand against her mouth, she weighed her options.

If they were a neighbour, they'd be astonished—to say the least—if they found her hiding. Crazy was not a reputation she yearned for, even if it was true. If the intruder wasn't a local, she needed to find out who they were and what business they had trespassing. If the stranger saw her hiding, she'd lose all credibility as the legit wanderer of the forest realm.

She had to protect Kuutamo. And Helmi. What if a stranger saw them? A biologist would notice they were far from ordinary. Sini peeked enough to see movement. They were still advancing! If she didn't confront them head-on, she'd lose the game. She had to make them understand they were in the wrong place at the wrong time. At that moment, she wanted to kill the stranger for putting them at risk.

Standing up and brushing off the loose snow, Sini moved as fast as she could towards the path while keeping her dignity. She might have looked funny, but all she felt was the adrenaline surge heating her body. She put on her stern face as she turned towards the incoming intrusion.

Her heart stopped beating as she tried to interpret the apparition closing in on her.

It was…Kuutamo?

She recognised his way of moving, but… It was him, yet it wasn't. Her heart started racing again.

He wasn't wearing his bulky cloak. With it gone, he looked half the size he'd been. Chills went through her body. He appeared so different. His movements were so free, effortless.

The male approaching her wore a blue outfit, and it looked tailored. Neither ice age nor cave style. It was more like ice prince. Sini was painfully aware of her being the bulky one and carrying more bulk under her arm and on her back. In order to look less stupid, Sini started walking.

Hello. I have been waiting for you. He was beaming.

Hello. I… It was so cold, and I was afraid. I didn't know…

Sini stopped before she reached him. Kuutamo came right up to her.

When she looked up, she forgot to think. He was stunning—no—he was mesmerizing. He looked amused, or so she thought. He must've sensed her lack of intelligible thoughts.

Wow…you look well. She knew she had a question about that, too, but somehow, she couldn't get a hold of it.

She had to know if he was real. Captivated by the vibrant figure in front of her, she raised her hand and placed it on his chest. He was solid. She put some pressure on her palm. Solid. She pushed some more…then more.

She got him to take a step backwards.

So… She struggled to find the question. *Never mind…*

Sini forced her eyes off Kuutamo. His eyes as bright as the sunlit sky. There was nothing more appealing than a man in his element.

You clearly seem well with this weather, but I brought this. She held up the big bundle that was the sleeping bag. *To keep me warm.*

Yes, very good. I know you do not feel well in the cold, and I am sorry I cannot help you.

It's OK, Sini replied and meant it. His hair seemed to have grown again. It might have something to do with the temperature. *Why is your hair longer?* Of all her questions, that was the one she managed to spit out?

Yes. The colder it is here, the more I am myself, the one I am in my world.

Sini imagined being much more herself in a pair of shorts and a sleeveless top, somewhere hot.

Kuutamo's mouth twitched. *Interesting…*

Sini frowned and looked at the greyish ornate swirls on his chest. Either she had to be more careful with her thoughts, or she had to be honest about everything. He was no ordinary human, and she guessed she had nothing to lose.

I don't know how long I can stay. The air hurts my lungs even if my body is warm. It pained her to admit she couldn't be with him when he was at his most comfortable, but it was better that he knew that, too. *What do we do now?* She thought the question before looking up at him, just in case. Else she'd forget.

Come! Kuutamo turned around and started walking at a comfortable pace. Sini took it all in. The contrast between them was striking, as if they were in different worlds. He was the ice prince in an enchanted winter forest, and she, she wasn't even fit to survive in her own world.

Kuutamo's outfit left nothing to the imagination. He had broad shoulders and a narrow waist, he was tall, and in perfect shape. His arms appeared well equipped, and she wondered if he was stronger than a human his size. When he was that solid, did he have all his normal strength? Yes—those were not the questions she'd prepared. But she was no more than human, a human woman who'd been without for too long, and with that perfect male in front of her…

Kuutamo deviated from the path and began ascending a little hill. Despite his slow pace, Sini thought she wouldn't make it. Kuutamo turned around, and his patient smile gave her the courage she needed.

OK, I can do it, but not too far, please. She trudged on, trying to keep her temperature stable.

Sini should've been relieved by how the threatening situation had turned out, but she felt neither calm nor content. Kuutamo turning into an ice prince of an adult fairy tale was beyond unreal, but stranger than that was her reaction to there being an intruder in the forest. Where had that rage come from?

The possibility of people invading their sacred world had never crossed her mind.

After a while, Kuutamo halted and motioned for her to step up beside him.

It was beautiful. The sun managed to cast warmth through the trees and onto the white ground. She glanced at Kuutamo, who seemed to glow. There was a time she'd thought he didn't like the light, but he'd been merely a shadow then.

Do you like the sun? Though obvious, it seemed contradictory to the cold.

Yes. The sun is an important element of our existence.

Yes, I want to know about that. I want to ask you—

Kuutamo cut her off when he nudged her shoulder and motioned at the stone on the other side of him.

You can sit down, and we can talk.

Sini looked at the stone and pictured a soft chair with plush white cushions to sit down on and lean into. She fumbled with the little plastic lock that, together with the cord, closed the sack of the sleeping bag. Her massive mittens on top of her gloves weren't up to the task, but she wanted to keep them on. Kuutamo reached out his hands, and Sini handed him the bag.

With undivided attention, Sini watched Kuutamo put his fingers on the little device that, while simple, was a very modern invention. Although she sensed the little piece was foreign to him, it only took a few seconds of fingering it before he figured out the mechanism and pulled the cords through. He peeled off the sack and revealed the olive-green sleeping bag that hadn't seen the light of day in years. Kuutamo held it up in the air, careful not to touch the ground. He scanned the bag with a question that turned into approval. When he turned it around with an expression of *how does it work?*, Sini pointed at the zipper and motioned downwards. He touched the pull tab, grasped it, and pulled it down. The zipper sliced the bag open in one easy motion. He looked at her, cocked an eyebrow and then broke into that smile that scrambled her brain.

How to step inside without bringing a heap of snow with her? She didn't want to take off her shoes as the bag would be cold. She was about to reach for the bag, when she realised, he might want to help the lady out like any ordinary man.

Sini motioned for him to put it on the ground and against the stone. When he bent down and did as she'd acted out, she felt warm inside. If he was ease and elegance, she turned out to be the opposite. It was a struggle to sit down on the bag and then bring her legs with her and close the zipper around her body while sinking into the snow.

Sini was thankful the bag fit her and the clothes. She managed to pull the zipper up to her chest and looked up.

Kuutamo's expression showed either amusement or content at the result. She must look comical, but she couldn't know how he perceived her, since her world was foreign to him.

Do you think I look funny?

You are beautiful.

Sini laughed. *Surely not…*

Kuutamo's expression stayed the same—upbeat.

He sat down beside her with perfect grace, and the snow didn't give in under his weight. Sini was confused. If he was solid, the snow shouldn't be able to carry him. Or did he weigh nothing?

He sat so close to her, giving her all his attention.

Why…? How can you sit like that on top of the soft snow?

He looked at her sunken into it—still with an approving smile. *I want it to carry me.*

You tell the snow what to do?

He nodded.

So, he was the ice prince, but still… How was that possible?

She knew he sensed her disbelief.

Kuutamo swiped the surface of the snow with his palm, and when he raised the hand into the air, a cascade of loose snow followed and turned into a thin column. The snowflakes towered on top of each other in an impossible formation. Sini swiped at the snow that crumbled into its normal state.

Her jaw dropped. *What else can you do?*

Kuutamo's face lit up, and he lifted his arm in front of him. The fabric of his sleeve began to shimmer and then sparkle. The sleeve looked like it was made of glitter.

That's pretty.

Then the shape of the sleeve changed form. It widened into a more flowing fabric, and ornaments appeared. Intricate swirls meandered across the sleeve like liquid silver. The beautiful pattern was alive.

Sini couldn't believe her eyes. More than just being solid or not, he created his clothing with his mind.

Was that the way his people looked?

He was looking at her again, most likely trying to read her mind.

Those eyes…

The second she thought it, his eyes flickered. For a split second, his eyes became an even lighter shade than hers.

Although he was mesmerizing according to anyone's standards, she felt a little uneasy. He was so much more than she could imagine. Was that what he really looked like, or was it a facade, not to scare her?

Sini took a few slow breaths and calmed down enough to remember one of the questions she'd written down. *Do you have a family on the other side—I mean, in your world?*

He looked at her as if he didn't understand the question. Sini pictured him surrounded by others in a place where he felt happy.

I had a mother, I remember that. In my world, we are all family.

You don't have a wife…partner?

His face was motionless. Her mind went blank, because the only way she thought of conveying her question was to picture herself as his partner. *In my world, people live as families. It's typically a man and a woman, and they have children. They all live together, and the children grow up in the home, the house.*

Do you have a family?

No.

Why not?

I don't know. She did know. She yearned to be honest. *I haven't found my partner yet. From my world.* She hesitated, but then said what suddenly felt like a bad thing. *I live alone.*

Is that your choice?

She didn't know how to answer. *No. Do you miss your home? You're alone here.*

No. He smiled. *I am with you.*

Sini's heart melted. She looked at his face, trying to memorize every detail for when she'd draw him again.

Why do you feel sad?

I don't.

I can feel you. His eyes fixed on hers.

I'm just cold.

It is something else. Tell me. I want to know.

She thought of her sadness, and it wasn't about her being alone in that house, not even trying to look for a family of her own. What she wanted was in front of her, and she couldn't as much as touch him.

He'd become more real than ever, but they were further apart than ever.

She shook her head. He looked strong, vibrant, like nothing could hurt him. Yet she knew it only took a change of weather, and he'd become half the man he was at that moment.

Sini regretted the summer vision she had earlier. He probably wouldn't be there even as a faint shadow when summer arrived.

She looked away, trying to understand her emotions. She wanted to tell him, but she was afraid she'd hurt him. On the other hand, not being honest would also hurt him.

His question hung in the air.

⌘ ⌘ ⌘

Sini drew a deep breath, coughed, and turned to him.

It hurts my heart because I want to be close to you, but I can't. My body temperature hurts you. I want to touch you. She couldn't hide the sensation of her face blushing. It was more than just her curiosity for him. She wanted to be with him on a deeper level. Reading his mind and emotions was great, and it should've been more than enough. Awesome and unheard of. Instead, she was upset she couldn't touch his body. Hold his hand just for the sake of holding it. She knew she was in love, and she wasn't quite able to admit that to herself, that she'd choose an impossible love instead of something real, with a real human.

He searched her eyes, and she didn't know how much he'd caught of her rambling. Half of it was meant for him, the other half she wasn't able to conceal.

She looked into his eyes for the longest time. She didn't sense her fears in his thoughts. He seemed more concerned for her than for himself.

When he stood up, Sini feared their time was over. It should be. Even the sleeping bag couldn't keep her warm, but it had granted her more than double the time with him.

Kuutamo stepped closer, and leaning his hand onto the stone, he sat down on his knees beside her.

Do what you want to do.

No. For real?

Yes. I will be safe. Do not fear for me.

Sini freed her hands from inside the sleeping bag.

She could sense he was stronger. *Why do you touch the stone? Does it give you energy?*

My body is not like yours. Where I live, we are of a different vibration. To be visible to you and for you to touch me, I need to lower my vibration. The stone helps me know the vibration of your world.

Because the vibration of the stone is so low?

Yes.

That was so much new info she had no chance of grasping all the implications. *But it hurts you when I touch you.*

No, it does not. It only affects my vibration. The warmth.

The way he said warmth. He didn't seem to think of it as something negative.

But if the warmer temperature hu— I mean, if it makes it more difficult for you to be yourself, why aren't you afraid of it?

I want to learn. I want to know more.

Sini frowned. *Are you here because you want to learn about my world? Why?* If the people of his world were like him, it meant they were more evolved than humans.

Sini felt him closing up. He didn't want to tell her.

She looked at his chest. He wasn't breathing. *Don't you have to breathe?*

Like this? His chest expanded towards her in a perfect simulation of an inhale, and when he breathed out through his mouth, vapour filled the space between them. It was so strange. She should feel alarm. Instead, she laughed out loud.

Do you like it like this?

Yes, please. If you want to be even a small part of this world, you have to look alive. But I like it better without the vapour. I like that you are the ice prince.

Ice prince?

Their time was coming to an end. She removed the mitten, reached her hand towards him, and gently put her palm on his chest. She loved how the steady rhythm of his heaving and contracting chest felt under her touch. He seemed fine.

He closed his eyes.

Does it hurt? She sensed the hesitation. Then he opened up again.

It is a little difficult. But it also feels wonderful when you touch me. It is new to me.

You mean, that someone is touching you, or me touching you?

I have not been this physical before. It is so different in this world.

Although he didn't mean her specifically, she was the first human who'd touched him.

She didn't want to dissect the meaning of it. She just let her sensations flow to him. He was so otherworldly that it had been petty to act like a typical human wanting to shield herself.

How to touch him without it appearing sexual? She moved her hand gently onto his shoulder and let it slide down his upper arm. She felt hard muscle under the soft fabric.

Something moved inside her stomach, and she was sure he couldn't grasp why it excited a female that a male had strong arms. She fought back the vision of him without the shielding cloth on. It was an impossibility that she didn't want to bring up for discussion.

Sini gathered her reckless thoughts and regarded his face. His eyes were still closed. She wanted to touch his face, to know what it felt like. Would his cheeks be soft? Would his hair feel like human hair? She wouldn't mind if it didn't. She just couldn't bear the thought of him disappearing because her touch made it impossible to keep his physical shape.

Do not be afraid. You can touch me now. The colder it is, the easier it is for me to be here.

Sini took the mitten and glove off her right hand and resisted the urge to blow warm air on it. She wasted no time pressing her palm against his chest. At first, it felt cold. After some seconds, it felt like burning. Then it started to ache. As much as she wanted to, she couldn't keep her hand on him longer.

Once again, Sini refrained from blowing on her hand and shoved it inside her already cold glove.

Wait. She eased herself closer. As if it helped her keep her own vibration at a high level, she leaned with her right hand onto his thigh and then put her bare left hand on his cheek. She struggled to describe what she felt at that moment.

It was familiar, yet it wasn't. It was as if he listened to her mind and tried to mimic the sensation she expected. His skin was firm, but the feeling of touching ice made it unnatural. She gently traced the flawlessly sculpted cheek, happy to be touching him, but trying to decide whether or not it felt good.

The cold stung her fingers. She didn't care that they were freezing, but with every second, she sensed less because of the increasing numbness of her skin. She looked at his inviting lips. Did he know she thought they looked perfect?

She couldn't feel her hand anymore and gave up. She put the fingers to her mouth and breathed warm air on the skin that began to sting.

When he opened his eyes again and there was pleasure in his expression, Sini swung recklessly between happiness and despair. There was no way they could ever get physical. She was looking at someone she couldn't have. *Thank you.*

I liked that.

Did he pick up on her feelings? Was he sorry that touching him hurt her? She swallowed her tears as she smiled at him. He was so perfect and out of her reach. *I want to stay with you. Like always. But I have to go home. Will you walk with me?*

Of course.

Kuutamo stood, and as a reflex, she extended her hand to him. She felt his tentative grip on her hand, as if he was estimating the correct amount of power needed. When he pulled her up, he did it without effort. He looked pleased at getting the physical thing again.

He didn't let go of her hand, and she didn't want him to.

When a shiver rippled through her body, he let go and started heading down towards the path. She was stiff from being still and only managed to take a few steps.

Do you need to be assisted? He stopped and turned towards her.

No—I mean yes. She reached out her hand, and he helped her descend the little hill. Chills seeped through her mitten and glove, but his hand wasn't much colder than the air. She felt the energy, though.

A peculiar current that ran through their connection and made her body tingle.

14 STAY WITH ME

Sini oscillated between smiling, intoxicated, and being terrified of having stayed too long.

It was stupid to go out in extreme cold. She hated winters and longed for the vision of her in summer clothing in that faraway paradise. But then, if it meant being with Kuutamo, winter might as well last forever.

Despite being inside the house, she was cold under her clothing, it prevented the warmth from reaching her body. Sini wrestled herself free from the impressive number of gloves, socks, shirts, and trousers and let them drop to the floor. Grandmother's knitted shirt had been a success. She spread it over the chair. She grabbed the thermos with the juice she'd totally forgotten and took a sip. It was still hot and burned her tongue. She imagined kissing Kuutamo would be like that, alternating burn and freeze. Would her tongue get stuck on him, like when they were children and someone would trick them into licking a frozen metal pole?

She wanted to laugh and cry at the same time.

Sini revelled in the pleasure of warm water cascading down her chilled skin. Or was it the thought of him sitting so close to her and wanting her to touch him that made her buzz? At least Kuutamo liked her—right? Not just because she was human and thus interesting to him? Everything he'd done that day was sweet and considerate, perfect boyfriend stuff. He'd helped her with the sleeping bag. Answered her questions. Helped her up and steadied her. He'd said she was beautiful.

He'd revealed things about his special abilities, but she still didn't know his true motives.

Kuutamo wasn't dangerous, and that was the most important thing—wasn't it? But falling in love with him might be. Then again, what did she have to lose?

Sini sat down in front of the fire with a big mug of cinnamon-spiced hot cocoa and laid the quilt upon her legs. She opened her newly found notebook and looked at the list of questions running up and down three pages. She'd gotten answers to a few of them, and knowledge of things she hadn't thought of. Would it be safe to write it all down?

She couldn't read the scribble in the notebooks of her own ancestors, and if someone read her scribble, they wouldn't think of it as truth. It would resemble plotting notes for a fictional story. Her notebook might be secure in the magic drawer, but she had no way of knowing. How would she make sure there, in fact, was a protection spell on it?

Sini decided to write about their time together—her feelings included. One day, she might want to read it herself. Although it would be impossible to forget someone like Kuutamo, the mind of an ordinary human was faulty. To be on the safe side, she wouldn't draw him in the book.

Other than appealing looks—and at times otherworldly beauty—what was it about Kuutamo that made her risk her health and even consider living through an eternal winter? Was she walking towards eminent disaster, wanting to be with an advanced being that most likely wouldn't stay?

Falling for Kuutamo wouldn't help her return to society and have a normal life.

Sini was aware she was in a dream.

Her grandmother had died years ago. The woman standing in front of her looked much younger, maybe thirtyish. Her hair was dark brown, and she didn't have wrinkles. Her clothes weren't grandmother-like either. She appeared healthy.

Pure joy flooded her senses. Her whole body was tingling. The longing for her grandmother had been much stronger than she'd dared feel.

"Grandmother, I miss you so…" She wanted to run into her embrace, but she was stuck. She looked around the room. The only detail she could make sense of was the black rocking chair.

"Satu." The voice of her grandmother was so familiar but lacked the gentleness.

"Yes, I know it's you, Granny." Tears rimmed her lids. Why was she just standing there, looking at her?

"Satu!" The tone of her voice was firm, as if trying to wake her up to something important.

Why was she repeating her name? Sini was sure it was a younger version of her grandmother, perhaps the form she'd taken in heaven. They regarded each other. She looked so vibrant.

"Sauna!" Satu was near to shouting now. She turned her head to her side as if looking at someone. Sini also looked but didn't see anyone. It was just an obscure room bathing in dispersed light with the rocking chair she thought was the one in her house.

"Grandmother, please, I need you." Her joy of sweet reconnection changed into desperation. She reached out her hand, wanting her grandmother to come to her as she was still unable to move.

It was still early.

Sini tried to linger in the dream, but it made no sense. She was unable to recreate the intensity of it. Even though her grandmother had felt distant in her lack of loving attention, it didn't take away Sini's love and longing. She'd never dared feel such deep emotion after her grandmother passed. Seeing her again was a warm reminder of how important their connection had been. The relationship between Sini and her grandmother was the only one in her life that had been based on unconditional love.

After a while, Sini gave up on trying to decipher the dream and opened her eyes to the dim light emanating from the kitchen. She wanted to remember the dream. She grabbed the notebook on the nightstand and wrote down every little detail. Once again, opposite emotions tugged on her. Happy to see her beloved grandmother but distressed by not understanding why she'd repeated her name over and over. And then, sauna. Did she want Sini to take a bath? She hadn't in a while, but she didn't want to prepare the sauna when it was so cold outside. Getting it warm would take longer than usual, and she wanted to use the wood only when necessary.

Why was the appeal to take a sauna more important than saying something nice? Why hadn't her grandmother hugged her, told her she'd missed her granddaughter? Wasn't that what spiritual reunions were supposed to be about? She wouldn't have given the appeal so much thought if the dream hadn't been so lucid. It wasn't the same as with her dog when she'd believed it was alive. She'd known her grandmother wasn't part of the living world, and Sini had never seen her look like that. She'd been aware of dreaming, yet she hadn't been able to influence the direction, let alone the outcome.

Was grandmother perhaps upset Sini tried to read her notebooks? She didn't want to believe that. If she had an important message, why couldn't she make it clear? The meaning of the words was such a strong mismatch to the intensity they'd been spoken with. The reunion had lacked warmth. In fact, she wouldn't call it a reunion. It had been more like a delivery of an important message.

Sini got up, and when she checked the thermometer against the dark of the dawn, she jumped with joy at the fact it was still cold as hell. She opened the fridge. One thing that would help her keep warm was pumping a lot of fuel into her body for it to burn into heat. She'd start right away.

Sini thought she was prepared for splendid Kuutamo.

When he walked up to her, her breathing became shallow, and she couldn't think of a thing to say. To break the spell, she offered her hand.

Kuutamo walked in front of her, holding her hand gently. She prayed the soft grip would let her hold on to him longer.

They did the ritual with the sleeping bag, and she made sure to drink the warm juice.

She'd memorized her questions so that they were easier to recall when she got bedazzled.

The question that came to her mind, though, was not *why here, why me,* or simply *why?*

"Sini."

He looked at her like he'd witnessed something fascinating.

She pointed at herself and repeated, "Sini." She pointed at him.

"Sini." It was her turn to look at him in awe. His pronunciation was perfect, but the voice… It was so melodic. Not the kind of masculine she'd expected. She pointed at him again.

"Sini."

She giggled. He said her name! He could speak! *Good. I like that.*

I like it too. Do I sound human? He must have picked up on her confusion.

Sini tilted her head from side to side while cocking her eyebrow.

He smiled. *Tell me.*

How to explain it if he'd never heard a man's voice? *It must be deeper—stronger—than mine.* She uttered her name in a normal voice and then lowered it, and then lowered it as much as she was able to.

He said her name again. Oh, how she loved hearing that. But it sounded only a bit different.

What if you breathe in and then use the air and pressure to make it stronger?

Sini felt superficial for wanting to change him into someone else, but they were just having fun.

Kuutamo's chest heaved, and when she heard her name the moment after, she nearly fainted.

She pointed at him again.

"Sini." Even deeper.

She had to let him know the effect it had on her. She opened her mind and let him feel how she sucked on the word like a delicious candy.

That is my name. What is your name?

His mouth opened, and she heard him say something, but it sounded so strange she couldn't recall it.

Please, can you say your name again?

She concentrated hard, but the result remained the same.

I don't understand; I'm sorry. Can you say it in your mind? Her disappointment was a fact when it sounded the same in her head. It was either too advanced for her, or they had very strange names where he came from.

I'm sorry. I cannot understand your language at all. Do you want to know what name I have for you?

Kuutamo…

You already know? She couldn't recall saying his name.

I have heard it many times when you think about me.

Dear Lord. Was he listening to her a lot? She was that schoolgirl again who got caught daydreaming about the coolest guy in school.

I like it. What does it mean?

It means moonshine. The first time I saw you was in the light of the almost full moon. I love the full moon.

That was not the first time I saw you. Kuutamo's cheeky smile told her he knew more about her than she was aware of.

It was that day when I was lying in the snow, and I saw the owl. Did you see me through Helmi's eyes?

Maybe.

"Don't tease me." She poked him in the chest.

"Sini. Don't tease me."

The butterflies. To protect herself from being even more open and vulnerable, she poured herself another cup of steaming juice.

She sneezed. Shit. Having fun with Kuutamo made her forget about the cold. She looked at him. *I can't get sick again.*

It will be warmer.

Sini caught him alternating between sadness and feeling relief for her.

Kuutamo pulled her from the snow, wrapped the sleeping bag around her, and began leading her back towards the house.

Back in the safety of her warm home, the relief was short-lived.

Checking the cupboards, she considered it amazing the groceries had lasted that long. She still had a few days' worth of food if she ate the pasta and canned meat she'd had for ages. Being with Kuutamo demanded frequent meals of good quality. Staying warm and sensing Kuutamo's thoughts had her exhausted, as it were.

She hoped Kuutamo was right about the temperature rising, even though he wouldn't be that magnificent, super-solid version that made it easier for them to get to know each other.

A wave of warmth flushed through her as she recalled how he said her name. The way he looked at her, always listening to what she was thinking. His eagerness to try new things with her. The complete lack of an attitude of supremacy. He wanted to learn things about humans, just as she wanted to learn who he was.

The days of extreme cold had been so much fun, despite the only brief moments they'd had together. She got to ask him some questions, and even though she learnt a lot, there wasn't much she actually knew. Little snippets here and there, but the pieces were too scarce to shed a light on the puzzle that was Kuutamo.

Sini poured the last bit of juice and drank. No need to let it go to waste.

Damn! She needed to get that car fixed. How could she drive into town to replenish her food stash when the risk of getting stranded in the middle of nowhere was bigger than ever? What if she had to call for help and her phone didn't work in the freezing cold?

She couldn't call her parents. Imagine if she told her mother she didn't have the money to fix the car and had to drive into town but that there was no guarantee she'd arrive in one piece? Sini walked over to the chest of drawers opposite the vestibule and checked the little message board. A couple of old receipts had been pinned to it, along with a school photo of her as a child. The only phone number was the one she'd tried earlier and that no one had answered.

Sini tapped the number of the landline phone and let it ring before she had a change of mind. Her heart, beat faster as she listened to the ringing tone. She imagined an elderly person picking up at any second, but nothing happened. Realising no one was going to answer, she closed the call. She hoped the number belonged to one of the neighbours. Then again, if it belonged to a friend or a relative, she might have the chance to ask them about her grandmother.

A second try later in the afternoon gave no result. It might be that the person was at work, especially if they were a farmer, and no one else was at home. By the evening, when the third try turned into another miss, Sini had almost made up her mind that she didn't dare leave the house before she found someone who'd come looking for her if she didn't report back from one of her trips.

What was wrong with everybody?

Sini knew without checking the thermometer that the weather had changed.

Clouds covered the sky, and the light escaping them was scarce. She was grateful it was still ten degrees. It was an anomaly they'd had no days when snow turned to rain and ice began to melt.

It didn't matter to her that Kuutamo wouldn't be the ice prince or that touching each other became more difficult. Not being tongue-tied from looking at him might even be a good thing.

Going out was easier. Less clothing, more freedom to move. Her face didn't hurt, and her fingers didn't numb. She didn't have to fear losing her toes.

She found Kuutamo at the beginning of the path that looked well used. Even Kuutamo's footsteps were recorded in the snow.

He'd bulked up again, but to her delight, his dull cloak was dark blue. She imagined it would match the colour of his eyes.

I want to see your face, please.

He wore the hood again. A nasty shiver sliced through her as she at long last understood the reason for the bulk covering his body. Kuutamo wasn't protecting himself against the cold like she did—he was trying to shield himself from her and her world.

Sini smiled with relief when he pulled down the hood and revealed his face. It was him, but different. He looked more human. The splendid Kuutamo took her breath away, but the cave warrior made her yearning strengthen.

How are you feeling?

Why do you like me like this, if the way I looked yesterday made you without thought?

Where was that coming from? She hadn't sensed pessimistic thoughts before. *I love the way you look, no matter the temperature or vibration, you know that. When you're like this, you're more like me, and that's easier for me.*

The smile she was waiting for didn't surface.

When you look like this, it makes me want to take you to my home and make you my family. She'd meant it as a joke to make him feel better, but the words stung her heart.

Come, let us go to your favourite place. He didn't take her hand when he began walking.

She knew he was leading her to the grove.

They sat on the stone altar, she inside the sleeping bag and he with his fingers digging into the snow.

"Kuutamo."

"Yes, Sini?"

She'd never tire of hearing it. His voice was a little fainter but still had her favourite amount of roughness.

You showed me a vision of your world. At first, it was wonderful, but then it changed into something horrible. She reimagined the dread she'd experienced. *I dreamt about your home before I knew you existed. And the same thing happened in the end of my dream. What does it mean?* She turned her face and observed his reaction.

I want to tell you.

Yes?

He looked at her, searching her face as much as her emotions. She sensed his hesitance, as if he felt concern for her.

It's OK. Please tell me.

She was stronger than before, and she knew much more of what it was about. Back then, the visions had taken her by surprise, and she hadn't been able to handle them. Seeing him so suppressed made her want to reach out.

He turned to her with reluctance, but there was agreement in his eyes when he held out his hand. Sini turned to face him and removed her glove. She carefully placed her hand in his cold palm and closed her eyes.

When the energy began flowing, his hand felt less cold. Their connection was like pure energy that was neither hot nor cold.

Sini grinned when the bright light surrounded her and she could make out the snow and ice. Kuutamo's devotion to the place was clear in her mind. She couldn't see herself or Kuutamo, but she felt his hand holding on to hers. She breathed in the pure air, and like before, it didn't hurt her body.

The uneasy atmosphere set in. Her instinct was to brace herself for the horrible nausea that soon would be upon her. Instead, she chose to calm herself and accept what was coming. For Kuutamo's sake, if nothing else.

She perceived the disintegration before she felt it. Her head was dizzy from the discord between her internal sensations and the optical serenity of the place. She didn't know if her head was spinning, or the whole place. The ground turned unstable, and her feet sank into the snow. As if it was melting. Then the ground shook. She assumed it was one of those earthquakes she'd read about.

She saw that a riverlike funnel had appeared in the distance and that it was widening by the second. The clear water sparkled aggressively in the sun, indicating rapid movement. The ice was melting.

Sini clenched Kuutamo's hand tighter. Then she felt the agony and heard the screaming. The staggering pain and the end of it all didn't overwhelm her like it had last time. Her body became heavier and heavier, dense.

She lost her energy and then her will to live. Her body bent in on itself until her very cells, her molecules, began to scatter. Into nothing, into the ground, into the air. She'd kept her mind composed through it all—she could handle the vision, the lucid dream—but when she sensed Kuutamo going through the same transformation into nothingness, she wanted to scream.

Sini fought to get air into her lungs. She was stuck in a nightmare and couldn't wake up. It was dark, and she was alone. What was left of her.

Open your eyes.

She tried.

Open your eyes!

No, I don't want to see it. Something tugged at her. Her face felt cold. It felt good.

She opened her eyes, and the first thing she saw was Kuutamo's, filled with concern.

I'm OK.

He held her face in his palms.

She released herself from his hold. *I'm fine.* She didn't want him to disappear on her. *Something is happening to your world?*

He nodded.

It felt like it was disappearing. Why?

It is because of you.

Me? Sini shook her head.

Yes. There is something in your world that will have this effect on my world.

Sini was confused. *Right now?*

It is happening, and it will keep happening.

You mean the existence of your world depends on what happens in my world?

Sini felt the emotion that was the answer. His calmness surprised her.

Tears filled her eyes, and she couldn't stop them from rolling down, burning her cold face. She couldn't imagine him leaving her, never mind cease existing?

You are sad.

Of course, I'm sad. What did he think of her?

You do not like the cold. Or winters.

Yes, I know. She searched her feelings. *No, it's not because I don't like winters. I used to love them.* More tears followed the trails of the others. If there'd ever been a time when she needed the comfort of his embrace, that moment was it.

Don't leave me.

I will not leave you.

But your vision?

That will not happen soon. I am here now.

You mean, in my lifetime?

Yes.

Kuutamo didn't understand when the words that were supposed to console her made her heart ache more.

Sini filled her lungs and let out a long sigh, trying to calm the flow of tears. She must be freaking him out.

You are right. I do not understand why you are so sad.

I'm lonely. I have no one. Her voice broke. He was the most important person in her life, and she'd just told him her biggest secret, the thing she didn't want to admit even to herself.

I know.

You do? What did he mean?

I am lonely.

But you said in your world you were all family?

Yes, we are. I want more. Something different.

Sini forgot about her tears. *Is that why you came here?*

Yes, I think so. Then his mind closed.

He was still looking at her attentively, trying to decipher her reactions.

You want to explore the human world? Is that what you mean? You want to have a connection with humans?

She read the hesitation in his mind. He didn't want to tell her.

Sini smiled.

Kuutamo smiled back.

Yes! *I love your smile.*

His eyes flickered into that crystal shade.

You know what? I don't feel lonely anymore…when I'm with you. And when I'm at home, I know you're here. You mean so much to me. Such simple words, but they contained the most profound declaration of love in her life.

I feel the connection between you and me. It feels good. But I do not know all your thoughts, and there is so much I do not know about you.

You don't? She thought they must be really connected in his world.

But I like that.

You do?

Yes. It is more challenging, like revealing small secrets.

Sini eased herself closer. She was getting cosy. For once, she wasn't preoccupied with the freeze, and she thought she could stay with him for hours.

It is interesting to lower my energy to your level. It is difficult, but I am getting better.

Butterflies.

At touching you. Kuutamo lifted his hand to her shoulder and let it run down her upper arm.

Shivers.

Are you cold?

No. Did he notice those too?

I have to guess what your reactions mean sometimes. So much is unfamiliar. I feel different when I am more like you. So much is new to me.

Thank you for coming to my forest. Whatever the reason. She wanted him to know how much he meant to her.

She was afraid he'd leave. How could he possibly stay? But she didn't want to think more of it. The moment was perfect. She stroked his arm the way he'd done to her.

Even though she couldn't feel him through the bulk of their clothing, it was enough for her.

Back in the light and warmth, Sini contemplated what she'd experienced.

Being with Kuutamo and hearing him say strange things about himself and his world had become part of her normal day. If he left, she'd be lonelier than ever. She hadn't connected like that with anyone else. Not her own family, not her friends, and not even Martin.

Everything had flowed with Martin. Their relationship had been quite effortless. They never had deep discussions about life. But they didn't need to. They had so much going on in their lives, and they knew where they were heading. But then, when disaster struck, the bond was severed so easily.

She was finally able to admit she yearned for a connection that was deep-rooted and would last a lifetime. To have someone she trusted—one hundred percent—to always be there. Because nothing else in the world could replace it.

She didn't want to be replaceable anymore.

Not so long ago, she'd have been thrilled at the chance to get out of there, move to a distant, warm place. Somewhere she could start a new life. But then her life had changed, and she was loving the cold and the snow and didn't know what would be left of her life if there weren't winters. Although she'd resented the winter season, she'd never entertained the thought that winters might disappear. Winters got warmer, yes, but the effects on ordinary life were merely less scooping snow off the yard and fewer skiing days.

Even though she hated when the cold killed beings in nature, there was a beauty in resting so that they could have new life in spring. The snow covered living and non-living things and protected against the freeze. The temperature underneath the snow cover remained stable, close to zero degrees, while the air above would change from mild to extreme cold. It provided shelter for small mammals that could go on living and reproducing despite harsh weather. The microclimate also protected fungi that provided nutrients for plants in spring once the snow melted. It was also a fact that a period of dormancy enhanced the flowering and growth in plants when conditions turned beneficial again. She'd learnt all that when she'd wanted to find positive effects of snow tucking away all living things.

She'd refreshed her memory with the facts about winters being a result of the Earth's tilted axis causing the altitude of the sun to decrease, and the presence or absence of ocean winds along with the elevation and precipitation in the area. It was basic school knowledge of things that had always been— at least for the modern human—but that could change in the future. As a winter sports athlete, she should've been more mindful of the threat to winters, but she hadn't taken the warnings of ecology scientists that seriously. Sure, she'd felt concern, but she'd never imagined that it could affect her on a personal level. That it would take away something she held so dear, even if it didn't happen in her lifetime.

Sini took a big sip of her cocoa. Would her lovely hot drink be such a treat if it was always summer? How many animal species would disappear, having to migrate North? And what about other consequences? If it was always warm, birds wouldn't fly south in the autumn to return in spring. Humans would never experience the joy of nature coming alive after being hidden away. The first birds to return, the first flower to bloom, the first day of the sun feeling warm on the skin.

Winter didn't kill things—flowers survived as seeds that bloomed anew, and fresh generations of birds and mammals always appeared. It was the loneliness and isolation that was the hard part. Being in the cold and dark was unbearable, but would she trade the wonders of an always changing nature for forever-warm days?

A vision appeared of a grumpy bear that didn't have a reason to sleep for months anymore.

She might find some comic relief from the situation, but the threat to Kuutamo's world was no laughing matter. Humans would prevail in a world that changed, but the vision had been clear; no one in his world would survive.

His people were different. She didn't know their exact location, but their existence seemed to depend on the actions of humans. But didn't ice ages come and go? Why were humans the threat, according to Kuutamo?

If what he said was true, there was no hope. Humans didn't care about their own world, not their own winters, and they wouldn't care about someone else's either. And why would they care when they didn't know about the ice world? A vision of Kuutamo being on display for humans to see horrified her. She couldn't bear the thought of her people hurting him.

Kuutamo had said he was lonely, too. She found it hard to imagine. OK, he was alone in that forest, but that was his choice—right? She hadn't got the impression he was suffering. He was looking for something. But if he was interested in learning about humans, why did he choose to stay in a forest in the middle of nowhere? The only reason she'd spent time there was she missed her dog and wanted release from her anxiety.

He'd shown her the vision the second time they'd touched. Letting her know seemed important. Other than make her freak out or feel responsible, what good did it do to show her? She didn't have any answers for him. Heck, she didn't even understand how he existed in another world that existed in the ice age but still existed in present time. She knew she liked the ice realm, and she loved being with Kuutamo, but other than that, she didn't know anything.

She was nobody.

15 OUT OF REACH

Sini woke to the gentle spattering on the roof.

The day she hadn't dared think about had arrived, and all she wanted to do was to hide under the covers. Close her eyes and pretend things were as they should be.

In what felt like another life, she would've rejoiced in the warm weather and the promise of at least some of the ice and snow melting.

Zero degrees and raining. She didn't want to comprehend what it meant for Kuutamo. As soon as she'd stopped swearing and throwing things, she'd sent him a question. She'd sensed he was there, but nothing more. The connection was so faint—as if he was out of range.

Would he return to his world? She hoped he would, even though the thought of him being somewhere else pained her. Taking a walk might have been good for her anxiety, but there was no way she'd be able to go to the forest and find herself completely alone. She'd have to make good use of her spare time. It needed to be good to take her mind off the rain and the empty forest.

Ice age. She didn't know much about it, only that it ended over ten thousand years ago, that the geography of her country had changed a lot since then, and that the ice had sculpted the surface and moved around big blocks of stone. She couldn't imagine anyone living on a thick bed of ice that covered the whole country and neighbouring areas.

Sini put two bags of mint tea and honey in her biggest mug and seated herself by the computer.

The internet told her that Earth, in fact, was in the middle of an ice age. The Quaternary glaciation, an alternating series of glacial and interglacial periods, had begun over two and a half million years ago. The Last Glacial period, that people actually meant when they spoke of the ice age and that in fact was only one glacial period among others within the ice age, had begun more than a hundred thousand years ago and had ended more than eleven thousand years ago. After an ice age, there'd be a greenhouse period with no glaciers at all on Earth.

Sini took a sip of the aromatic and sweet drink. Greenhouse periods didn't sound fun. Not that kilometre-thick ice sounded like a party, either. Or being chased by the ice that, at some point, would cover the entire nation. As the ice moulded the topography of significant parts of the country, it destroyed all evidence of the stone age cultures that might have existed.

She scribbled down numbers and facts in her notebook. She wondered how prepared humans would be if another ice period was incoming. Would they be able to develop technology to aid them to survive on such a thick ice sheet for thousands of years? She hadn't seen any such technology in her visions of the ice world.

Was there an intrinsic meaning to the ice ages? Nature did nothing by mistake. Everything had its purpose, such as yearly floods bringing in nutrients onto land or forest fires clearing areas for new growth and habitats. Apparently, the last glacial period had created mountains, lakes, and pressed down extensive areas in a short time period on a geological time scale. It had also caused changes in winds and ocean currents.

Scientist estimated that the next glacial period would occur in fifty thousand years, but because of human influence, it could be delayed by another fifty thousand. Some scientists were of the opinion they'd cease coming altogether. The thought of returning mammoth glaciers was frightening, but surely mankind would be prepared by then—assuming it wasn't already wiped out. The fate of the returning glacial ice wouldn't be known in the near future, but what about the existing ice that was diminishing as she sat there?

As if it wasn't dreadful enough to see big blocks of ice breaking off glaciers into the ocean and emaciated polar bears looking for food close to human settlements on TV, what about the effects that reached across the globe? Big river systems that supported billions of people flooding and drying, landslides, rising of sea levels and air temperature. Volcanoes erupting, earthquakes… Glaciers were melting, and some had already vanished, and there seemed to be a consensus among the scientists that it was because of human impact.

Kuutamo appeared to be right about humans being on a path to destroying the ice on Earth, but what was the connection to the ice world, and why did he think she was a representative of the human species?

The more she read about it, the sicker she felt. She'd succeeded in taking her thoughts off the horrible weather and not being able to go to Kuutamo, but when she realised rain in winter had implications not just for her, but for the entire world, she had to turn off the computer. Rubbing her aching eyes, Sini leaned back in her chair and moaned.

What was wrong with the world?

The longest days of her life came to an end when the temperature at last descended to a decent level.

It had rained for days, and it had been the end of the world to Sini.

Absence makes the heart grow fonder. She'd never experienced that with someone. Had he missed her? Would she dare ask? She laughed as she wrote down the question in her notebook that was already half full of her thoughts and comments. Apart from what she'd learnt about him, the writing consisted of her feelings for him, and her wondering about his feelings for her. How could she still not know? However, why would he be interested in a kind of relationship? He'd, without doubt, be the reasonable one.

She could sense him again, and she was happy he was safe. She closed her eyes and took a deep breath. If she already felt that nervous at home, how would she come across close to him?

When Sini saw him standing further away, up on the little hill, she gave him a virtual hug. She sensed surprise, delight—with a little confusion. Maybe they didn't hug in his world.

Hi, I missed you. Her heart, beat too fast.

Come here.

Sini looked at him standing there, expecting her to wade through the snow that still lay there in marvellous amounts.

Come on!

Sini took a step into the thick snow. It didn't give in when she put her weight on it. She took another small step. The snow carried her.

Yes! Thank you, nature, rain, and freeze. She took more steps to be reassured and then walked straight to where he was waiting.

She scanned the surroundings. With the snow carrying her, she was able to go anywhere. Places she didn't visit even in summer. The forest looked so different—like a new, fascinating world.

So, did you miss me? She stood in front of him, wondering whether he might be upset she hadn't visited.

I am glad you are here. I know you do not like to be out in the kind of weather you saw in the vision.

Being without him for days had left her wanting to open up more. *Do you know what I mean when I say I miss you when we're not together?* She regressed to the bittersweet memory of her wanting to be with him but not being able to.

I do like it better when you are here.

It wasn't the answer she'd hoped for, but she tried to think of it as a good one.

He looked well, so she stepped closer. She felt tiny and vulnerable next to him.

She reached her hand towards his stomach that was hidden by the lapels of the cloak. She slid her hand between them and hoped she wouldn't hurt, offend, or embarrass him. But she needed to touch him again. He appeared solid to her. He didn't move. She didn't dare look him in the eyes. She mostly felt her own glove against her skin.

Sini ripped off the glove and put her palm against his lower chest. She felt the stiff fabric of his jacket underneath. Then it gave in, and she saw him flicker. It was as if her hand tried to find resistance in a couple of heavy curtains.

He'd said it didn't hurt, but she retrieved her hand and put on the glove. When the temperature was much more bearable than thirty degrees minus, he wasn't solid enough for what she wanted from him. She knew it was wrong, but she needed him to be physical for her. She already felt like crying when he spoke the dreaded words.

We can never be together the way you want. I do not exist in heat, and you will not survive the cold.

She knew it was true, she'd always known it, even so, she fought the hardest battle of her life against the tears.

Breathing became difficult. Her chest turned so rigid. She needed to distract herself. She didn't want to burden him with her emotions.

Sini began walking, and Kuutamo followed her wherever she wanted to go. She wanted to explore the whole forest. Before, she'd thought there was nothing to see as everything was covered in snow, but suddenly, the wintry forest had never been more intriguing. She led him from boulder to boulder, wanting him to recalibrate his vibration so that he was comfortable. The snow on the spruce branches reflected the light of the day in thousands of crystals. It was so quiet. It was just the two of them.

The snow was no longer a pure, untouched white. Scattered across the ground lay debris that the winds had beaten off the trees. Needles, cones, pieces of bark, little twigs. She told him the folklore of how it was the god of the forest, *Tapio*, who sowed seeds of the forest. She didn't tell him that people also used to say summer came nine weeks after the sowing. Kuutamo smiled at her new eagerness to explore. She didn't know if he might believe the forest had its own gods and goddesses.

She was looking for a special place. At last, she found it on the highest mound in the forest. It was the largest boulder she'd seen, and it overlooked an open space towards where the sun should be if they could see it for the clouds. She scooped snow off the wall, sat down on the sitting pad she'd brought, and leaned into it. At her request, Kuutamo sat down beside her.

Since she could take a break from coveting her romantic nonsense, she'd ask him more questions.

Why did you show me the vision of your world dying? Why did you come here? Why did you choose my forest of all places? Why me? Since you don't want to be with me...

She couldn't help blurting them all out. She didn't know which one to ask first, which one was more important—the one about the annihilation of his home or the one about what he wanted from her.

Sini. You are special.

She rolled her eyes. Wasn't that what all women wanted to hear?

Kuutamo took her hand in his. He didn't let go as she fidgeted. He wanted her to look at him.

This forest is a very special place. It is important. You are important.

To whom?

To me. To everyone.

Sini shook her head.

"Sini."

"What?"

I need your help. There is a reason why you see the threat to my world. You told me you saw it with your own eyes before you sensed it through me. Before you knew me.

He was talking rubbish. Nonetheless, it made her uneasy. She tried to retrieve her hand, but he wouldn't let go. He grabbed hold of her other hand.

How am I supposed to help you? I don't have any power in this world. I can't tell people to stop what they are doing because it is destroying our world. They don't care about themselves, how are they supposed to care about you?

He still wouldn't let go of her. *I do not know this world. I know you. You are the one who can help me.*

No. I am no one. Don't you see I'm all alone out here? Do you think people would have stopped caring about me if I was so important? Maybe I could tell you who to talk to if you want to. But even if saving your world is the most important thing, I don't believe the people of this world can help you.

You are the one, Sini.

Who!

He didn't answer, but the look in his eyes told her everything. That he was desperately asking for help from the wrong source.

She looked down at his hands. They looked exactly like human hands. The skin was flawless, but they looked strong and able to do anything. Except touch her. She couldn't grasp what he requested of her, only what he'd denied her.

Sini closed up.

Kuutamo let go of her hands.

The day had gone in the opposite direction from what she'd expected.

Instead of having a lovely reunion, a rift had cracked open between them. She stood on one side with dreams of him being her boyfriend, he on the other side with illusions of her being some sort of saviour.

The hot water felt good on her skin, but it brought no ease.

He'd never see her naked. He'd never help her soap up her body. She looked out the small, square window. All she could see was the black night. Was he curious?

Sini felt guilty for imagining him looking at her. She felt a tingle between her legs. Could he feel her touching her wet body? Did he sense what was on her mind as she worked the soap onto every inch of her skin? Did he understand her vision of his warm body pressed against hers?

She did the forbidden thing, what she had tried so hard not to, and thought of him without censoring as she touched herself.

No one had touched her since Martin. She had wanted no one. She had needed no one. Wasn't it just her bad karma that when she found the one she would've given herself completely to, it was the one who literally couldn't take what she had?

Sini took a deep breath, rinsed the soap off, and let the water run down her hair and face. She wanted to drown her desires, to let them pour out and down the drain. It was no use torturing herself with wanting the impossible.

Using her fingers to help her get rid of the soap was a mistake. Her body reacted to the pressure, and she had no choice other than answer the aching.

Forgive me…

Supporting herself by leaning her palm against the cool brick wall, she gave in to the desire of her body, thinking of him all the way through. If he was listening, he was getting a profound lesson on how the human female body worked.

She couldn't help herself. Compared to him, she was an animal ruled by her physical craving. Knowing he'd never be hers, she had nothing to lose. At that moment, she wished he was as human as she was.

Lying in bed, still undressed, it was the first time Sini didn't want the hours to rush by so she could go back to him.

Things had changed.

She wanted him with her body as much as with her mind, and she didn't know what could become of them except heartache.

For both of them.

16 HIDDEN

Sauna!

The word popped into her mind, accompanied by that demanding tone.

Sini couldn't imagine why it was important. Yes, the sauna united her and her grandmother, but the word only resurfaced the memory of her grandmother washing her hair when she was a child.

It was time for a sauna, though, and it wasn't that cold outside.

Sini got up and walked to the kitchen, pulled away the curtains, and checked the temperature. Same as the day before. She didn't bother getting her robe. She wasn't chilly. All that time in the forest made her more resilient. Instead of being weakened by the illness, she felt healthier than ever, and she knew to appreciate it. It was the perfect temperature for going out, but she didn't want to.

She couldn't.

Even though their days were numbered, she had no choice but to waste one. If she went to him, she'd only feel the sadness, and she didn't want that.

How could she explain she liked him so much it made her sad?

He had bigger problems than her lovesickness.

Sini hummed as she headed to the sauna. She was trying to push out the thought that she was walking in the wrong direction. It was supposed to be a cheery tune, but a melancholic tone grabbed hold of it and turned it to something murky.

She scooped away the snow from the front of the door. It opened with a little creak, and the familiar scent of birch leaves and old wood welcomed her. She stepped inside and looked around the changing room. The almost burnt-down tea lights from last time still lay on the table. The window let in a sufficient amount of light. For some reason—probably economical—the sauna hadn't been linked to a power line.

Sini decided to carry wood in and sweep the floors.

She opened the door to the sauna room and looked at the old benches, wondering who'd built them. The wall, floors, and bench wore signs of time and wear. It was clear many generations had bathed there. Why didn't she know more about her ancestors? She knew the property had belonged to her family for an extensive period of time and that the house she lived in had been built to replace an older one.

Sini loaded the sledge with enough wood to last for a few occasions and pulled it across the yard. Physical work did wonders for her restless mind.

She carried the wood inside the sauna and piled the logs into a neat formation against the wall. After getting the dust and debris off the floor, accompanied by, little by little, jollier humming, she eyed the walls of the changing room. That tapestry on the wall might need a dusting. The large, dark fabric was draped on a wooden pole above the bench. On it were circles and spheres of varying sizes stitched into a simple pattern that complemented the old, dusky atmosphere of the room.

Sini walked over to the tapestry and touched it. She hadn't given it much thought before. In her eyes, it was a dull, old-fashioned piece of decoration. The tapestry felt soft against her skin. Trying not to scatter the dust around, she carefully pulled it off the pole.

When Sini took the cloth outside and spread it open, she noticed that it wasn't an ordinary tapestry. She turned it around in her hands. The other side was a dark grey, and when she turned the cloth, it reflected the light in a way that made speckles appear. It felt like the softest suede. The other end of the cloth, the part that had been hidden, was sewn together. She turned the cloth around again and thought it looked like a hood.

Sini grabbed the end part and lifted it onto her head. The cloth wrapped around her body. She noticed a loop on the left side and a wooden toggle button on the right side. When she united the pieces, the tapestry turned into a cloak that reached all the way to the ground. She turned around and watched the hem graze the snow in a flowing motion.

Awesome! Now she too, had a cloak.

She took off the cloak and scrutinized it. There were no signs of wear. She didn't know if it was meant as decoration or if it had actually been used by someone. Turning the fabric in her hands, she liked the way it came to life. It couldn't be new, but it didn't look old, either. Rather timeless. Precious.

She returned inside and laid the cloak on the table. Were there other things hiding in plain sight?

Her eyes swept over the walls and the floor. She raised her gaze to the ceiling and noticed a line in the corner above the bench.

Sini took her phone from her pocket and turned on the flashlight. She made out two lines that united in a straight angle and then a third. The elusive square looked like it might be a hatch, but it lacked a handle. She stepped onto the bench and pushed at the ceiling with her free hand.

Nothing happened.

She put down the phone and pushed with both hands. There was a slight upward movement of the ceiling. The piece felt heavy, but it was definitely loose. She stepped down and pulled out the stool from under the table so that she could stand higher.

Next time she pushed, the square gave in and revealed an opening. Dust cascaded down, and she had to turn her face away. She slid the hatch along the upper floor, waited, and looked up. The space was dark, but she discerned wooden structures of what appeared to be the roof. Her pulse broke into a gallop as she wondered when the last time someone had been up there. She couldn't leave it unexplored.

She had to find a ladder.

Sini returned with the ladder and her headlamp.

Climbing the few steps, she didn't know what to expect. She hadn't known of the little attic's existence, so it was either empty or the best of hiding places. She didn't know which option she hoped for.

Entering the opening and looking around, it was quite what she'd imagined. Joists and rafters running across the space with insulating material in between. No floor except for a few planks to step on.

Some big cardboard boxes were placed at the far end. She'd bet on used clothes or Christmas decorations if the space had been more accessible. Instead, they might be filled with more of the insulating material.

Sini managed to stand up and almost hit her head on a ceiling beam. Balancing on one of the floor joists, she reached the planks and walked with careful steps up to the boxes.

The first one was filled with old building material. Sini laughed at her hopes of finding a hidden treasure. The second one contained fabrics that appeared to be curtains. She flipped through the stacks all the way to the bottom, but there was nothing she might want to use, and nothing was of the same quality as the cloak.

The third box was the biggest. Better go through them all and then have peace. She bent open the flaps of the sturdy box and looked at what seemed to be more fabric. When her light hit the surface, it looked like the lid to one of those old big wooden chests that people used to keep their belongings in long ago.

It looked too old to be her grandmother's.

Sini felt the excitement build up again. Either the chest and its insides were as worthless as the other boxes, or it was a clever disguise. She pulled the chest with its protective box away from the steep angle of the roof to get better access.

Sini expected the lid to be locked, maybe even protected with a spell, and when the lid opened without problem, her heart sank.

Clothes.

Thick, knitted scarves, mittens, and hats. She picked up one of the mittens at an arm's length, expecting it to be moist and dirty. She turned the mitten around in the light. It might be a treasure after all, as it felt dry and soft. Perhaps the box was to protect the clothes from moths and the like.

Sini brought the mitten closer and inspected it. It smelled of wool and old wood. It looked old; used but whole. She picked at the other pieces in different shades of grey and brown, knitted in traditional patterns. Maybe someone had wanted to store them in the attic because they neither wanted to use them nor throw them away. A family heirloom too ugly to keep in the house. She wondered whether the chest had been brought there when the sauna was built or when the roof had been renewed. Either way, it hadn't happened without effort.

Caution gave way, and she tried on a hat and a pair of mittens. The hat fit, and she was enveloped by instant warmth. The mittens were big even for her, and she'd easily fit a thinner pair underneath. Sini saw herself walking in the forest wearing the cloak and mittens and scarves and all the stuff. A pair of socks peeked out from under some more mittens. No one seemed to care about the ancient clothes, so she'd put them to use. They wouldn't hold up forever in the chest, anyway.

Rummaging through the small pieces of clothing, her hand hit something solid. Shoving the clothes away and getting a grip on the object, she pulled it out. It was a book. The cover of the book was a velvety dark brown with swirling leaves and flowers in a light-sand shade. Two ornamented latches kept the book closed. It looked like something from the past. Not ancient, but perhaps from her grandmother's childhood.

Releasing the latches and opening the book up in the middle, the scent of old books was released. It wasn't mouldy, but quite pleasant. The text was ornamental calligraphy. The font looked beautiful, but the slight unevenness told her it was handwritten. On the next page was a coloured illustration of a little house at the edge of a forest of tall trees.

Sini grabbed as many pieces of the clothing as she was able to carry together with the book and closed the lid and the box. She hoped the interior of the book would reveal why the best place for it was hidden under old handicrafts.

Back down, she felt the urge to put the hatch back in place—better keep the attic a secret.

Sini hung the found clothing to air on the clothesline outside the house but took the cloak with her inside. She wanted to study the book but told herself she'd benefit more from preparing the sauna and having that relaxing bath.

Besides, heating the sauna and the bathing water would take the entire afternoon.

Keep her busy.

Sini lay comfortable and tired on the top bench of the sauna.

The temperature was perfect, and the moist air pleasant to breathe. She was alone, but knowing that generations of her kind had bathed there helped her feel at ease. Her grandmother must have been lonely, too, but she'd never given that impression.

Her grandmother had always looked busy and up to something interesting, although Sini hadn't understood why when she was younger. She seemed content with her fate. As if she had a mission.

Sini closed her eyes and tried to empty her mind of thoughts of her ancestors, secret books, and Kuutamo. Except she couldn't push him away. He was always there. As if her mind was his natural habitat.

She hadn't sensed him since the day before. Lying in the dark room with only the fire as a light source, she thought no one could see her through the window that was at the same level as her. Was it luxury or just another testimony to her secludedness to have the sauna all to herself? Was it a privilege or a failure?

Slow breathing, thoughts on the warmth. She began slipping away.

Are you happy now, Grandmother? I have spent all day doing things in the sauna. At least she'd done her best. She envisioned the smiling face of her grandmother.

She was tired. A good tired. The warmth caressing every part of her skin made her feel safe, shielded from the cold world. Weightless. No thoughts. She managed to cease all thoughts. Then she fell through a gateway. She was somewhere else but still aware—awake and in a dream. She was falling and falling and falling. A part of her was afraid, and another part welcomed the abyss. Peace. Rest. Time stopped.

Kuutamo…

Where was he?

Sini jerked into consciousness. She wanted Kuutamo by her side. She opened her eyes and became aware of her surroundings. As she tried to get her body to work again and into an upright position, a thought crystallised in her mind. She wasn't prepared to let Kuutamo go.

But if she insisted on not wanting to help him, he would give up on her and leave her.

Sini put on the bathrobe and wrapped herself in the cloak.

The sensation of shelter washed over her again. The long cloth and the hood had protected her from the cold and the winds as she'd crossed the yard, carrying water. Knowing it had belonged in the family made her feel connected to the ones who had done the chores before her.

Sini grabbed her clothes and boots and pulled up the hood. Walking barefoot in the snow, she hurried towards the house.

The first steps were OK, but then every step more and more burned the soles of her feet, and the pain spread to her ankles. Halfway across the yard, her feet hurt so bad she regretted following her impulse, but it was too late to turn back. The snowless porch gave some relief, but her feet had turned into icicles.

Inside the house, the wooden floor felt hot for a change. A welcomed peace had entered her in the sauna, and she wanted to preserve the sensation. Instead of changing into clean clothes and going on as she did every evening, she grabbed the old book and sat down in the armchair, still dressed in the cloak.

She wasn't into old fairy tales, but she wanted to know if the book held any clues to her grandmother's life history. What was her childhood like, and what were her parents like? Sini couldn't believe she knew next to nothing. Those stories were meant to be passed on to the next generations, but Sini had no one to tell her. She didn't want to hear them from her parents as she was certain they'd be negatively biased.

Sini flipped to the first page and felt the soft, grainy texture of the thick paper. The font proved a bit difficult to interpret, and Sini feared it would be as unreadable as the notebooks. She relaxed as she saw the language was a bit archaic but fully recognisable as her mother tongue. It was a fairy tale about a family a long time ago. There was a father, a mother, and a daughter who lived in a little house in the country, far away from people. The mother's father lived with them as well, and one day the little girl found out that her grandfather was the guardian of a magical forest. He told her of a secret in the forest that needed to be protected from other people for always. A little chill ran through Sini.

She wondered who the book had belonged to and who'd made it. There were the initials S. K. again on the inside of the front cover. It could've belonged to her grandmother, but who'd written it? She suspected the book might be a lot older than she'd thought at first, but it was well preserved. The illustrations were idealistic in the typical style of children's books. But the vibe she got wasn't juvenile. Although the story was simple and typical for the genre, there was something touching about it. As if it had been written by someone from her family for her family.

What triggered the thought was the illustration of the grandfather wearing a cloak that resembled the one she'd found. The grandfather wore the cloak while he showed the granddaughter magical things of the forest. There were secret markings on big stones that only he could see and interpret. He told her there were portals that led to other worlds.

It was just like Sini and her grandmother playing.

She wanted to go to the forest the next morning to try out the cloak and the old clothes.

Sini looked up from the book. What time was it? She put the book away and stood. The cloak was too warm for comfort, and she folded it on the armrest. She realised she'd forgotten to pull shut the curtains, and she hurried to close out the darkness from all windows. When she got to the kitchen, she startled.

In the darkness, the light from the kitchen lamp was reflected in a pair of round eyes. The eyes were aimed at her. She tried to catch her breath as her heart sprinted.

Sini hurried to the vestibule and put her boots and jacket on. She'd seen no cats around, but if there was one out there, it needed shelter from the cold. She hastened out and down the steps but slowed down when she reached the corner of the house. She didn't want to frighten the animal.

Coming to the second corner, she took a peek. She saw nothing on the ground, but there was something on top of the birdfeeder. A small, round figure that flew away as soon as she revealed herself.

Helmi?

17 THE LINEAGE

Sini finished off the peculiar outfit with the cloak.

Posing in front of the mirror, wearing the old hat, mittens, and scarf that clashed with her modern jacket, she resembled a model from a knitting magazine.

Walking across the field with the hem of the cloak swirling on the snow, she felt like an aspiring superhero. She was glad no one was there to see her and laugh. Not that she cared. She'd been through worse. Kuutamo, on the other hand, would approve of it. They'd match each other better.

Sini pulled the hood over her head as she reached the forest. She hoped the new outfit would take the attention off the shower scene. A surge of embarrassment washed over her. She wouldn't be able to explain if he asked. He might be in shock, for all that she knew.

She looked around, but all she saw was white, and more white.

He wasn't there.

Sini started walking. He would be. He always was.

Walking towards their grove, she pictured him leaning against the altar boulder. Before she could reach the circle of spruces, she sensed he wasn't there either. There were no recognizable footprints in the snow. New snow had filled in the indentations of their feet.

Instead, she sensed something else. A whisper so silent she couldn't hear it, as if the trees themselves had a message for anyone who listened.

She played with the snow on top of the boulder. As she drew her hand along the edge of the snow, it crumbed and scattered to the ground. A part of the side of the stone was still free from snow. On it grew lichen in round patches of grey.

The formation was pretty, and as a child she might have pretended it had a secret meaning.

He wasn't there. Where else might he be? She knew he wasn't playing *Hide and Seek* because she would've felt his energy close to her. She turned back to where she'd come from.

Except she couldn't find her trajectory through the snow.

She looked around. Her footprints were nowhere.

How peculiar. The wind wasn't strong enough to blow snow into her footprints. The whole situation was eerie. Kuutamo wasn't there, she heard the trees whisper, and it looked like she wasn't there either. She was ninety-nine percent sure she wasn't dreaming.

Returning to the path, she turned around for a last glance. There were no traces left in the snow in the direction she'd come from. Sini walked back towards the boulder and then returned.

Nothing.

She planted her foot in front of her and saw the clear, normal indent in the thin layer of new snow. She walked forwards and turned around. The indent was gone. Nothing.

Either she'd turned into a kind of spirit being like Kuutamo, or something else had changed. She walked back towards the path, looking at her boots squashing the snow and then behind her, where the evidence of her boot prints had again disappeared like magic. The hem of the cloak was like the long train of a charcoal wedding gown on the snow.

Sini gathered the cloak in her arms and walked forwards again. Her boots left recognizable traces in the snow. She let the cloak down and watched it dance on the snow cover, leaving nothing but a perfect uniform layer of snow behind her.

Either she was hallucinating, dreaming, or her cloak was magical. It was of her world, belonged to her, and covered up all her movements in the snow.

Whatever the reason—it was fun!

Sini ran with light feet up the hill and did loops while she checked that all her footprints were swiped clean.

A laugh of pure joy surfaced.

Sini walked to the other place special to her and Kuutamo. Maybe she'd find him there, contemplating the sense of their relationship. Disappointed in her primal reaction to him and his quest.

He wasn't there either.

Sini sighed and bowed her head. There was still a noticeable indentation where she'd been sitting in her sleeping bag, leaning against the stone. She moved to the back side of her seat. There were those markings again on the bare, grey surface. Simple dots of lichen in different sizes. They must be random, but to her eyes they seemed again to make out a distinct pattern. Though she wasn't able to pinpoint the construction.

Driven by a new thought, Sini sought out the biggest boulder. She expected it to be filled with those signs, and maybe the pattern would give a clue to its secret. Disappointment was apparent when she found nothing special. The square, vertical surface was the perfect canvas. It had spots of different sizes, but nothing coherent, and some were fragmented.

Sini looked around. She was half expecting to see Kuutamo standing there, regarding her enthusiastic exploration of the stone messages. He wasn't. She began to understand he wouldn't show up.

Sini told herself it was fine to have fun on her own for once. She wasn't sure she wanted to tell him about her findings. She also told herself that it was fine with her if he didn't like that she'd been avoiding him. Instead of being a supportive friend, she'd only thought of herself and her desires.

Was it Helmi she saw last night? Was it Kuutamo checking up on her? Sini shook her head and moved on.

Her new accessories seemed to be working well, as they kept her warm and comfortable. At first, she'd felt like an oddball in the cloak, but she'd soon gotten used to the fabric draped on her body. It was as much a protection against the world as it was the weather.

Without Kuutamo to talk to, and with nothing special to do, Sini wandered the forest, looking at the signs on every boulder she found. She hadn't come to any conclusion when she found one with a pine tree growing next to it.

The boulder had a pointier top than the other ones. The pine stem grew so close to it that the bark merged with the rough stone surface. Beneath their union was a gap between the stone and the ground that looked like the opening to an animal's den.

She didn't see any animal tracks. It looked as if the pine kept the boulder upright so that the opening to the underground wouldn't close.

On the stone above the opening spread a big round sphere in light grey. It was, without doubt, lichen growth, but to Sini, it looked like a sign, a *place your hand here* to open the gate to a secret destination. Although it sounded funny, like a children's story, she didn't dare place her hand on it.

Sini walked around to the other side. Snow covered half of the stone. On the bare spots were small and slightly bigger circles of the same colour. She brushed away the snow and squinted at the pattern. Somehow, it looked familiar. She grabbed the lapel of her cloak and studied the lining.

What had seemed an irregular pattern of circles in different shapes looked like the patterns on the stone. In fact…

Sini looked through the hand stitched figures and found a match. A wave of cold travelled her spine. Holding the cloak by the part with the eight circles arranged in a constellation-like pattern, she hunched down by the corresponding spheres on the stone. Beside the formation on the cloak was an upright line. Checking the other clusters of circles, she found all had a group of lines beside them.

The number of lines was different for every cluster, and there were nine clusters in all. That would make the pattern on the stone number one. She was reading the lining of the cloak upside down. That way, she could read the pattern the right way when wearing the cloak.

She longed to tell Kuutamo about it, but intuition told her it was something to be kept within the family. Always.

Sini stood up and looked around to check no one was watching. What she'd discovered was too fantastical to be real, but if Kuutamo was real, then anything could be.

A few steps from the path, Helmi flew past her. Sini put up a hand to get her attention, but it was too late. The owl continued along the path and headed for the exit. It astonished her the owl hadn't reacted.

Closing in on the exit herself, Sini was disappointed that Kuutamo had chosen to stay away.

Sini took off the cloak the second she stepped onto the field.

The chance of some stranger seeing her wearing it was slim, but she didn't want to risk it. Earlier, she'd felt embarrassed wearing it, but after she learnt how unique it was, she didn't want anyone to know of its existence. It had been on display in plain sight in the sauna, but nobody had recognised its value. She folded it into a tight bundle under her arm.

Walking the familiar trail across the field, Sini felt more and more dejected, almost naked and vulnerable without the cloak. Another lonely evening and a long, dark night were all she had to go back to. She should've been more considerate towards Kuutamo. It wasn't his fault that he talked about his challenge with the wrong person. Would he leave the forest when he didn't find what he was looking for? Not even Helmi had paid her any attention.

She wished she could tell Kuutamo about her findings, to ask him if he knew anything about the boulders and the symbols. She hadn't gotten the chance to ask more about Helmi, to understand why there were drawings of her from a long time ago.

Sini was about to reach the porch when a shadow swooped by. She jumped but was relieved to see Helmi landing on the railing.

"Helmi!"

She wasn't completely ignored, after all.

The bird zoomed in on her with unblinking eyes. She couldn't know what went on in its head. Although the bird always looked a little surprised, it might be wondering where she'd been.

"Kuutamo—where is he?"

Speaking the question out loud, she heard the concern in her own voice, and fear hit her. Had something happened to Kuutamo?

Kuutamo? Sini opened her mind to find his energy.

Sini!

Is something wrong? Where are you?

You are at home? Are you safe?

That was the question she was supposed to ask. *Yes, of course I am OK. I didn't see you in the forest.* She didn't want to admit she was afraid he'd stayed away on purpose. Why had she thought he'd act like a simple human?

I am here. Please come to me.

Whatever she'd told herself in the forest about being fine on her own, it was bullshit. She'd go to him as soon as she could. *I will.*

She looked at the bird and smiled. He'd asked the bird to look for her, hadn't he?

The little owl fixated on her, and Sini returned the gaze. After what felt like minutes, it did a slow blink and jumped into flight.

Sini watched as the bird headed back to the forest and disappeared between the trees.

Seated by the fire, Sini battled the urge to stuff herself with a bag of candy.

When she was with Kuutamo, she hadn't even thought about needing sugar as relief. One moment she was giddy in love, the next wanting nothing to do with his purpose. Then, experiencing the familiar feeling of abandonment and trying hard to deny the effect it had on her. It appeared he'd been worried about her, not knowing why she hadn't gone to him the day before. She wasn't fit for a new relationship—it was painfully obvious. On one hand she was being selfish and single-minded, on the other she didn't want the ups and downs, being on the peak of bliss only to fall into darkness the next. How did she manage to mess things up with someone who shouldn't even exist?

Sini smoothed the velvety lining of the cloak with her fingers, seeking comfort in something tangible. Finding a footprint-sweeping cloth in her sauna made no sense. Her grandmother had been right in letting Sini know there was something special with the sauna, but it still made no sense. Too much was happening at once. She had no one to talk to about everything. She'd never have anyone. Her grandmother was gone, and there was no chance she could ever mention things to her parents. She could ask her father about her relatives, but only if she did it without any hint of weirdness. How relieving it would be to get even the simplest corroboration from her next of kin that what she'd experienced was real.

Sini suspected her father had been coaxed by his wife into diverting from his mother. Sini's mother was the opposite; she thrived in urban settings, valued career success, and was not one bit spiritual. Sini had never admitted to herself earlier that she could be interested in the supernatural. None of her friends had been into those things, either. It was becoming clear that she had a kind of gift to see things hidden from others. And…she had a strong suspicion she wasn't the first in her family.

Standing up and approaching the kitchen to grab something to eat, she swirled around and headed for the notebook drawer. If she'd found the connection between the markings on the cloak and the rocks, she might have a chance at deciphering the scribble.

"What the heck."

Sini sat down with a sigh and pulled a row of notebooks out onto the table, checking that all curtains were pulled tight. One by one, she flipped through them, not knowing what she was looking for.

She had an eerie notion when she took the plain and worn black notebook in her hand.

"To the reader.

You know whether it is your place to read these notes. It has been my purpose to write down what is not known in any other book. Not all knowledge can be held in the memories of persons, and there can be times when the chain of telling them is broken. It is with the utmost importance that these facts are told to the next one on duty.

S. K. 23rd of October 1920"

That S. K. again. She must ask her father if there'd been a fixation with names beginning with *S* in the family. The words seemed to be written in plain Finnish. Relieved at finally understanding some of the notes, Sini flipped the page.

A list of people, like the ones in church books, with birthdates beginning from the seventeenth century. The first and all other names were Kataja. If those were her relatives, it was illogical that they'd all inherited the name Kataja, since the wife, by tradition, took the last name of the husband.

Every entry had the place of birth and death noted. Sini flipped through the rest of the pages. More of the same kind of entries. There was nothing extraordinary about them except for the two words that figured in most of them. Witch and guardian. What in the world?

Sini looked through the following pages. Most people had the word guardian in their entries, fewer had witch. The witch thing seemed to have a pattern of skipping generations. How long was the list? Why would anyone admit they were a witch in those times? Wasn't it forbidden by the law? At one point in time, being called out could mean a death sentence.

Her fingers fumbled with the pages as she tried to find the last entry.

"*Sinikka Kataja.*" Had her grandmother written it? There was her birth date and place, and then…

Sini rubbed her eyes. It was nonsense. In her entry, someone had written witch and guardian.

Wow. It must all be rubbish—childish games.

It was one thing connecting to Kuutamo and finding a cloak that swept the snow, but there was no doubt she was neither a witch nor a guardian. A guardian of what? She'd never felt drawn to witchy stuff, even when it had become popular and kind of accepted.

Out of nothing else than pure curiosity, Sini read the entries of her family. "*Matti Kataja*", her father, had been left without titles, so something was accurate. "*Satu Kataja*" had been a guardian. Her great-great-grandfather Simeon had been both witch and guardian.

Sini thought of the fairy-tale book. Had someone for real written it about them?

No wonder her grandmother seemed a little eccentric if she'd really believed the stuff.

Jesus…

Sini closed the notebook and tossed it onto the table.

Sini stood up and walked to the kitchen to look for what she just remembered was tucked away in the pantry. The big box of chocolate-covered cherries that her mother had sent for Christmas and that had been too sweet even for her was perfect to numb her from the weird things pouring into her life.

She knew she'd never leave. She'd die there, alone and half-crazy, like her grandmother.

Like all the other witches and guardians before her.

According to the book, none of them had left that place after they got there.

Something, a well-concealed mental disease perhaps, seemed to run in their family.

18 DESTINY REVEALED

Sini's mind emptied, and her body went soft when she laid her eyes upon Kuutamo.

He was waiting for her, standing tall on her path like any other time, but in her eyes, he was more gorgeous than ever. Maybe it was his looks that fogged her rational mind. She was probably predisposed to it—falling for magical beings—by the burden of her genes.

It didn't matter, because being with Kuutamo always felt right.

Hi. Sini hoped they wouldn't get awkward.

Hello. I searched for you yesterday. There was a moment I did not sense you at all.

A moment? You mean you sense me all the time?

Yes.

Whoa. She knew their connection was extraordinary, but... Wait... Sini thought about the time she spent studying the stones, and then closed her mind. She didn't want him to find out about the cloak or the stones. It wasn't because she didn't trust him, but because it wasn't her secret to give away to outsiders.

Did you send Helmi to look for me?

Yes.

Were you worried something bad had happened to me? She was fishing for affection.

Kuutamo stepped closer and looked at her with eyes that were too serious.

You are very important, Sini.

To you? The question slipped out, but she wanted to know.

To everyone.

OK, back to square one. It wasn't going in the direction she wished for, but she had to be careful not to reject him. *What do you mean? Who is everyone?*

Everyone who lives in our world.

Sini frowned. *Do you mean your world or my world?* In her opinion, neither would care, but she'd try to understand where he was coming from.

Kuutamo held up his hand and waited for her to take it. When she reached for him, there was something that wanted to hold her back, as if it knew there was no return if she did it. When the other option was her living alone and day by day becoming insane in that house with no one knowing, she had to take the chance.

Sini put her palm in Kuutamo's gloved hand.

Nice mittens.

Thanks, they're family heirlooms.

I know.

What, how do you...? Sini tried to retrieve her hand and demand clarification, but he wouldn't let go. *Fine.*

Sini sighed and let him hold her hand. It was nice, but she was beginning to tire and succumb to the stress.

Relax. Breathe… Your world… My world… We are all the same.

She felt the calming energy coming from his body and tried to open herself to receive it. With every inhale, she imagined letting the soothing vibe enter her body, and with every exhale, she released the aggravated energy gnawing at her.

Good… keep breathing…

Sini's mind emptied, and the blood flowed through her body without effort. There was only comfort, and she was warm all over. She fought the urge to close her eyes. As he was before her again, she wanted to look at him. She lost.

Kuutamo's calming voice in her mind was hypnotizing. Sexy. In her relaxed state, she couldn't help images of her pressed against his body floating up. Shit… She tried to fight them off.

Kuutamo squeezed her hand. *Relax. It is fine.*

To her relief, the visions didn't get more graphic, but faded away as she accepted their existence.

Show me. I know you want to tell me something.

Sini felt the mitten slide off her right hand and then Kuutamo taking it into his bare palm. Just as the sensation of her skin on his started to excite her, the familiar vision of his world opened before her. Sini felt at ease. It was both due to the return to a place she'd come to appreciate and that it was intact again. She breathed in the scentless air.

Kuutamo was there, standing beside her. He turned around. She followed his gaze and turned around herself.

Sini gasped.

A female figure stood farther away. She didn't seem to notice them, but when Sini tried to get a closer look, the figure turned. Sini drew a sharp breath. The face of the woman was both beautiful and intimidating. Her hair blazed from a ruby to a garnet red, and it cascaded down her back in a hundred thin braids. It was like blood on her white cloak that looked like feathers flowing down her back. Her most dominant feature was her striking eyes. They were the same crystal blue as hers and Kuutamo's—only the power behind them was exponential. Dark shadows gave the impression of both authority and responsibility. Sini believed the woman could read a person's soul just by looking at them.

Sini forced her eyes off the most striking figure she'd ever seen and noticed others behind her. She couldn't distinguish their looks, but they weren't of the same stature. She sensed that the woman was their leader. The leader of Kuutamo's people.

She almost wished the woman *would* see her.

Sini's heart ached at the beauty of Kuutamo's world. It was so simple but so powerful. It was pure. She wanted to know more about them.

She thought they appeared more angelic than human. Then, she felt a little uneasy.

Please, don't make me go through the destruction again. I can't take another round of it.

Everything is fine, Sini. This is the way our world is now.

But I feel it. There's something wrong. She felt like crying, but she didn't know why.

Something gently squeezed both her hands. The ice world got blurry, and the vision scattered into a mist that slowly dissolved. Kuutamo's chest came into her view. He was still holding her hands. Sini lifted her gaze to his face.

His face had softened, and he seemed more relaxed. *Thank you.*

For what?

For wanting to see our world.

Our world. She wished he'd meant his and her world. *Who's the female? She seemed very strong.*

She is our mother.

Your mother? Sini was confused. *Are you saying you're all her children?*

We are all her children, in a way. The way it is in our world.

Sini looked down at their hands. Her bare hand had begun to hurt. She would've held on a little longer, but Kuutamo let go of both her hands. He pointed at her pocket where he'd tucked her mitten.

Sini grabbed it and put it on. Her hand warmed in an instant. She looked at him again. She couldn't interpret his face. The little smile clashed with the tightness of his eyes.

I do not want to hurt you.

I know. You *seem to be fine.* Would she ever stop fearing he would disappear?

I am fine. I am surprised you see so many things. It is a good thing.

She was intrigued, but she wasn't sure whether Kuutamo saying that it was a good thing was a good thing.

Sini's mind was full.

All she saw was the female, who embodied both strength and knowledge. She looked fierce. Not in a scary way, but as if there was no match for her in any realm. Sini was convinced of her power, as if the knowledge of the woman had been imbedded in her genome.

If someone should be called a witch, it should be her. Sini didn't have a clue to what being a witch meant, but the female looked like she might have invented witchcraft.

Sini dragged herself from the comfort of the warm chair and sat down on the sofa. She picked up the dictionary and flipped through to the part about witches.

"Witch was a name used for the Finnish shaman."

Sini felt a compilation of chills surge through her body. Shaman was something she could grasp. She pictured the red-haired female wearing deer antlers on her head and power animal figurines pinned onto her white cloak.

Too many things had happened, and Sini thought she ought to quit thinking she was crazy. She couldn't have invented it all. Her imagination wasn't that vivid. A question that once again surfaced was whether someone else knew about the ice world. She couldn't be the only one, but then again, Kuutamo hadn't wanted to involve other people. Not that she was aware of.

Why him? Was he a messenger? They couldn't all be her children—he must've meant she was a mother figure to them. She didn't look old enough to be Kuutamo's parent, for one thing.

Sini thought of the black notebook. Could the word witch, in fact, mean shaman? She'd much rather be a shaman, although she didn't feel more shaman than witch. Her grandmother *should* have been there, telling her what it all meant. If anyone had the answers, she would've. There was no one else to ask, as it had been established her experiences and findings mustn't be revealed to others.

The only ally she had was Kuutamo, and she was already keeping secrets from him. But chances were he'd been keeping secrets from her as well. What was that comment on her mittens being familiar about?

Sini couldn't stop yawning. The day had sucked out her energy.

Our world… We are all the same…

The words haunted Sini in her dreams.

She wanted to be the same with him. But she didn't have the talent. She tried to understand… He wanted something from her. They all wanted something from her.

Kuutamo telling her she was important. Her grandmother repeating words she didn't understand. Her mother asking her to come to her senses and turn into an adult. Then there were the other voices, the whispers from the darkness.

She tried to turn away from them, walk off, but they followed her everywhere. They didn't understand that she couldn't...

Sini came to while trying to kick the covers off her body. Why couldn't they leave her alone already? She didn't have the talents...

Battling the exhaustion that tried to drag her into unconsciousness again, Sini worked her heavy body into a half-sitting position. If she could only keep her eyes from closing.

Still drowsy and in the atmosphere of her dreams, Sini thought of how she'd seen the female leader of Kuutamo's people and felt the connection. He'd never described the female to Sini, or even mentioned her.

Sini saw Kuutamo and was able to touch him. What about listening to his mind and answering without speaking? She did have some talents. What if she was a witch of her time?

Or a shaman...

What differentiated the shaman from other witches and seers was the ability to journey to other realms as a soul. She'd never crossed to Kuutamo's world on her own—it had been via dreams or through him.

If she really was supposed to be a shaman, she must be able to do it by will.

Sini placed her apple chunk and cinnamon-topped oatmeal porridge on the kitchen table and sat down.

In front of her lay the old fairy-tale book she'd camouflaged with the jacket of a book on interior design. Chewing on the anything-but-inspiring oatmeal, she opened the book to a random page. She hadn't finished it since the ornamental, old-fashioned writing turned out to be a slow read.

The grandfather was explaining to his little granddaughter that she'd someday be in charge of taking care of the forest and its secrets. Sini thought the little girl was too young to comprehend the gravity of such a message. She pictured herself exploring the forest with her grandmother. She didn't remember her grandmother saying anything similar to her. In the light of all things uncovered, she should've—shouldn't she?

If it hadn't been for Kuutamo, she wouldn't have taken any of the scribbles seriously—never mind, literally. Sini flipped through the pages towards the end. Just as she hoped the illustrations might give some clues, her eyes fell upon an image that made her almost choke on the porridge.

She'd seen that picture before! She grasped at the fuzzy memory fragment of her grandmother showing it to her.

In it, the grandfather held a box in his hands. The lid was off, and he stood in a dark room. The insides of the box cast a soft golden glow onto his face and the surrounding air. The way he regarded it and the darkness of the location made it clear that the box contained some kind of treasure.

Sini read the writing on the page. There was no mention of what the treasure contained, only a fragment with the words *treasures of the sun*.

Maybe her grandmother had read her the story after all, and she'd forgotten about it. But the picture of the treasure box had intrigued her enough to make a lasting print in her memory.

⌘ ⌘ ⌘

Sini leaned back in the kitchen chair and closed her eyes. If her grandmother had read her the story or showed her pictures from the book, why did she only remember the one with the treasure? Regressing back to her childhood, she pictured herself lying in bed late in the evening. Her grandmother sitting next to her on the bed, holding that same book in her hands. A low, calm voice speeding up as she got to that page. Yes, she could see a little girl propping herself up, leaning closer to get a peek at what was so exciting.

Her grandmother had smiled as she tilted the book so that Sini could get a good look. Sini had laughed, excited at the good news. Who didn't like a treasure?

It wasn't the first time her grandmother had read her bedtime stories. Sini opened her eyes, disoriented at the familiar sight of the kitchen but knowing she wasn't that child anymore. Yes, her grandmother *had* told her stories like the one in the book. Why hadn't she remembered?

She leaned onto her elbows, massaging her temples as if to call forth the missing part. Her father.

Her father!

It all came back to her. Her father had been upset with his mother for telling Sini damaging stories. He'd been so angry that Sini had believed him. He'd actually called them crap. Sini had been ashamed. Her head spun as she tried to retrieve more memories. As if pulling a never-ending strand of magician's handkerchiefs from a pocket, repressed memories were fast becoming new knowledge.

It made no sense other than him not wanting his daughter to not believe in fairy tales. Her parents hadn't read her bedtime stories. Until that moment, she'd never reflected on how strange that was. No wonder she'd forgotten about the book.

What did *treasures of the sun* mean? Wasn't it peculiar that such a compelling image wasn't better explained? Sini read the chapter again, but she found nothing that shed a light on the purpose of the glowing box. It rather seemed to have been inserted into the story like a piece from a different puzzle.

Despite that, or perhaps because of that, the image had stuck in her memory and lasted through time. It was the only one that had survived her parents' efforts to keep her from knowing.

She looked at the image one more time before she closed the book. If she remembered correctly, her grandmother had been quite enthused herself.

Sini gazed out the window at the peaceful winter scenery, wondering what else she'd forgotten from her stays at her grandmother's.

Sini had stopped checking the thermometer in the morning.

One peek outside the window and checking her mood, she just knew. Her new old clothes seemed to keep her warm enough, no matter the temperature. She'd decided to wear the cloak, and she'd told Kuutamo she was on her way. She wanted him to be waiting for her.

Sini hoped the walk across the field would clear her mind. That the fresh air would dissolve the atmosphere of her dreams. Despite being awake for hours, she still suffered the anguish caused by the demands of everyone—and everything—around her. Though Kuutamo had become her life's biggest joy, his requests had affected her the most. She feared he wouldn't go easy on her in the time to come, either.

Crossing the barrier between the ordinary world and the enchanted forest, she pulled the cloak tighter around her chest. As expected, Kuutamo stood in his usual spot, looking at her.

She paused at the entrance. She waited for a minute, but he didn't come up to her.

Kuutamo?

No reaction.

Sini shouted his name as loud as she could in her mind. Still no reaction.

He didn't see her, and what was even stranger, he didn't sense her at all.

She walked closer. With all her willpower, she fought the urge to walk up to him and spy on his irresistible face. His gaze travelled between her house and the exit. Sini grinned and indulged in some forbidden fantasising before putting the hood down and unfastening the cloak.

She pulled the cloak off her body and folded it with care under her arm before looking at him. She'd expected him to be baffled, surprised, but the joke was on her.

Kuutamo had a shrewd smile on his face.

What's so funny? She felt like the child whose parent wasn't at all in awe of her hero costume.

It pleases me to see that you are realising things about yourself.

The chance to keep her legacy a secret vanished. She couldn't do it for long with him, anyway. *That day when you said you couldn't sense me, I was walking around here in the forest. I didn't see you.*

I am sorry. I did not know where you were. I did not look for you in the forest.

It's OK. So, you can't sense me at all when I'm wearing this? She held the bundle in front of her, but not close enough for him to touch it.

That must be the reason. Did it belong to your grandmother?

I don't know. I don't know anything about this, because there is no one here to tell me.

Come. Kuutamo started walking through the forest, and Sini followed, walking by his side. It dismayed her she couldn't wear the cloak in his company, when they at last had something in common.

He took her to the secret grove. He sat down on the stone altar.

I want to try something. Sini unfolded the cloak and wrapped it around her neck, kept the hood off, and folded back the lapels over her shoulders. *Can you see me now?*

There was static, as if he said something, but she couldn't make out the meaning. She put her hand on his shoulder. Kuutamo reached out and took it.

I sense you now.

That's good! I want to keep it on. It keeps me warm.

Kuutamo indicated for her to sit down beside him. Sini arranged the fabric, sat down on it, and faced Kuutamo.

I'm supposed to be descended from a long line of protectors of this forest. I don't know what that means. Why is this forest to be protected? And how am I supposed to do it?

Still holding her hand, Kuutamo's expression lit up, as if he'd been waiting for that question.

This forest is the only one of its kind. It is the link between my world and the human world, and it must be protected at all times.

Protected from whom?

From everyone, except me and you.

You and me? Are we supposed to fight the rest of the world? Worlds…?

It is not like that. No one else can find out about its existence.

Then you are…?

Yes, I am the guardian in my world. The ice realm.

I understand that humans can't be trusted, but what about your people? They are not a threat to humans, are they?

Our worlds are not supposed to be connected. The portal in the forest is not meant to be used.

Sini's breathing got faster. *But you came here.* She was afraid he might suddenly see he'd made a mistake. She wanted to tighten her hold on his hand, but she feared hurting him. *Why did you come?*

I am the keeper of the gate in my world. There has always been someone from your world who has been the keeper of your gate. I saw that, before you came, there was no one keeping guard.

You mean after my grandmother passed away?

Yes.

How did you know? Have you been here for long? Somehow, Sini guessed he wasn't the same age as her.

I have eyes and ears. He looked up at the trees, and soon a hoarse whistle sounded.

Helmi!

Yes. She can go through the gates.

You mean she stays with you in the ice realm, too?

Kuutamo nodded.

Cool!

Sini, I came here to see you. I needed to find out who you were. I sensed that you were not aware of your task. He pressed her hand gently and rubbed his finger over the back of it. Even through the thick wool, it felt heavenly. As if that wasn't enough to stoke her energy, he smiled while staring her down with his sapphire eyes. *Sini, you are special.*

She felt special at that moment.

You are the one. You are the guardian.

Sini's arising smile faded. *The link has been broken. I have no one to teach me.* Plus, she didn't want to be the one.

There must be someone on your side. There is no one but you.

Do you even understand what that means for me? That I'm supposed to walk this forest and live in that house until I die?

His smile didn't disappear completely, but there was something in his eyes. Was it sadness?

There is no other way. This is the fate of the keepers.

She sensed the wave of deep desolation that rolled through his energy. He was alone, too, on the other side. He'd been keeping the secret for much longer than she would ever have to. Without thinking, she raised his palm and pressed it briefly to her lips. There they were, two beings tied to a fate so vital that no one else must know, and no one would be there to comfort them.

He'd never be hers. He was never meant to be hers. Yet the fate of the world needed her to sacrifice her life to keep a secret she knew next to nothing about.

Kuutamo turned on the seduction again, and she steeled herself.

Sini, there is something more to you. I can feel it.

I don't know about that. She didn't want to talk about the alleged shamanic heritage.

You can help me. Help me save my world.

It broke her heart to pull her hand away from his.

Sini.

Sini shrunk into herself, wanting to once again hide from the world.

She couldn't hear him, but she knew he was calling her name. She watched him. He was so close, yet so far away. He was well aware of the effect he had on her, and he'd used all the tricks to reel her in. To convince her to give in to her fate. The price for meeting that magnificent male was losing her freedom. And she'd pay it. What else could she do?

He wasn't angry. He just sat there in stillness, gazing into the forest. She believed he had the time to wait her out.

Sini pushed the cloak off her shoulders.

Pulling her feet up and putting her arms around them, she rested her chin on her knees.

Her vision unfocused as she thought that even though he didn't care for *her*, she'd do it all for him.

Strange how someone's life could flip in an instant.

Her home didn't feel like a refuge for the wounded outcast anymore. Instead, it had become the prison whose bars were invisible to everyone but her. A place she could never leave, because someone might, out of the blue, get the idea that somewhere in an unheard-of part of the Finnish forest existed a secret passageway to an even colder place.

She wanted to ridicule the whole thing, but deep in her heart, she knew she was supposed to stay. Even if she didn't understand. After all, how could she be certain her predecessors had known more than she did? She doubted Kuutamo had socialized with the others or showed them visions of the other side.

All her plans for the future were smashed apart and thrown in the garbage. Living alone in that house wasn't supposed to be for forever. She was supposed to mend her wounds, gather strength, and start over somewhere else. In civilization.

Sini threw herself onto the bed. She let the tears come. She had the right to mourn. Mourn the family of her own that she'd never have. Even if someone proved to be crazy enough to live with her there, she couldn't see herself with anyone else. She'd lost her heart to the one who would never give her the heir she presumed was to be the next link in the chain of keepers.

She was too young to be trapped there. It was supposed to be her father's turn to keep watch. He most likely had no clue what obligation he'd avoided by not having the gift.

She got hot in her outdoor clothing, but she didn't care. She wiped the tears in her mittens. How many before her had infused them with their despair?

Maybe she was the only one who couldn't embrace her calling? She had turned out to be the outcast in the world of keepers as well. The one no one had bothered to prepare for what would be the end of her life.

Sini...

Leave me alone.

He wouldn't understand. Did he know how short human lives were? Did he understand what it meant to be isolated from one's own kind? Uninvited loneliness was the worst fate a human could suffer.

That night, drenched in tears and regret, she thought of Martin.

Sini remembered the good times with her friends, how they'd talked about their future as if it was set in stone. She could've been a winner, and after that, she could've passed on her knowledge. She would've been among like-minded, life-loving people with good things on the way.

It had been taken away from her. Maybe fate had been so cruel that it had snatched her away from the life she wanted. She'd never have chosen to move to her grandmother's house if her people hadn't pushed her away. The more she thought about it, the more she became convinced that only something so monumental as a tragic accident with her as the perpetrator would've succeeded in ripping her from her own choice of life.

She'd give up her future, and no one would know of her sacrifice.

Her own grandmother had set her up.

19 A WAY OUT

The weather fit her mood.

On that day, she was thankful for the rain. She wasn't ready to go out there and pretend she didn't resent her destiny. The best part of it was that she had Kuutamo on the other side. The worst part was that he was on the other side.

She was desperate for something to distract herself with. There was no need for more research. She already knew enough. Walking up the stairs to the attic, she was disappointed at herself for being relieved he couldn't sense her. As their telepathic connection was out of order, she didn't need to explain why she wasn't up for a forest walk.

Very much doubting she'd find what she was looking for, Sini opened the door to the sideboard beneath the window. Old magazines, both for children and grownups. Some old toys, tablecloths, napkins, miscellaneous decorations, candles. Nope. Nothing in the closets either, except clothes and stuff she wasn't planning on using. They were all that was left from those who'd lived there before, so she wasn't going to throw them away, either.

The box wouldn't be downstairs. She would've found it already. She'd began the search in the house because it was most convenient. Next, she was heading for the sauna, that was her best bet.

The wet air felt oddly warm. As she stood on the porch, she looked for the little owl, but she couldn't see a living thing.

Carrying the ladder, Sini crossed the yard to the weathered little building. It was silly to look for a treasure based on a fairy tale, but the excitement built up with every step she took. The other things had been true, like cloak-wearing keepers of a secret in the forest and a task that was passed on from one generation to the next. She got to the little attic and searched the cardboard boxes to see if she'd missed the little box last time. Nothing.

Sini straightened herself and searched every nook and cranny of the space. The box might very well have been slid in between a rafter and the insulating material or placed in a corner difficult to reach. The room was both dark and lacked detail, like the one in the image. Was there another secret hatch somewhere? After three rounds of looking and groping at every surface, Sini gave up. If something had been hidden there, it wasn't meant to be found.

The next place would be trickier since it was full of things. The garage was neither very dark nor lacked detail, but a lot of time had passed since the creating of the fairy tale. Perhaps the box wasn't hidden where it had once been? Thinking she had nothing better to do, Sini checked every box, lifted every object that might shield a smaller one, lit up every dark corner, but found nothing that resembled a box with a lid. No treasure anywhere.

She needed to find it. The more time she spent searching, the more she wanted it to be real. The picture with the secret treasure was the only one she remembered seeing as a child. Her grandmother had been excited too, and she'd wanted Sini to find and read the fairy-tale book. Her name, Satu, meant fairy tale in Finnish. No wonder Sini hadn't understood why she repeated her own name in the dream.

Still, no box, no treasure. It had to be in one of the buildings. If it lay buried in the ground, she wouldn't know where to look.

Sini wiped her forehead with her arm. She was getting tired and hungry, but if she paused, she'd lose the benefit of daylight. With no time to lose, Sini headed for the last buildings on the property. She didn't believe it would be in the gazebo, but she checked under the benches, nonetheless. While the garden shed wasn't messy, it was crammed with gardening tools like shovels, buckets, pitchforks, sacks... She moved them around to check nothing important had been hidden behind them, and as she grabbed the shaft of the apple picker, she remembered how her grandmother had always talked about...

...harvesting and storing the *treasures of the sun*. She'd said that—hadn't she? She'd called the apples, berries, vegetables...the treasures of the sun, because the sunlight was what made them grow. It wasn't a coincidence. The treasure *must* exist.

She just couldn't find it. The box wasn't in the garden shed either. Sini stood, regarding the objects linked to the only clue she had apart from the dark space. Dark space...

Where had her grandmother stored her treasures of the sun? In the earth cellar. It had to be there! Sini had flat-out forgotten about its existence. She hadn't used it since she hadn't grown anything. The cellar was a room half dug into the ground, and the top half was covered with earth that grew weeds.

Sini exited the shed and strolled to the cellar, trying to look like nothing special was going on. She released the hook of the door, opened it, and brought a heap of snow with her as she stepped inside. The air was heavy with dirt, but it wasn't the scary place she remembered from childhood. The cellar was ageless in its simplicity. Dusty and, for the most part, empty wooden shelves lined the walls. She found shrivelled potatoes and carrots in a couple of wooden boxes. Glass jars containing grandmother's apple jam.

Not allowing for sentimentalities, Sini let the light sweep over every surface. She was about to proclaim the cellar another fruitless venture when her gaze locked onto the darkest spot of the room. Just above the door, where daylight never entered, a potential hiding place presented itself. Reaching her hand onto the wooden beam and tracing the rough surface, the only thing she felt was soft tissue that without a doubt was cobwebs and dead insects.

Then her finger hit something solid that budged.

Sini's hands shook as she held the wooden box in her hands.

She traced her fingers along the carvings of the lid. It wasn't that heavy. She guessed birch. A zig-zag pattern carved in thin lines traced the borders of the lid. Enclosed in two circles on top was a six-pointed shape that looked like a mix between a flower and a star. Countless intricate shapes of tiny flowers and leaves within geometrical grooves told her it would contain neither gardening tools nor screws and nails. As with the other things she'd found, the box had been made with love by someone a long time ago, and it saddened her she didn't know who. The contents made no sound as she carefully shook it.

Sini put the box inside her jacket and exited the cellar. She couldn't believe she'd actually found it. Whatever the box held inside, she hoped it was worth all the hype and search effort. Some kind of heirloom perhaps? A magic tool like the cloak?

Sini secured the old box in gentle hands as she got inside the house. She put it down on her grandmother's desk and drew the curtains on all the windows. No human was watching, but she wasn't sure about other creatures.

Sini sat down and beheld the box. It was her moment with her ancestors.

The lid came off without effort. Inside lay a package wrapped in what looked like plain grey linen cloth. She lifted the package with caution and placed it on the table. Sini expected something exciting since it had been hidden that thoroughly as she took hold of the other end of the cloth and unwrapped the contents.

Oh…my…God. Sini's jaw dropped. When imagining the treasure, she didn't expect it to be an actual treasure.

There were four rolls of banknotes secured with cotton twine. There must have been thousands of euros, probably more. Then there was a small black pouch with a string closure. She took the velvety fabric in her hand and felt lumps of various sizes. She carefully widened the opening and peeked inside.

Something gave off dim sparkles. She poured the insides onto the linen.

They were small yellow nuggets.

Gold.

At some point Sini remembered to breathe again. She felt faint-headed.

Who…?

Why…?

She looked inside the box for a clue, and there lay an envelope on the bottom. It was closed with a seal.

Was she allowed to open it?

She took out the envelope and flipped it around.

"Sinikka"

It was her grandmother's handwriting.

She could feel her heart beat, and her cheeks heated as she reached for the top drawer and took out the letter opener.

Sini sliced the envelope open and took out the folded piece of paper.

"My dearest granddaughter Sini,

I write this letter today with both joy and sorrow in my heart. The joy is from my love for you and my knowing that you have the gift that has run in our family since times no one can remember. If you find this letter without me, you must realise that you have the ability to see things others cannot. You are strong, powerful, and you have the light inside you.

It is a great privilege to be the keeper of something so sacred, but also a great burden. You will have to give your all to it, but it will also give you a sense of purpose. It saddens me that I did not have the chance to school you for your task, but I have all the faith that you will conquer any fears and obstacles along the way. You have the ability to see, so do not feel alone, but connect with nature and its beings.

The contents of this box is for you to use when needed. Nature will always provide for us as long as we honour it. It is tradition that keepers keep the box plentiful, so that the assets can be used when required.

You must begin your journey towards embracing your calling. Only you can comprehend what it will entail. Trust your heart and your inner wisdom. You must also find someone to love, for I do not wish loneliness upon you.

I do not know where my afterlife will be, but I will do my best to guide you through spirit when needed. One day, you will have to write a letter like this to make sure that the contents of the box will fall into rightful hands. For reasons I cannot reveal in a letter, it is imperative that you have a child that carries the blood of our ancestors, and I pray that you will have the chance to prepare her for the assignment that must be passed on in the future as well. Have faith in life, as I have in you.

With love, Satu."

Tears had begun rolling the moment she started reading, and by the end, she was snivelling. Inside the envelope was a photograph of her together with her grandmother. They were sitting side by side; her grandmother looking at her smiling, and Sini looking up at her grandmother with an expression of pure love. She might have been six and didn't remember the occasion, but she remembered that love. She still felt it.

Sini pressed the letter and the photograph to her heart. Reading through the letter again and again, each sentence made her cry. She hadn't had the chance to prepare Sini, and Sini thought she understood why. Her inconsiderate parents were without a doubt to blame. If they weren't so ignorant, she might have believed they'd wanted to break the chain on purpose.

Satu wanted Sini to find love. Had she found love herself?

The letter didn't give specific clues to her destiny, but it had been safest not to reveal details in a letter that might be found by an outsider. She looked at the seal. Pressed into the red wax were the initials S K, and underneath it a hand drawn star with eight points. Sini identified the shape as the octagram, the symbol used for protection in the past. The magic lay in drawing the octagram without lifting the pen from the paper.

Sini shook her head and sighed at the faith her grandmother had in her.

Her grandmother was just like Kuutamo, seeing things that were not in her. But it meant so much more coming from her grandmother.

As Sini paced around the house, she didn't have a single coherent thought.

What did it mean? Did it mean she could stay in her home without the fear of having to give up and sell the house? Was she allowed to get the car fixed with the money? Or was it supposed to be saved for extreme emergencies only? She could buy better outdoor clothes—right?

To find something to do with her hands, Sini began preparing coffee. She was too scrambled to eat, but having coffee instead was very likely a bad idea. What if she got herself a bigger stash of food next time she went into town? A real doomsday haul.

Sini grabbed the mug of coffee and sat down. She hardly noticed the coffee burned her tongue as every possible scenario ran through her mind.

Her grandmother wanted Sini to carry on the task that had begun ages ago, and she owed it to all her ancestors that had given their lives to it. That wasn't enough for Kuutamo. He wanted her to set herself up for failure again. She couldn't run a career as a simple skier, so how was she supposed to become the saviour of the winters?

If she took a thousand euros from the stash, it wouldn't put much of a dent in it. No one would notice that a couple of notes were missing. It would be enough to get that one-way ticket to the place far away she yearned to go to.

She imagined how the warm sand felt when she dug her feet into it. No need to put on three layers of clothes when going for a walk. Instead, the sun was shining from an azure sky, and the mild breeze caressed her bare skin as she strolled down the beach promenade. Watching the beautiful people walking towards her, not knowing her or judging her. Not one of them knew what she'd left behind, nor did they question her preference of diving into a summer-warm ocean rather than staggering around in freezing winter. Goodbye, soul-sucking darkness.

Sini pulled two five-hundreds from one of the rolls and put them in the envelope together with the letter. She walked over to the bookshelf, pulled out the book about shamans, and switched out the bookmark for the envelope. Glancing back at the treasure box, she thought it was safest to put it back where she found it. She wished she had a protection spell to put on it.

⌘ ⌘ ⌘

Sini pulled the duvet up all the way to her chin. She had the means required for getting away for good. Her prayers had been answered. At last, she'd gotten her chance at freedom. The only thing she had to do was choose a destination and date. She pushed away all thoughts of what would become of the house, as she couldn't very well sell it.

With her eyes closed tight, she envisioned her new life.

Her new freedom.

Waiting for sleep to come, she'd never felt more at ease.

Looking at Kuutamo, her heart hurt.

She wanted a new life. She couldn't imagine telling him she was leaving. But if she stayed, would he be there with her still? What if…

She couldn't think the thought anymore.

You are sad. Why? Kuutamo's question wasn't grounded in sympathy, but rather curiosity.

Sini felt she was about to break. Too much pressure had been laid upon her, and she had no answers. She didn't want to start crying in front of him. In that moment, she cared about only one answer, and she was desperate to have it.

If I give up my own dreams and stay, will I get something in return? As she'd expected, Kuutamo's expression was blank.

What do you mean?

She prayed honesty was the right path to choose. *What do you want from me, Kuutamo? Would you care for me if I didn't have the gift?*

I want only good things for you.

Sini sighed. Of course, he wouldn't understand. *You want me to help you, but what if I can't help you? What if I don't have that power you think I have?* She had to take the leap. Inhaling the fresh air, hoping for it to give her strength, she continued. *I care for you,*

Kuutamo. I care for you in a way you might not understand. Before you told me you wanted things from me, I believed you might care for me too.

Sini waited, ready to give him all the time he needed.

It must have been minutes when she reached out her hand and touched his chest. If she could only know what was in his heart.

If I told you I can't help you, would you still stay here with me? At least now and then? What else could she say to make him understand? *Do you like me?*

Kuutamo grinned. *Yes!*

Sini's heart jumped, but she wasn't convinced. With so much at stake, she couldn't take another day not knowing.

Come. Kuutamo grabbed her hand and started walking. The forest had never been that serene. The beauty of the trees covered in white cloaks hurt her. In her heart, there'd be no other emotion than love towards winters for the rest of her existence.

It was bittersweet. She wanted all or nothing. She'd go insane walking the forest wishing every day—or perhaps every year—that Kuutamo would care for her the way she wanted.

Kuutamo took her to the giant boulder in the middle of the forest. His ascension to the top lacked effort. Sini looked at the ice prince portrayed against the pale sky. The blue backdrop or the magnificence of the forest couldn't compare. As with her mind, he dominated her field of vision. He took his cloak off and let it fall on the snow.

Then he stepped to the edge, hunched down, and extended his arms towards her.

Ah… Sini woke from her trance, reached out her arms, and soon rose through the air, pulled up by her hands as if she weighed nothing more than that cloak.

She felt a bit unstable standing on top of the boulder, high above the ground. She was able to see much further. The untouched snow expanding in all directions, as if there was nothing else left in the world. A black silhouette of a bird landing on a treetop in the distance. Quiet black-and-white pines and spruces stood as sentient beings passing time in the never-ending circle of life.

A miniature hoot echoed from nearby. She laughed. There was something about Helmi that always elated her.

She turned around and saw that Kuutamo had sat down and was arranging the cloak in his lap. He pulled part of it up on his chest and looked up at her. When he extended his hand towards her in a gesture that left no question, she swallowed.

She took his hand, and when he pulled her towards him, she got down on her knees. Encouraged by his gentle tug, she moved closer in between his legs and turned around on the cloak.

Kuutamo reached one arm around her and pulled her to his chest. She eased herself backwards and leaned in. When he wrapped the cloak around her body and put his arms around her, she felt nothing but calm. Her back tight against his chest, she rested her head on his shoulder and closed her eyes. With a sigh, all anxiety and overwhelming feelings melted. With the next inhale, she was weightless.

Lying in Kuutamo's embrace, she was immersed in a stillness she hadn't felt in ages. Maybe never. Her breaths grew deep and slow. The sensation of his equally slow heaving chest brought a smile onto her lips.

Minutes passed. Perhaps hours.

She tried to sense what lay on his mind, but he'd gone silent, too.

I love you. In that perfect moment, she loved everyone. It was simple human love.

She felt him lean his chin on her head. *You love summer as well.*

I do.
Show me.
Summer?
Yes.
How?
Think of it, as if you were there right now. How it feels. What you would do.

Sini opened her eyes to the blinding whiteness. *But, will it not hurt you? The heat?*

Of course not.
Do I need to hold your hand?
No. Do you want to?

Sini smiled. *Yes.*

Wrapped in his embrace and holding his hand, her life was complete. Slipping into the dream of a perfect summer's day was easy. She imagined everything around them becoming green. Dark green as the wild rosemary and the spruces, lighter green as the occasional birch and the new bilberry leaves. It was sunny, the warm light of summer, and she was wearing knee-length shorts and a sleeveless top. She felt so bouncy.

Can you see it?

Kuutamo squeezed her hand.

Bird song filled the forest. There was movement in the tree canopy. She sat on a stone that was warm against her skin and turned her face towards the sun. The bright light penetrated her eyelids, and she soaked it into her whole being. She let her hand slide over the soft moss and stiff lichen that adorned the top of the stone.

She wanted him to understand why she loved summer.

Then she stood on the beach. Perfect dunes of beige, fine-grained sand heaved behind her. She walked into the clear water where sunlight danced on small waves and sparkled in the swells. The cool water gave relief from the hot sun. She looked down at her body, exposed except for the two-piece bathing suit. She let her fingertips glide through the surface of the water that belonged to an entire ocean. The cool liquid made her skin knot. When she let herself submerge, she felt both alive and weightless.

Just like she felt there with Kuutamo.

Do you like it? She had no idea if he had any concept of summer other than her visual cues.

I do.

A shiver went through her body.

I feel cold. She thought it was the contrast between her vision and the reality, but when Kuutamo let go of her and moved away, she felt the freeze release its grip. She wrapped his cloak tighter around herself and pressed her nose against the thick fabric, slowly drawing in the mild scent. If she hadn't known better, she would've thought it reminded her of the promise of summer.

She glanced at Kuutamo, who sat beside her. He looked like he'd experienced something enjoyable, but his face contradicted with the vibe she picked up. The contrast between his expression and his emotion made him appear human.

She didn't want to break the spell, ruin the perfect moment they'd had together, but she had to ask. She knew he cared for her on a level he hadn't revealed before, and she was ready to know.

You want to know what summer is like for me, because you will not be here when it arrives.

Pain. She sensed his pain.

She studied his profile, more than ever wanting to memorize his features. She preferred him like that—almost human. Still too good to be true, but with an edge that earthly hardship brings. *You are going to leave me, aren't you?*

He felt her pain, because he turned to her and took her hand. *I have to go home. I am needed there.*

She needed him too, but she wouldn't tell him that. She imagined more people needed him in his own world, and he'd been with her all winter.

Will you come back? To see me? She still harboured hope that he could make a short visit in spirit despite warmer weather.

I will return when next winter arrives.

She counted the months. It could be eight or even more. How was she… Sini gasped for air. *How am I supposed to manage here all alone?* He'd go back to his people. She had no one.

Sini, you do not have to be all by yourself to keep your task as the keeper a secret. It would be good for you to find people to connect with.

Find someone to love, perhaps? She wanted him to care enough to feel possessive of her, but she knew he wouldn't vibrate that low. He'd tell her to find someone like her, who could give her what he wasn't able to.

Will you wait for me?

I will. Of course, I will. As she promised him, she remembered the thousand euros envelope hidden in her bookshelf. The dream of an easy life in a warm climate had been unattainable, anyway. At least she'd had one fleeting moment of believing she could have it. *Please, can you hold me again?*

Kuutamo opened his arms, and Sini crept into his lap. She looked at his hands that held her tight and thought he was awfully good at hugging.

Do you do this in your world? She guessed what she wanted to know was if he had a female there. *Do you hold each other?*

No. It is different in my world. We are not physical like this.

You're getting really good at it. Touching me without disappearing.

I like it. It is new, but I am learning. Thank you for giving me the chance to learn.

Kuutamo?
Yes?
I wish I could help you.

20 DEPARTURE

Walking towards the end of their day together, Sini felt hollow.

She didn't want to be alone anymore. Not when she knew what being in his energy felt like.

I don't want to go… She wanted him to understand how much he meant to her, but she also didn't want to be needy. She wanted more, but she didn't see how it could be.

When they reached the exit, Sini stopped and turned to him. She didn't know how to say what was in her heart without ruining their perfect day.

Kuutamo's eyes lingered on her face.

As he fired off his striking smile, her melancholy dissolved like mist in the morning sun. He looked up and held out his arm, and soon Helmi swooped down and landed on his hand. Helmi ruffled her feathers and settled onto her belly as if his energy had the same effect on her. Sini took off her mitten and gently stroked the belly of the bird.

Helmi's feathers were softer than they looked, like petals of a flower.

He looked at the bird with a tenderness that left no doubt about how important Helmi was to him. Although they were perfect opposites—Kuutamo tall and inconceivably strong and the bird fragile with the weight of a hamster—their union was beautiful. She wished she could have such a connection to an animal.

Take her with you tonight.

Are you sure? I'd love to. Can she come inside the house?

If you want her to.

I do. Can you see through her eyes?

Do you want me to?

She felt butterflies. *Sure. I'd love for you to see my home.*

Bring her back tomorrow?

Tomorrow it is.

In a normal world, it would've been the moment for a goodnight kiss. As much as she loved him, she didn't want to kiss his icy lips. The difference between them would become more tangible than it already was—and too much for her to handle. And heaven forbid, what if her moist lips got stuck on his?

Regardless, she wanted to do something special. And he wanted to learn about humans. Sini stepped close and tried to avoid breathing on him. She raised her hand to his face and brushed his cheek with her fingertips. When her fingers only just touched his skin and she didn't linger, he didn't feel that cold. Her fingers ended up on his lips, feeling the soft curves she'd never taste.

She smiled.

He closed his eyes.

Encouraged by his reaction, she continued exploring his face.

Then her fingers numbed.

As he'd sense her reaction, she avoided thinking of the cold on her hand and shoved it into the mitten.

Sini exited the forest and crossed the field. Looking back, she couldn't see Kuutamo. She was digging herself deeper into a hole without walls by getting closer and closer to a being that broke her heart every time she left.

Soon he'd be the one to leave, and she'd be left with the memories.

By the middle of summer, she'd find it hard to believe he'd been real.

Helmi passed her and headed for the house. If only the lit windows had still looked inviting. Humming her favourite sad tune took the sharpest edge off her desolation.

Sini reached the porch and raised her hand. Helmi appeared from a nearby pine and landed on it.

"Just let me know if you want to go outside, OK?"

Sadness morphed into excitement as she escorted the little owl inside the house. Without kicking her boots off, she walked to the armchair and suggested the backrest as a place to perch. Helmi hopped onto the chair with a little encouragement. She wondered if the bird was hungry, but realised she had nothing to offer. There were no mice, frogs, or small birds in her food stash.

Taking off her clothes, she took care not to frighten the bird that watched her every move. Was that the bird or Kuutamo? She turned off all lights except for the floor lamp. She had to manage without a fire, as the room temperature most likely was already too hot for Helmi. It was a shame she couldn't keep a window open.

Wherever she went, the little head turned to look. It was surreal. To keep herself grounded, she began telling the bird what she was doing. She told it she'd sit in that chair and look at the fire. It was funny how her slow and uneventful life might be too detailed for Kuutamo to grasp. She couldn't tell him how she watched TV or used the computer to pass the time. When she went to the kitchen to prepare dinner, the bird followed and landed on the backrest of the kitchen chair. It was definitely Helmi, as she seemed quite taken with the raw chicken slices. Sini didn't dare offer any as she guessed human food would be bad for the digestion of a wild animal.

Helmi watched her as she ate, and she imagined a marvelling Kuutamo behind those huge, round eyes. Helmi's head bobbed, and her eyes darkened every time Sini picked up a piece of meat on her fork and raised it to her mouth.

Sini tilted her head backwards and laughed. How wonderful to have dinner company. She was as peculiar as they got— preferring the company of an owl and its fairy-tale snow prince of a master.

Sini tried to go about the evening as usual but found it difficult to focus. She caught herself glancing at the bird, either to admire its beauty or check that it wasn't just her imagination. TV was out of the question, since it would startle Helmi and spoil the magical ambiance. She tried to read her library books, as she didn't want to reveal the notebooks or other secret manuscripts.

She was a natural at being a good keeper, suspicious of everyone as she was.

As bedtime arrived, she contemplated how to go about getting ready. Maybe it was best not to overthink it. What was the harm in him seeing her take her clothes off? It was a human taboo, and why should she hide a part of herself in the name of decency? If he wanted to watch, she'd let him, and if he didn't feel like it, it was OK. She wouldn't ask him about it later.

The more she deliberated it, the more she wanted him to know everything about her. It might widen the rift between their realities, but she wanted him to understand why winter made a harsh environment for a human. She offered her hand to Helmi and watched the bird step onto it. She didn't care that the talons dug into her skin.

Sini carried the bird to the bathroom and put it on a folded towel on the washing machine. She left the door open and took her clothes off as if the bird was just a bird that didn't care about human anatomy. She stepped under the reviving warm spray of water. Soaping herself up, she felt like she was in a soap commercial. Her thoughts turned to that day when she got her release in the shower, but she didn't feel aroused.

She brushed her teeth and braided her hair. She carried the bird to the bedroom, where it flew on top of the wardrobe. Propped on a couple of pillows, she wondered whether it was Kuutamo who helped it remain so calm. A little lamp was still lit in the living room, and she could see the contour of the bird and the light gleam in its eyes as it continued to watch her.

Or watch over her.

Sini thought she'd be up all night regarding the creature beneath the ceiling.

When she came to and realised it was late morning, her gaze went straight to the top of the wardrobe. No owl. Awake in an instant, she scrambled out of bed. She pulled up a chair, climbed up, and peeked at the empty and a bit dusty space. There were prints in the dust where the owl had sat, so she hadn't imagined it.

Sini wiggled down and began looking for the bird that was nowhere to be found. Kuutamo had said that Helmi was real—unlike him—so she couldn't have poofed herself away. Hopefully it hadn't gotten hurt—or crept inside some hole in the wall she didn't know of.

She looked everywhere. And then she looked through the same places with more attention.

"Helmi?" Her voice was harder than intended. She called out again, softer.

A faint whistle sounded.

Sini cocked her head.

Did it come from the vestibule? She walked over and looked around, still not finding it.

Another whistle came from the hat rack. Sini looked up and then tiptoed. Only the top of the bird's head was visible.

"Good morning, Helmi." As owls were nocturnal, she didn't ask if it had slept well. She opened the door to Helmi's natural habitat and saw the bird's head stretch into sight. She grabbed her coat from the hanger and put it on. It didn't protect against the cold air, but she wanted to stay until the bird left.

Soon Helmi revealed herself from behind caps and gloves, eyed her, and without a sound, flew out the door. Sini felt a tug on her heart as she stepped outside and watched as Helmi headed for a pine. Maybe she'd rest there until dusk. Sini monitored the sky for potential threats. Raptors and large owls were Helmi's natural enemies.

She prayed she hadn't put Helmi in jeopardy by taking her into the house and having her spend the day in an environment that wasn't as safe as the forest.

⌘ ⌘ ⌘

Sini got cold trying to make out the owl among the trees. Helmi's plumage would camouflage her from the sharpest of eyes. That she was protected and in her natural habitat was a good thing. So why did emptiness fill her chest? It was more than fearing for the safety of Kuutamo's companion. She yearned for it to be hers as well.

Sini sighed and closed the door. She was thankful for the first guest she'd had in a couple of years. For once since she'd moved to her grandmother's house, she hadn't felt alone. Her parents had visited her soon after the move, but only to talk her out of the silly notion to settle down there.

She knew the bird would be fine. Warmth washed over her as she thought of how Kuutamo had gifted her the company of his precious confidant for the night, trusted her with the little spirit animal.

She hoped Kuutamo had enjoyed their evening together. How did he regard her home? She looked at her simple, spartan living room. It must be the opposite of his dwelling. Would he find her way of living interesting or off-putting? Other than having read things about it, there were no indications of shamanic practices or the task of a protector in her home.

Maybe he'd seen how simple her life was and thus realised her non-existent chances of making any kind of difference in the world. Him seeing her humble reality might, in fact, be a blessing.

Sini took off the jacket and forced herself to stop obsessing about the owl. She had no reason to dwell on negativity. Her heart picked up the pace at the idea of doing the same thing again. She'd go to him in the forest where they'd have a sweet moment, and then he'd visit her via the owl. She should make her home more functional for an owl—perches in every space, lower temperature, owl food… Could it be a solution that granted them more time together?

She knew the sweet moments between Kuutamo and her were rarities, but she permitted herself to be hopeful, if only for a day.

The day came too soon, sooner than she'd expected.

Neither she nor Kuutamo could do anything to prevent it. Sini would've prayed to the gods of weather if she believed they existed. She tried to convince herself the rising temperature was momentary and that freezing, harsh winter would return. Indeed, she'd endure the tormenting existence of sharp frost as long as it meant he could stay.

She was unprepared. He hadn't warned her. Maybe he did it to spare her. Maybe he didn't understand what him leaving would do to her.

Sini.

No. She didn't want to hear what he was about to say.

I am returning to my realm. It is not good for you or for me if I try to stay. I have been away for a long time, before I came here, and I want to return to my family.

You said you didn't have a family.

Not the way it is for you. Our connection is of another kind.

When?

Tonight.

Sini fought for air.

Can I be with you when you go? Merely saying the words was painful. She pictured herself watching, becoming hysterical as he disappeared into some hole in the ground or evaporated into nothing. No, she wouldn't be able to handle it.

It is not possible. It will be difficult if you are there with me.

I know. Sini pressed her body tighter against his. Kuutamo strengthened his embrace.

Sini. I do want to stay with you. This has been a very good time for me.

You mean that? Sini gazed into his eyes. She didn't care whether they were dark from emotion or bright with enlightenment, only that the wonder she felt was reflected in them.

You are as new to me as your world is, but there is something in you that I recognise.

I know what you mean. I was never afraid of you when I should've been.

You think that I am more special than you. To me, you are very special. I want to learn more about the human world. I want you to show me.

Sini chuckled. There were many things she wanted to show him, none of them possible to turn into reality. *I could show you how to ski.*

Kuutamo laughed out loud.

You laughed! I taught you that—didn't I?

You have taught me many things. I want to thank you for that.

Please don't forget me.

Why would I do that? His surprise was genuine.

That's what humans do. I can't know what you will think of this world when you're back with your own people.

If that is what humans do, will you forget me?

Sini pushed away from his embrace and punched him playfully in the chest. *Don't be silly.*

Then she felt like crying. She needed to be watchful of any emotion that could send her over the edge. After he left, she'd have all the time in the world to mourn.

I want to give you something to remember me by. Close your eyes.

Sini closed her eyes.

Think of summer. You sense the warm sun on your face. You see the beautiful flowers and hear the birds singing. Your body is warm and comfortable. Light, and joy.

Sini concentrated hard on conveying the memory of summers she didn't miss anymore.

She felt his hands on her arms, pulling her closer. *Do you feel it?*

Sini nodded from her vision of sunbathing. Something soft touched her mouth. Something as warm as her own skin.

It was his lips. She didn't know how, and she didn't care. She lost herself in the few seconds they united in a way she hadn't thought possible. A thousand chills rushed through her body. Her energy turned into a sea of sparklers.

You are cold. He was pushing her away.

Believe me, I am not cold. This is what happens when…something feels really, really good. She forgot why she was sad. Opening her eyes and seeing the gorgeous male in front of her, she fought the urge to push against him and demand more of those kisses. Instead, she realised how much energy kissing her had drawn from him.

Thank you. I will remember it forever.

You are getting colder. Let us walk through the forest so that your body gets warm again.

Sini wanted to revisit the places they'd been during the winter, and every time she saw something familiar, she sought to relive the moment with joy in her heart.

Kuutamo was getting a practical lesson in the turbulence of human emotion. When they reached the grove, she could no longer repress her sobs. He was going somewhere she couldn't reach. It wasn't like she could phone or text him and ask how he was. He wouldn't visit her before the next winter. And she knew enough about life to understand that things could change in a heartbeat and that there was no guarantee she'd see him again. *Hold me, please.*

She dashed into his embrace without waiting for permission and wrapped her arms around his waist. She wanted to nuzzle her face in his neck but settled for his shoulder. Kuutamo's gentle arms folded her in a heaven on Earth.

The closer she was, the faster she'd get cold.

It didn't matter. She couldn't let go of him.

They became motionless like the old trees surrounding them. Little snowflakes began falling, and she watched them become a thin blanket on their shoulders. By focusing on the snowflakes and his body, she was able to clear her mind of her fears. As long as he held her, she stayed intact.

Still, after so many weeks of getting used to the freeze, and despite layers of warm clothing, the chill was reaching her skin too soon. If she stayed absolutely still, she wouldn't feel it. She tried so hard to ignore the limitations of her body. In the end, she couldn't control the trembles that forced her muscles into motion.

Sini. It is time. He began letting go of her, but she couldn't ease her grip.

Please, a little more.

Again, he tightened his hold around her, giving his all to the moment. He laid his hand on the back of her head and leaned his face against her temple.

She was so cold. But she didn't care.

You must go. You know I cannot carry you home if you get too cold to walk.

His words made her feel so fragile. Not even he could help her if something happened to her.

She knew it was to protect her that he began prying off her hands.

I can't. She felt the hysteria, maybe even shock, rise in her, and the shaking didn't make it easier.

Kuutamo cupped her face in his palms. *Listen.*

She tried to focus on his troubled eyes. A sensation of calm flowed into her. A soothing mist that choked her rampaging mind and ended the trembling.

Sini sighed. *Thank you.* She managed to smile. One last time, she surveyed every part of his face, measuring it, etching it into her memory. *See you soon.* She wished time passed faster for him than it would for her.

She didn't dare touch him. No calming spell would help her then.

You need to be the one to leave first. You know I can't walk away from you.

Kuutamo nodded. *Goodbye, Sini.*

She turned around and waited. The landscape became a blur. She sensed the moment he wasn't there anymore, glanced over her shoulder, and began walking. She hastened down the slope, and when she reached the path, she started running.

She didn't remember how she got to the house.

She took off her clothes as if in a dream. Perhaps the spell was still in effect. Perhaps she didn't dare feel at all. That night, she didn't pull the curtains. Knowing he'd still be there in the forest for a while provided some consolation. Her mind tried to transform it into hope. More than once, she played with the idea of going back, but she didn't want to hurt him by hurting herself.

She'd have to manage. She'd been left alone before. She'd survived. And there she was—the hero shaman keeper of a little house by a little magic forest. What more could she wish for?

Sini turned on the computer and opened the drawing software. She'd spend their last hours in the same world honouring him. The combination of having to focus while spending time with a version of him was perfect. She pulled the quilt from the armchair, wrapped herself in it, sat down, and began sketching.

She drew him all night. Every minute detail she could recall. She captured his features from every angle. Perfecting the details gave her respite from emotions. Sadness and despair were not what she wanted him to remember her by. She placed the notebook in front of the computer clock so that she didn't see the hours pass.

He didn't call out to her, but she imagined sensing when he left. She preferred not knowing the exact time. It kept her intact.

Only after she began nodding off and a chill got beneath her skin, she gave in and went to bed.

Waking up the next day, Sini was convinced it had all been a bad dream. Like those other lucid, troubling ones. It was still March, and that month was still cold on her latitude. Her heart sank as she noticed she'd slept in her clothes from the day before and that she'd only partly managed to cover herself.

She found no reason to get up and start the day.

She rose anyway, did her things, and walked to the forest. It might not be the best idea, but she was closer to him there than any other place. The crust of the snow didn't carry her as well, and walking took a bit more effort. New snow had fallen and covered up their footprints. No matter how hard she looked, she couldn't find fresh ones. Every time she saw movement in the trees, she searched for the little owl. She thought she heard a faint whistle.

He wasn't there, of course, and neither was Helmi. It comforted her that at least they had each other.

Her heart galloped as she approached the stone altar where she'd seen him for the last time. Despite the thin blanket of snow, she could make out the spot where they'd stood embracing each other.

She fought back the tears. The right thing was to choose to be grateful. Her experience had been amazing, incomparable, unique. Even though their physical connection would never be more than what it had been, being able to sense someone from within was so precious.

Standing there in the memory from the day before, she saw something peeking out from under the thin layer of snow. It looked like it might be a twig, but when she picked it up, she realised it was something much more valuable.

Dangling on a dark grey string was the stone pendant. It was Kuutamo's pebble of granite that he'd used for grounding himself to a lower vibration. She tugged the zipper open, put the string around her neck, and closed it back up.

Never had she imagined the worthless stone could make her so happy.

21 THE CALLING

It was officially spring.

Sini had trouble getting used to the sun being so high in the sky and how its glaring brightness called for a more celebratory state of mind. The light revealed everything, but there was nothing to see. The forest had lost its mystery.

The equinox had passed a while ago. Most snow had melted, revealing the evergreen vegetation, the big boulders, and most of the path. She should've been relieved the snow was gone and nature was heading back to normal. Except she'd changed her mind. Plants and moss and pine needles had become dull, whereas snow represented magic and feeling alive.

She stood on a large patch of thinned snow that the sun hadn't been able to melt. The snow had become porous and infested with debris and dust. It lacked the fierceness that had commanded so much respect a while ago. The once pure and fresh snow had turned into the corpse of winter.

She hunched down and put her palm on the snow. The air wasn't freezing anymore, and she was curious how long she could keep it there before it began to hurt. The snow melted a little, becoming water that transformed the snow into a slippery crystalline surface. It wasn't that bad.

Kuutamo knew how to command the snow, and he used the energy from the stones of the forest to change shape. She didn't have any magic powers, but was she able to control how her body reacted to the cold?

Sini took off her boots and unzipped her jacket. She'd done crazier things. She laid the jacket on the snow and sat on it. Piece by piece, she took off her clothes, trying to hurry before she changed her mind. She kept the socks and underwear and Kuutamo's pendant that she always wore in the wood. The air chilled her skin as expected.

She stood and sat down a bit farther, lay down, and rested her head on the jacket.

Jesus—it stung!

She grinned and breathed between her teeth. Her skin began to burn, and she fathomed it was what lying on a bed of nails felt like. Except lying on icy snow must've been worse. She told her brain that it wasn't dangerous, just her skin against the cold and her body trying to warn her of the consequences. She also told herself she did it for Kuutamo. To be closer to him.

As the pain strengthened and spread through her whole body, she could think of nothing else. Instead of hissing at the freeze on her skin, she worked on slowing down her breath. Composing herself. The pain morphed in her mind. It still hurt like hell, but she accepted it. Accepted that it ruled her body and mind. Thinking of nothing else was a relief. Not thinking of how lonely she was and how her days didn't have meaning anymore or of how she forced herself to eat when she felt nothing but emptiness inside.

She turned her mind towards the icy landscape of Kuutamo's home. Though she'd never felt cold in the visions, it helped her visualise the landscape clearer than ever. Kuutamo next to her. So close. Her hand touching his face of ice. His hand taking hers.

She felt joy. Only joy. His face was so vivid. She was at peace.

As she was finally able to think of Kuutamo without the accompanying sadness, she didn't sense her body anymore. She was light as the air, no longer a part of the excruciating human realm. She hovered somewhere in between. In a good place.

It took a lot longer than she'd expected before her body started to clash with the extreme cold. Her skin had numbed, but when a nasty chill ran through her body, she struggled into a sitting position. The cold air had stiffened her arms and legs, but it was bearable. Her fingers were slow, and putting her clothes back on took some time. The cool fabric gave no relief. The shirt stuck to her moist back, but she didn't care. Besides, the iciness granted her more of that thought-smothering relief.

Standing up, Sini looked down at the faint imprint her body had left on the hard surface of crystals. She realised it was such a shame the snow was about to disappear as she could've started doing the exercise to harden herself.

The better she got at resisting cold, the longer she could stay with him next winter.

The last evidence that there'd ever been a winter was erased as the little lumps of snow hiding in the darkest parts of the forest melted.

The temperature hovered above freezing, and the sun climbed higher on the sky each day. Winter had surrendered its reign to spring.

The dull wait for summer began. Springs tended to be an extended period of cloudy days and grey landscapes. The green didn't show up earlier just because snow disappeared earlier. Sini visited the forest once in a while. She should've gone every day to check things were in order, but she knew there was nothing going on.

When tiny snowflakes began descending from the sky, Sini took it for a hallucination created to soothe her. Sitting at the kitchen table with a book in front of her, she watched the ethereal scene unfold outside the window. It was beautiful. Knowing the mistaken snowfall would soon cease, she intended to enjoy it while it lasted. Fantasise a little of how winter had returned because *he* wanted it to.

It kept falling, and Sini stood at last and saw the ground remained as dark as before. The snowflakes melted as soon as they touched the ground. They didn't stand a chance. She carried on with the day, did her chores, watched a little TV.

When the snowfall thickened and began painting the earth white, Sini rushed to the forest with a foolish hope that he indeed would return to her. She had to go, because the only thing worse than him not being there was that he'd be there—and she wouldn't. As she advanced through the scenery that, with a magic wand, had changed from ashes to a fantastic ball, she was aware that the chance for the snow to remain was slim. A tiny moment with Kuutamo would be enough. To see him again—if only to tell him she missed him—would be enough to carry her through summer.

She sat on the altar stone, watching the snow cover up the ground more and more. With her eyes closed, she emptied her mind. She sensed him, but it was the memory of him, a trace of energy left behind. It was like inhaling the scent of a lover left on his pillow after he was gone.

April. Seven more months, and it wasn't even summer yet. How could she love summer anymore? How could she enjoy anything? She was addicted to him. Their love story would most probably end in tragedy. She couldn't see the other end of the spectrum, how it could ever work.

She shouldn't be hard on herself. Who wouldn't become addicted to something so magical as Kuutamo? It was her job to keep close tabs on what happened in the forest. They were more or less colleagues. She'd done wrong when falling for a co-worker. A relationship like theirs wasn't built on a healthy foundation. To be honest, it was a good thing winter had left and put an end to their self-indulgent adventure. He wanted to *learn about humans*. And she wanted to date someone who literally was too good to be true.

Guarding the forest wasn't the problem. She'd more or less been doing it long before she found Kuutamo and the various notebooks. Her grandmother's idea of her being a shaman was off the rails, though. She had no idea what it entailed and what it would be necessary for. There was nothing witchy or shamanic about her.

Sini held out her hand and watched the snowflakes land and melt on her palm. She barely felt them. As he'd been gone for a while, and the wound from losing him wasn't gushing anymore, she reflected on how essential he'd become to her in such a short time. Was it her loneliness that had made her susceptible to his charm? Would she be able to live without him? Was the crazy attraction a direct result of him being out of reach? It was easier to fall for a dream than a reality weighed down by the burdens of everyday life.

Sini cocked her head and let the snow land on her face like ghostly kisses. Her mind was still a mess.

⌘ ⌘ ⌘

When night came and the temperature refused to sink below zero, the rational thoughts she'd had in the daylight were gone. She missed him so much!

Like any other night when melancholy held her in its grip and she couldn't focus on anything else, she sat down by the computer and drew him. Sometimes, she'd include herself in the image. She saw her own improvement. There was more emotion in his expression, more depth in his body language.

She thought anyone would be able to perceive her devotion.

The day the first roses bloomed was the first time she heard the voices.

She'd accepted the irreversible arrival of summer—the faster it came, the faster it would be over with. In the midst of it, she had to admit she enjoyed the warmth. She could walk barefooted in the garden, lie down with a book on a quilt between the apple trees and the currant bushes. Being outdoors was effortless. Life buzzed all around her. Birds, bumblebees, beetles, ants, butterflies.

Her days got better. She tended to the garden with the notion that *nature will provide*. She had ample possibilities to grow all kinds of vegetables in the soil that so many generations had worked before her. Garden chores kept her busy during the day. On hot days, she worked late in the evening. The sun dipped below the horizon late in the night and got up again in less than no time, providing enough light to do everything outside. And there were fewer mosquitos.

She was digging up plants with decorative foliage in the front yard to split the roots and plant two thirds of them elsewhere when she lost control. The plants were called *lily of the moon,* and even though the link to Kuutamo was weak at best, something inside her ruptured.

Her feelings for him were true, valid. Why should she have to stifle them just because he wasn't meant for her, or because he wasn't *real?* She loved him with her whole being. When the tears came, she couldn't hold them back. She'd reached the point where it was easier to stop resisting. What she didn't expect was the wailing sound coming from her mouth. Her shoulders shook as she let it surface.

Screaming out her pain, she didn't care that she was ungrateful and selfish. She opened her heart and let her bottled-up emotions pour out. The censored yearning for his embrace, the silenced need for him to always be with her. The wild flood of invalidated love flushed her empty, scraped her insides raw. She was honest at last.

After an eternity, her wailing became crying, and crying ebbed into sobbing. Her legs had gone numb.

When the activated feel-good chemicals muted the pain and her mind cleared, she heard it. *What are you doing?*

"What?" Sini looked up and around. She wiped the tears off her cheeks. She was so used to hearing Kuutamo in her mind that she hadn't considered it strange to hear a voice come out of thin air.

What are you doing?

Who was it? She couldn't see anyone.

What are you doing?

What the…? It was as if someone was playing a joke on her that didn't make sense.

What are you—

"Shut up!"

The voice in her head paused.

Only to continue in the evening when she tried to settle down and do therapeutic drawing.

"Who is this?"

You shouldn't be...

"What do you want?"

You should be...

She felt confident they weren't her own thoughts, that she wasn't going crazy. It had never happened to her before. Perhaps in her dreams, but never while awake. Maybe becoming sensitized to Kuutamo's thoughts had left her wide open for vicious spirits?

Go away...

By the next morning, she knew what was happening. She hadn't slept much, as the voices followed her into her dreams. She'd seen shadows and unfamiliar faces. After a while, they'd annoyed her more than scared her.

Answer the call. She woke up to that—and knew.

They were calling for her to step up to the task that she'd been designated for by some unknown authority before she was born. It was her ancestors, the ancient shamans—or the garden gnomes for all that she knew—who were calling out to her, demanding her to do the thing she didn't want to.

You have to.... You have to...

"Shut up! I don't owe anyone anything. Just leave me alone."

She'd read in the books that spirits would haunt and tease their gifted victims for weeks or months on end when calling. It was a relief no humans would witness her arguing with them. Shamans might have been revered by their community in the past, but the present day wasn't a good time to claim to be harassed by spirits.

Or claim to be a shaman with actual abilities.

⌘ ⌘ ⌘

Sini sang louder than a student choir at a party. The singing made them shut up. It drowned out their repetitive words as long as she performed it with enough enthusiasm. Songs from childhood, hits from her youth, the national anthem.

It was the battle of wills. It was one against the rest. But they weren't real. And they were just as delusional as Kuutamo, assuming that her answering the call would bring something good to her world.

Her world was not worth it. Nothing would change. People wouldn't change. At least not in the near future. If it was OK for the majority of people that winters disappeared—what could she do about it?

Answer the call…

She wasn't fit for the task. Wasn't her half voluntary seclusion proof that she didn't get along with people? If she was incapable of handling conflict with her own people—her own friends and family—what kind of world-changing skills did she have?

Protector…

Fine, she might try to put protection spells on the stuff in her house as soon as she discovered how, to protect the secrets of her family, but that was it.

She could sense the voices getting agitated when she ignored them. When she fought them, they became persuading, almost seducing.

That made her even more suspicious.

What made the constant calling worse was that it reminded her of Kuutamo. He'd requested something from her as well.

Answering to the calling meant giving in to his request.

She was sure of that.

⌘ ⌘ ⌘

Sini took pride in her resilience.

Knowing that she wasn't mad gave her strength. She got better and better at putting their demands on the worry boat and letting them sail away. Singing was still the best antidote. The problem was she couldn't sing all the time. She got skilled at the singing also, always coming up with a new tune. Old lullabies remained her favourites. Their melancholic melodies matched the mood of her soul.

The voices were relentless, but she'd sworn to be the exception who wouldn't give in. She wouldn't let them break her. She wouldn't crack under the pressure. Everyone had the right to free will. Then came the third week, and she was getting tired. Another night of sleeping poorly, and she was as happy as a trapped wasp. She looked out the window. It was a picture-perfect day of early summer. The sun high in the sky. The garden a plethora of light green. Twenty degrees. Not cold, but not too hot.

She pulled the curtains close. The light hurt her eyes.

She'd been working until late in the garden. The more she accomplished, the more she found new things that needed to be done. Emptying the compost. Cutting apple trees. Turning the soil in the vegetable plots and pulling out the weeds. Fertilizing everything and finding out which fertilizer best suited which plant. The deadline for when the unemployment money ceased was imminent, but the more she thought about the money stash she'd found, the more she wanted to refrain from using it.

After Kuutamo left, she hadn't been able to force herself to look for jobs, and when she at long last acknowledged and released her pent-up emotion, the voices started tormenting her. Not the optimal circumstances to look for a job. She had to get rid of them before she tried again. The good thing was she could focus on producing food.

Except for meat, she'd get most of what she needed from the garden: potatoes, carrots, lettuce, beans, apples, herbs, and berries. If she got even more into it, she could start collecting wild plants like willowherb and dandelion.

Perhaps she should get some hens and a rooster. For eggs and company. Then again, having to put them down when necessary didn't sound like her thing.

Working late and being bullied in her dreams was a bad combination.

She pulled out a bag of potato chips and a bag of candy from the cupboard.

She'd been able to keep her sugar addiction at bay for so long. It was so much easier when Kuutamo was there, but he was gone, and there was no one else to support her. Her current situation was an emergency, and the sugar was the medicine she needed. And she'd risk going into town to get more.

Planting herself on the sofa with the bags of promised release, she put on a violent movie to make sure the noise drowned out the voices.

Halfway through the movie, she couldn't take another bite of the chips, and all the candy lay in her stomach. Sini got up, took her wallet and phone, and got into the car. She'd stock up. It was a terrible idea, but the only one she had.

Going into town proved to be a big mistake. Instead of getting a day's vacation from the ranting, it just wouldn't end. She had to be on her best behaviour. She must have looked as tired as she felt. That time, they actually stared at her in the grocery store. It could've been because her cart was full of chips and sweets and soda instead of the usual selection of proper food. Or it could be that she couldn't distinguish when she heard the voices, or a real person was talking to her. The cashier had asked her if she wanted something else, and Sini had ignored her and then inquired whether she'd said some-thing.

Back at the wheel, she had serious challenges to stay awake. The day was bright and clear and the road dry but staying in her lane had never been more difficult. She could've let go of the wheel and ended it all, but she'd promised Kuutamo she'd wait for him. Provided she survived the voices, there were a few months left until dark and cold would once again reign her world.

"Shut the fuck up, or I will drive this car off the road and into one of those lethal concrete culverts. Who's gonna watch the stupid family secrets after that, eh?"

Sini cackled at the trailing silence.

The moment Sini put the four bottles of red wine in the pantry, she regretted her purchase.

Why would she spend her little money on alcohol when she probably wouldn't use it? She'd panicked and bought the bottles because it had been a good idea at the time. She'd walked by people and when they'd turned to look, she hadn't known who'd spoken, the people or the spirits. Had they said anything at all? The idea had been to get drunk and forget about seeking refuge among normal people. She'd better stay at home where she was secure, not act like someone who needed psychic care. But as she gave it another thought—what kind of horror hallucinations would she get when drunk, as those spirits already drove her nuts?

Anyway, answering the call would make her even crazier. She didn't intend to start traveling to the underworld or battling bad spirits any day soon. They'd give up any moment. Not once had she been tempted. They were running a sub-standard campaign—scaring her into submission wouldn't work. There were darker clouds in her sky. Like what would happen to her if Kuutamo didn't come back.

A terrible notion hit her. What if she'd accepted her task with all that it entailed, and Kuutamo wasn't needed on the human side anymore? Since she'd told him she couldn't help him, what reason would he have to come back and check whether she was doing all the keeper stuff?

Sini stuffed herself until she was nauseous. She felt horrible—but it worked. Her whole nervous system numbing felt awesome. She didn't have a clear thought anymore.

The world became flat. It was a terrible place to live, but at least in that state, she didn't think of potential solutions to all problems.

Sini was beyond exhausted.

She stopped trying to answer the voices weeks ago.

She hated that they tried to force her into surrender with incessant suggesting, begging, demanding, and, at times, threatening. The most difficult thing was she still didn't know what they expected from her. She felt no more witchy or perceptive than before. The only magic she'd ever experienced was when she was with Kuutamo.

Sini had tried draping herself in the cloak. She'd hoped she could create a protective barrier around herself. It had been quiet for three hours, and then the voices had returned. Either the magic of the cloak was faulty, or the voices came from inside her.

Nevertheless, she'd taken the cloak with her when she went to the forest. As she entered her refuge, she put it on. With the hood up and the lapels pulled tight around her body, she felt comfort. It took the sharpest edge off the headache. She walked straight into a sea of white. The wild rosemary was in full bloom. White clusters of delicate flowers dominated the forest floor.

It reminded her of snow. Of him.

She imagined walking through a field of fresh snow. A flock of tits foraged in the pine canopy. She listened to them chatter over food. If someone had seen her wandering about in the shrubs, they'd seen the image of a witch. She would've enjoyed it if she hadn't been so weak. Her eating habits had become a mess.

Walking to a part of the forest where they hadn't been together, she sought interruption from everything. A little getaway. She sat down in a patch of shorter and more open vegetation. The tits tweeted above her. Bumblebees hurried from one lingonberry flower to another, pollinating the treasures of the forest. Without their hard labour, there'd be no berries in late summer. A little bird appeared on the ground right next to her. The little bundle in plain brown and white jumped on quick little feet and pecked at the soil.

Forest birds were not tame, and she assumed it couldn't sense her through the cloak. It was a shame that wild animals feared humans. Was the knowledge of the evil nature of humans written into the genes of animals, or did they just sense there was something off? It was unfair, as *she* didn't want to hurt the animals.

Her gaze fell upon the little flower next to her. It was called *star of the wood* for a reason. Smaller than her thumb nail, white as snow, six perfect petals that ended in tiny tips. So innocent. A single flower on a stem thin as a thread hovering above a ballerina skirt of leaves. Growing in the otherwise robust vegetation, the little flower appeared oblivious of its own fragility. It had a sweet, positive outlook on life, and it had earned its place among the giants just by believing in itself.

She had to say *yes*, or she'd lose respect for herself.

Leaning her arms and head onto her bent knees, Sini tried to gather her thoughts. If she said yes, she'd do it of free will—not because she'd been driven to. During the difficult—hellish—summer, she'd had the chance to think about it. At first, she'd only found reasons not to. To her, answering the call would've been as appealing as trying to fly an airplane without getting lessons, as sensible as walking through a vast jungle without a guide. Then, flashes of how there might be a place for her in the world. A life mission tailored for her. Even if it wasn't something she'd chosen for herself, it was hers and no one else's.

With her eyes fixed on the little star, she untied the cloak and folded it beside her. With a sigh, she lay down on the soft forest bed. Her head spun. She adjusted the granite stone so that it lay on top of her heart. The brightness of the clear sky beyond the treetops made her squint. With the tall pines towering above her, she'd become the little star flower.

Shhh…let me think. The voices knew something was up. She'd gotten used to them, but their crescendo made her head split.

Abandoning her call meant abandoning Kuutamo, loving him only for selfish reasons. Answering the call meant admitting to Kuutamo's vision for her, even though she didn't know how to align with it. She'd been abandoned by those closest to her. How could she abandon the only one who stood by her side? No matter the underlying reasons, Kuutamo believed in her, and he'd said he'd return to her. She wanted to become a better version of herself, to have something to offer when he came back.

But it also meant forever. She could never leave once she accepted her place in the world. And she'd forever gravitate towards the love she could never have.

Grandmother… She envisioned her grandmother coming to her. *I don't know what to do…help me. You said you would help me.* She bent a wild rosemary stem down onto her face and smelled the aromatic scent of the flowers. A biology teacher had once told her the plant had been used as medicine and that it contained narcotic compounds. She buried her nose in the bundle and inhaled the scent to the bottom of her lungs and called on her grandmother again.

Look within you. It is all within you.

I'm scared…

You are not alone.

Maybe. Maybe she felt alone because she wanted to be alone.

Sini closed her eyes. She didn't want to fight life anymore. She wanted peace.

Peace of mind, peace of body, peace of soul.

It was quiet. Even the tits had moved on.

She turned her palms to the ground and felt the moss and pine needles and little twigs against her skin. The sweet scent of summer forest got more intense. She felt the ground both soft and steady underneath her back. Whatever happened, there'd always be solid ground under her feet. Losing her self, she let go.

I accept.

There. She said it. It sounded like the truth.

The dizziness got worse—or perhaps the whole world pivoted. The release of months-long torment and exhaustion plunged her into velvety oblivion. At last, it was quiet. The earth enveloped her in reviving energy. She didn't know if she was being infused with life, or if she was melting into the ground.

She tumbled, spun around her own axis. She fell into nothingness, but it wasn't that uncomfortable.

She'd entered a dream.

22 HIS HEART

Sini woke, a new person.

Light shone from the kitchen, but it gave no clue to the time of day. She might have slept for days, and she'd never slept that peacefully. The aches were gone, and she was in a good mood. Best of all was the silence. How she loved the silence. No spirits invading her dreams. She couldn't remember dreaming at all. It was a total reboot and recharge. Like waking up in a new world.

She'd slept in the forest, too. At least a couple of hours. She'd said yes to the calling, but other than that and the stillness, there was no change in her. She prayed the silence in her head meant the pressure was off, not that her tormenters were regrouping.

Sini got up, and as she walked into the living room, she saw all the empty plastic bags and bottles on the table. The sight disgusted her, but she chose to have compassion towards herself. It could always be worse. As she threw the bags into the garbage, she let the unopened ones follow. It was all or nothing. She'd either have to be without any sugar or accept she was never satisfied with only a little.

Throwing away what the day before had been her only way of escaping, she felt nothing but relief. Her cravings were gone. Not feeling any more special than the day before was a bit of an anti-climax, though. Was that what she'd been fighting all summer? On the other hand, she felt such relief. She was still herself, just a healthier version.

She should begin a new, healthier life—but how? Not having any books to go by—which ability did she wish most of all to better? What would be most effective at making her mission easier?

Her wish was silly compared to what she should aspire to. She wanted to train her body so that she wasn't as sensitive to cold. The ability to stay longer in the cold with Kuutamo motivated her more than meditating or attempting to change into the shape of an animal. The thought made her laugh. Magnificent snow princes might be real, but she'd never be able to morph into a bird. Those things were superstition from a long time ago. A time when people believed in all kinds of bizarre things.

But how to become less sensitive? Winter swimming would have been perfect if it hadn't been summer. Cold showers perhaps? She wrinkled her nose. Stepping down a ladder into an icy lake was more natural than stepping under an icy shower. What if she trained her mind to withstand pain instead?

Sini fetched her notebook and began scribbling down ideas for training her physical and mental abilities on a tight budget. She might use some of the stash money for training purposes.

Her breakfast got cold as she got caught up in the flow of thoughts and ideas.

⌘ ⌘ ⌘

She was in the forest again, but she wasn't alone.

In the back of her mind, she understood Karo wasn't alive, and the tears she dried from her face were happy tears.

She watched the beautiful black dog trotting up to her. His coat shiny and thick and his tail wagging. She hunched down to greet him. He stopped, turned around, and trotted away along the path. She stood and followed.

"Karo!"

The dog turned around and came towards her. Sini laughed as he jumped at her.

"My beloved Karo." Just as she was about to feel his fur against her palm, he turned around. Then he turned back and began the restless pacing about.

She tried to grab hold of him, but he kept evading her, coming up to her and then escaping her hands. When he began whimpering and whining, her joy turned into worry.

Karo was anxious, but she didn't understand why. Did he hurt? Was he afraid of something? She wanted to soothe him, to stroke away his fears, but he wouldn't let her touch him. She was working hard on keeping calm so she could help him.

He began barking.

"Shhh…"

No effect.

"What do you want?"

The dog stopped, looked at her, and then pranced off again. Did he want her to follow? She started walking, but he came towards her—only to refuse her touch again.

"What do you want me to do? Please tell me. Let me help you."

Her words were useless. Tears of desperation stained her cheeks.

"Please…" The agitation took hold of her, too, and she felt him slipping away. "No, please…"

⌘ ⌘ ⌘

Sini woke up clammy and knowing she'd failed the dog once again.

It was clear he wanted something from her. They said that recurring dreams were about unfinished things in life. She had no clue. Everyone wanted something from her. Why couldn't they just tell her straight what it was so that she could do something?

Maybe you haven't been listening?

Sini squeezed her eyes shut. The voice in her head didn't belong to ancient shaman spirits or her grandmother. It belonged to her.

It was true. While she'd thought she'd been seeking meaning in life, she'd shut out others and even herself in her quest for being left in peace. She'd been wounded and had wanted to tend to her injuries in total seclusion, trusting no one.

She'd been hiding for too long, feeling powerless and unable to work out a new direction in her life. If cruel fate had brought her home—to the place she was fated to be—she mustn't let her sacrifice be in vain.

Sini sighed.

She was still young. The time had come to make some tangible changes, and she already had a great idea.

Time to make that big purchase.

The night was warm.

The moon was full.

Finally! It didn't get dark in the middle of summer, and she'd missed the stars and the moon like crazy. Walking in the lit forest in the middle of the night had been special, but it didn't come close to walking in the light of the full moon. It was late summer, when evenings came faster, and the nights lasted longer.

She wanted to visit the little pond where Karo used to swim. In reality the pond wasn't deep enough to swim in, but he'd enjoyed splashing around. She used to throw him a big stick, and he never grew tired of fetching it. Thick and soft light-green moss covered the bottom of the pond and made it look inviting. Karo hadn't cared that the water was icy. The pond was really just melted snow and rain that lasted until it dried up as the summer progressed.

As Sini walked along the path lined with robust shrubs and continued up the slope, she found the forest beautiful again. In the soft air and gentle dusk, some of the magic had returned. Karo and the dream were on her mind as she reached the plateau in the middle of the forest. The forest floor sparkled. Sini slowed to a halt.

It must be moonlight reflecting from a watery surface. There was movement. A shadow. It had to be an animal.

Making no sound, she moved closer. It looked like a bird swimming in the pond. When it changed direction, its feathers caught the light of the moon. She believed the cloak hid her from the perception of the bird, but she needed to be careful. That was no ordinary bird, and she couldn't be sure who was able to sense her through the protective barrier.

She'd never seen birds in the pond. It was small and surrounded by tall trees. As she step-by-step eased closer, the scene got more surreal. The pond brimmed with water, and the bird floating on the black-and-silver surface took her breath away. Its body was a graphic masterpiece of black, grey, and white shapes. A strong and sharp bill perfected the streamlined, alert head. The thin white lines on the back and throat turned silver when struck by the moonlight. The bird was pure magic. It was a black-throated loon.

It wasn't real. Sini knew as fact that the loon needed a vast area of water surface to run on to get into flight and then several times longer space of woodless land to gain enough height.

She also knew the loon happened to be one of the most important spirit helpers of the Finnish shaman.

It must be a sign. Was she supposed to connect with the diver? Doing her best to stay calm, she walked over to the rim of the pond and eased herself onto a small stone.

Sini watched the ghostlike apparition glide on the water. Its red eyes underlined the otherworldly impression. Or should she say underworldly? Waterbirds were powerful animals as they could walk on earth, reach up high in the sky, and dive deep under the surface. Was it of the underworld or the upper world?

Maybe she could ask it?

Sini slowly raised her hand to the hood and pulled it down, unclasped the toggle button, and let the cloak, without a sound, fall onto the moss-covered stone. The loon angled its head, and she sensed the red eye observing her. Then, it no longer was.

Sini searched every corner of the pond. No ripples had appeared on the surface to let her know the bird had dived under. It was nowhere. Instead, another creature revealed itself.

It was seated on the bent birch arching across the pond with its feet immersed in the water. She knew what it was.

Sini felt unprotected without the cloak. As she inhaled, the breath stretched into a short eternity, as she decided whether she should use it.

She sensed the creature's attention on her, but she wasn't afraid. She should've been—everyone knew the price of being ignorant—but she felt only curiosity. As they eyed each other in silence, Sini was aware of the creature's interest in her.

She was the most beautiful being Sini had seen. The face looked innocent, childlike, and her hair was a shimmery silver, as if it reflected the light of the moon instead of having its own shade. The eyes were soft and the colour of the light-green moss. Her body was slim and had neither feminine nor masculine features, and Sini thought she might be beyond gender.

The creature smiled. The smile was contagious, inviting. As Sini smiled back from the brim of bliss, she thought of the stories parents told their children. The evil water spirit Neck lay in wait in ponds and lakes, wanting to lure children to get close enough to catch them and bring them under the surface. According to folklore, even adults were in danger.

Sini couldn't sense any evil intentions from Neck. Only curiosity.

To her own surprise, Sini began humming. Instantly, a delightful tone flowed from the creature that matched and elevated the song. For once, Sini sang a happy tune because she felt happy. Everything was so beautiful.

Neck wanted to know what made her happy.

What made her happy was the dog bouncing into the water, looking back at her, wondering why she didn't throw the stick already. Her grandmother making her a cup of hot cocoa and reading her a bedtime story. Kuutamo reaching for her and pulling her into his embrace.

Being there with Neck and uncovering her happy moments, she wasn't sad that she didn't have those things anymore. She felt only the positive emotions, the gilded version.

She looked at Neck.

What did she want from Sini?

Only to know what made her happy. In return, she would give something that meant everything to Sini. Neck raised her hand and invited her to come closer. Sini wanted to give in. Revealing the things she loved most of all to someone was freeing. Neck showed no judgement towards nor evaluated the worth of Sini's desires.

Sini stood up on wobbly legs and walked up to the edge. Her boots got wet, and she took them off. Barefoot, she stepped into the water and watched the moon reflecting on the black surface. The black and silver brightened gradually until it became a blinding white. She saw a figure standing in what looked like a palace of ice. As soon as she recognised him, his body focused onto the water.

Sini's heart ached with joy. She clutched his stone in her hand and thought of how she wanted to be there with him. Nothing could make her happier than seeing that he was well.

Kuutamo closed his eyes and put his hand on his heart.

God, he was more beautiful than she remembered.

As the image from the other realm dissolved into the depths of the dark water, Sini closed her eyes and lingered in the joy. She thanked Neck and sensed the spirit's satisfaction. She asked Sini to stay for a while. When the sun began rising and the light of the moon would fade, she'd have to leave.

Although Sini didn't feel the pain at that moment, she knew she'd miss the creature when it was gone. She sat down beside the stone and leaned sideways onto the cloak, looking at the wondrous thing dangling its feet in the water.

Sini snapped into consciousness.

The air was moist and fresh. She found herself wrapped in the cloak. It had kept her warm through the chilly morning hours.

Her eyes fell upon the pond that had no magic. The water wasn't more than a foot deep, and the birch looked like it couldn't hold anybody's weight. If the night hadn't felt more real than the most lucid dream and she hadn't found her boots and socks scattered halfway to the water line, she would've thought she'd imagined it all.

Sini peeled herself from the damp cloth and stood. It was a beautiful new morning. The magic of the night had vanished with the sunlight, but the forest was alive with a myriad of plants and animals. The pristine air of an untouched day filled her lungs as she took the longest breath. She found the path that cut through the forest and started heading home.

Since the day Kuutamo left, she'd envisioned him in his home, being at ease in his natural element, surrounded by the ones who loved him. She'd pictured Helmi, always by his side, dedicated to him.

Sini smiled.

She finally knew. Neck had shown her what she'd longed for to be true. Kuutamo cared for her enough to think of her on the other side. He missed her too. Their connection hadn't been severed on the threshold of a higher dimension. He'd known she'd thought of him.

He'd sensed her love.

Psyched by the magical night, Sini decided to set up her new training facility.

She'd ordered it online and paid loads to have it delivered to her backyard. Letting a stranger come to her house had been unnerving, but what could she do when she had no one to help her? She'd been polite but hadn't encouraged small talk, and she'd given vague answers when the guy asked if she lived there around the year or if it was her summer cottage.

Sini pulled up the garden hose and turned on the water. She put the hose end into the wooden hot tub and looked at the little wood-burning heater. A regular spa without heating would've been sufficient, but she'd decided she might enjoy a hot bath sometimes. It might be fun to heat it up some winter night and, floating in warmth and comfort, stare into the stars.

Waiting for the tub to fill up, she decided it was best to start out when the temperature of the water was still bearable.

Sini stripped off her clothes, threw them on the grass, and climbed up the three steps of the wooden entry stairs she'd included in the package. Putting her foot over the edge and down in the water, she realised it was going to be harder than expected.

The water was freezing!

Clenching her teeth tight, she commanded the other foot in onto the seat and stepped into the deeper centre. She could do it. It was child's play. What about the day she'd pour a bag's worth of homemade ice cubes into it?

Sitting down, Sini reminded herself how she'd endured much colder circumstances in winter. She forced herself to calm down and morph the hysterical ventilating into semi-normal breathing.

She looked to her forest. Winter was a few months away, almost around the corner, and she had to be prepared. She'd suffer cold water and do other challenges to make it easier for her to be with Kuutamo. She wanted to astound him, make him proud. With her hand on her chest, she touched her heart the way he'd done in the ice realm.

Neck had helped her realise what she hadn't dared think. She wanted to be with him in the ice realm.

It wasn't possible, yet it was what she wanted most of all.

23 THE LOVE LETTER

Sini looked at the image of Kuutamo on the screen. She'd managed to capture at least part of his beauty. It wasn't just a pretty face of an ice prince. The deep sorrow mirrored in his sapphire eyes made her want to reach out and do whatever she could to make him feel ease. She'd thought about it the whole summer when she'd been working on the images. Though he was her secret to keep, she wanted to share the uniqueness of his beauty.

She pressed enter.

The world would know, yet they wouldn't. The internet was filled with images of ice princes, fairies, and fantasy warriors. No one would think he was real. No one would know she was the person behind her username.

Publishing her drawings of Kuutamo was like sending love letters that would be read by anyone who cared.

ABOUT THE AUTHOR

H. S. Winter lives in the Finnish countryside, where the uneventfulness of the surroundings and everyday life makes her want to think of what lies beneath. She has a Master's degree in Animal Ecology, and her former career comprised of working out the delicate balance between exploiting natural resources for economical profit or recreational use, and protecting them. Her stories are inspired by thoughts on the meaning of life, an enhanced future for humanity, and finding the one.

Find out more about the author and her books at hswinter.com.